"*Restorations* by Charles Strickler begins with a failed bank robbery by a famous gangster in the 1930's, quickly moves to present day when Miles West acquires a 1928 Stutz Black Hawk Boat Tail Roadster as a classic car restoration project, and suddenly explodes into mystery, mobsters, mayhem, murder, a treasure hunt and personal redemption. Warning, make sure your schedule is clear before you pick up this book, because you won't be able to put it down again until the end."

—John J. Jessop, author of *PLEASURIA: Take As Directed, Guardian Angel: Unforgiven, Guardian Angel: Indoctrination*

"*Restorations* is a grand combination of mystery, adventure, and intrigue in the same vein as *National Treasure*.

"With a strong historical basis, and a string of prized antique cars, *Restorations* deftly bridges the gap between the 1930s and 2018 in a truly magical way."

—Nelson Gomm, author of *Overhead Assets*

"Charles Strickler creates an endearing, relatable protagonist in Miles West, and readers will delight in riding along on his quest to solve a Depression-era mystery via modern-day tactics. West and his charming friend, Bramley Ann Fairchild, deliver Strickler's cleverly-researched detail, light-hearted word play, and fast-paced plot as the two race to expose the mob boss at the center of the intrigue."

—Becky Morris and The Tales End Book Club, Richmond VA

"*Restorations* takes you on a wild, rollicking ride from a Midwestern 1920s bank robbery to a present-day NYC gang war, then perches you on a Southern front porch swing to catch your breath while enjoying a summer breeze and a glass of sweet tea. At the heart of it is a man trying to restore his faith in love and life as he works to restore a vintage vehicle. Throw in a little "MacGyver"-like ingenuity, fascinating American history, a smart, pretty auctioneer, and some witty banter . . . and you have the perfect escape novel. You'll want to devour it in one sitting, then you'll ask: what will Miles and Bramley do next?"

—Debra Thompson—Freelance Writer

R3storations
by Charles Strickler

© Copyright 2019 Charles Strickler

ISBN 978-1-63393-779-6

Published by

 **köehlerbooks**™

210 60th Street
Virginia Beach, VA 23451
800–435–4811
www.koehlerbooks.com

R3STORATIONS

CHARLES

STRICKL3R

VIRGINIA BEACH
CAPE CHARLES

To my wife, Mary—what a great adventure

CHAPTER ONE

December 5, 1930—Decatur, Illinois

"COPPERS!" YELPED THE DRIVER. "What do I do?"

"Calm down. Just maintain your speed and drive right past them, and DON'T look at them," replied Lefty Webber. He flipped the thick black collar up on his wool overcoat and peered out of the Auburn Phaeton sedan's rear window. The two officers must have just come out of the restaurant after eating breakfast. They were standing at their cars talking.

"Keep your head. They didn't even notice us," Lefty grumbled.

Lefty stared as they passed a strange octagonal building with a shingled handle on one end and a shingled spout on the opposite side. The roof was topped with a small, white, glass sign that said *The Coffee Pot*, which resembled the glass nob on the top of a percolator. The place didn't look very big and surely couldn't seat many people. Lefty had almost stopped in the last time he visited Decatur. He inquired about it when he was staying at the Hotel Orlando. A waiter informed him that it had been built the previous year and was drawing quite a few visitors from out of town as rumors of the strange building spread.

"Go on over to the Texaco. It's a new one on West Main Street. We can fill up before heading to the bank," Webber instructed his young driver,

Billy Hudson. It was the first time he used Billy as part of his crew, and he could tell the kid was nervous.

"Billy, you need to act normal. Stay calm. Don't be so anxious."

"Jack, when we get there, you fill it up and pay," Lefty whispered to the man riding beside him in the back. "The kid looks too wound up. Don't want him to spill nothing. He can play the part of the high-hat driver and just stay in the car."

The wind had picked up and the snow was coming down sideways. Lefty debated whether he should call the whole thing off. Heading out of town through driving snow could be problematic. On the flip side, the snow would limit visibility, making it more difficult for them to be seen. Given how far they traveled, he decided to stick with the plan.

The new white-and-green-trimmed Texaco station had just opened the previous August. The canopy over the fuel island connected to the building on the north side of the street, which blocked the frigid gusts. As Jack filled the car with gas, the white building seemed to disappear in the midst of the snowstorm.

The young driver was shaking his leg and tapping on the steering wheel, obviously nervous. "Billy, relax. You know the plan. Just stick to it," Lefty admonished.

They paid without incident and set off. With a couple more turns, they pulled up to North Park Street.

"Everyone ready?" asked Lefty. All nodded in assent. Two of the men exited the car on North Park Street. The driver quickly darted forward and paused momentary before taking a right turn onto Water Street where Lefty hopped out. Lefty looked up and down the street before turning to enter the Citizens Bank. Everything appeared quiet. The cold weather kept people indoors, and the people who were outside had their heads down as they navigated the city amidst the blowing snow.

Lefty entered the bank, drew open his overcoat and withdrew his gun. Then he barked, "This is a hold up. Put your hands in the air and don't move."

Lefty's compatriots, Thomas and Jack, had already strode in through the south-facing doors of the bank. They glared at each other when they spotted the policeman standing at the teller's window. In four quick strides they moved behind the cop and hit him in the head with the butt of a gun, confiscating his pistol from his holster just before he fell. The teller screamed.

"Quiet!" yelled Lefty.

His two accomplices herded the bank employees to the far side of the lobby, while Lefty cleared all of the offices and the washroom. Jack McDonald dragged the unconscious policeman by his feet over to the other bank patrons, who were lying facedown. Then he secured the lanky man with his own handcuffs.

Lefty cased the bank a couple of weeks ago and knew the layout. He had drawn up a plan and gone over it in great detail with his crew. Everyone knew what they were supposed to do and moved efficiently.

Lefty shoved the last straggler he found in an office toward the rest of the captives. "Who's the manager?" he demanded.

"I am," came a muffled reply from a plump man splayed out on the tiled floor.

"Get over here and open the vault," Lefty instructed.

The rotund bank manager pushed himself up with help from Thomas, who lifted the wheezing man by his collar.

"I can't. It's on a time lock." Lefty waved his Colt M1911A1 in the man's face. "Here let me show you," the petrified manager pleaded. He demonstrated that there was no way to engage the crank until the time lock was released.

What the manager didn't disclose was that he had a cold, and the previous evening he had sneezed at the moment he was setting the clock. The resulting twitch in his wrist translated to a two-hour delay for access to the vault.

Lefty was livid. When he cased the bank, it was mid-afternoon and the vault door was propped wide open. Inside were stacks of cash that had been delivered in anticipation of people cashing their weekly payroll checks. Lefty grabbed the manager's coat and pushed him back to the others on the floor. "Get back over there with the rest of them! Don't none of ya make a sound."

Not wanting to leave empty handed, Lefty barked at his crew, "Grab those waste bins and clear out the tellers' drawers and that little vault in the corner."

Thomas and Jack grabbed separate waste bins, dumped their contents on the floor, then started cleaning out the cash from each compartment of the drawers. Lefty moved so he could see the doors and keep an eye on the employees and customers on the floor. He had one gun pointed down at the mass of bodies and a second pistol aimed between the front and side door.

Ruby Green had been sitting in her car watching her husband, Edward, enter the bank to make a small withdrawal from their savings account. When he was just inside the door, he stopped and put his arms in the air, his bankbook extending from his right hand like a little flag. In that instant she knew the bank was being robbed. She looked around and didn't see anyone on the street. Pushing the door open, she braced herself against the wind and set off as fast as she could go. Her leather-soled shoes were horrible for snowy conditions; she wished she had heeded Edward's admonition to wear boots. She had refused because they would make her look ridiculous.

She had told him in no uncertain terms, "I am not going out looking like some ditzy tomato." Now here she was, struggling down slick sidewalks through the snow-covered streets trying to find help and alert the police.

As soon as the door moved, the motion caught Lefty's eye. "Put your hands up, then come over here and lay on the floor with everyone else." Edward Green froze, throwing his hands into the air, then joined the other hostages on the floor.

"Fellas, get a move on. On the jump now!" Lefty barked. "We need to go." He looked at his watch again. They had been in the bank for six minutes. They were supposed to be out the door in half that time.

"Everyone, just stay on the floor till we're gone, so ya won't get shot."

Ruby Green stumbled down Park Street and fell into the first open storefront she found. "Quick, call the police. The Citizens Bank is being robbed!"

"Hey, doll, no one's gonna rob a bank on a day like this," a man at the counter said.

"Don't razz me! My husband's in there with his hands raised at gunpoint."

Without another word he went to the phone on the wall and dialed the operator. "I need the police! The Citizens Bank on North Park Street is being robbed."

Thomas and Jack fled out the door to the car waiting for them on Water Street. As they dashed, the wind whipped at the waste bins and a lone bill flew out; in the next instant it was pitching and floating down the street with the snow. Lefty kept his gun trained on the people on the floor as he backed through the doors. Then he turned and dove into the back seat as Billy sped north on Water Street. Lefty had planned on capturing a big score of a couple hundred thousand dollars. Instead, the teller registers and the tiny vault yielded only about $30,000.

"What happened?" asked Billy. "I had to circle the block two extra times."

"Damn time lock kept us from getting into the main vault." Lefty dumped the few clothes he had in a worn canvas laundry sack onto the floor so he could empty the cash from the waste bins into the makeshift money bag.

They were doing forty-five as they crossed icy East North Street. An approaching car slipped and skidded sideways into their lane. When Billy hit the brakes, the two-ton Auburn went into a slide, careening directly toward the car in their path. It smashed the rear end of the little Model A coupe like a gnat, changing the trajectory of their own rapidly skidding vehicle. The rear end of the Auburn clipped a lamp pole and the car spun down the street like a top dancing over an ice rink. Its momentum slammed it up on a curb and into the Moran Funeral Home at the corner of El Dorado and Water Street with a loud crash. Everyone was stunned. The money was strewn throughout the car.

"Cabbage is spilt everywhere," Jack croaked. Thomas had been tossed like a rag doll against the door. The bottom of the metal waste bin caught his rib and snapped it in two pieces, one of which pierced his lung and sliced an artery. He was bent over trying to get a breath.

"Okay, boys, keep your heads about you," Lefty said. "We need another set of wheels. Billy, grab a heater and fetch the keys to that car." A 1931 Chevrolet hearse sat in front of the funeral parlor—with keys in the ignition.

"We're in luck," Billy yelled as he climbed in and started the hearse.

"Good," yelled Lefty. "Fellas, we need to get all this picked up fast."

Lefty and Jack grabbed handfuls of money and shoved it in the canvas bag as fast as they could snag it, but it was scattered everywhere. Thomas flopped over on the back seat with blood dripping out of his mouth. His eyes were glazed over; his mouth opened and closed, gasping for air and gurgling as blood filled his lungs. After gathering most of the money, Lefty and Jack transferred their stuff to the newly acquired vehicle.

"Get in. Let's go," commanded Lefty as he climbed in the front seat.

"What about Thomas?" Billy asked.

"He's done for," responded Lefty.

The funeral home's proprietor, Mr. J. J. Moran, stepped outside to investigate the commotion, watching in surprise as his hearse sped away. He darted back inside and called the police.

Lefty and his gang heard approaching police sirens before they saw them through the driving snow.

"Get a move on, on the jump now," prodded Lefty.

"Here they come!" hollered Jack.

Billy drove north as planned, which was the quickest way out of town. He looked ahead and saw a railroad wigwag arm moving back and forth while the bell clanged.

"No! No! No!" yelled Lefty.

A train was steaming down the tracks, blocking their path. They were trapped.

Officer Oliver Davies heard the calls for assistance over his patrol car radio. Police were told to be on the lookout for the stolen black hearse. Officer Davies was a block from the funeral home and spotted the hearse sitting at the railroad crossing.

"I've got you now," he said as he slid to a stop well behind them.

Lefty saw the police car approach. "Hold him off. Fire at the car."

Jack opened the rear-facing door and leaned out, then let go with a hail of bullets.

Officer Davies skidded to a halt, opened his door, jumped out and returned fire. He kept his shots low, trying to take out the hearse tires or get a hit through the back; he didn't want any of his shots to hit the train. He was slow and methodical with each and every shot. One of his shots landed home.

Jack yelped, "I've been hit!" A shot had gone through the back of the hearse and hit him square in the leg, shattering his thighbone.

"Go! Go! Go!" yelled Lefty as the train finally passed. He looked back and saw steam rising from the front of the police car.

"We must have hit his radiator," Jack said.

"I think he got our tire," Billy yelled back.

"Keep going as long as you can," Lefty said. "We will have to find another car. When you get to Grand Avenue take a right. We'll head northeast."

Lefty rubbed his wooden cipher like a talisman. He grabbed the piece of paper containing one of his messages and ripped it up, then let the pieces float out the window and disappear in the blinding snow.

"I think we might make it. I don't see anyone back there," Billy said.

Phone operators quickly spread the news of the robbery and escape. Several local residents responded, grabbing rifles and jumping in cars to help police catch the thieves.

After just a few miles, the flat rear tire on the stolen hearse started separating, the rubber peeling off the metal rim. *Whap, whap, whap.*

"Get in the middle of the road. Stop that truck headed this way!" ordered Lefty. He leapt out and waved his gun at the oncoming driver, who stopped. "We need your truck. Get out."

"Take it," said the grizzled old man as he climbed out.

Lefty and the two remaining crew members loaded into the old man's truck. Jack had ripped off part of his shirt and tied it over his leg, trying to staunch the trickle of blood.

A string of cars, some with lights flashing, appeared out of the blowing snow behind them. Shots rang out.

The old man dropped and rolled into the ditch.

Lefty was in the midst of completing a three-point turn to get the 1930 Ford AA truck turned around and headed north. The side windows shattered when a bullet plowed through both, just grazing Billy's head. Jack had the only machine gun. He dove over the thin metal sidewall into the back of the truck bed. Then, without looking, he pointed the gun over the tailgate and pulled the trigger, sending a couple of random-burst automatic fire toward their pursuers. The ad hoc caravan veered for cover and slid into ditches while the bandits made their getaway.

Lefty finally got his bearings through the blinding snow as he skidded away. He glanced at the dashboard.

"I can't believe this; we're almost out of fuel," he yelled.

In the lead pursuit vehicle were a pair of hunters. One was leveling his .30-06 Springfield for a shot. Just before the dark-green Ford Model AA disappeared, he managed to get off three good shots.

One shot went straight through the center of the back window. In its wake, it left a small hole with spiderweb cracks. A much larger hole appeared in the front windshield in the split second before it fell apart in a thousand pieces. The second bullet went through the passenger seat and hit Billy square in the back. He slumped forward. A third bullet drilled through the dashboard and made a ruckus as its fragments ricocheted through the engine bay.

"It's just you and me now, Jack," Lefty yelled out the window as he eyed the dead man next to him. He pushed the Ford for all it was worth. He could barely see with the snow coming into the cab where the windshield had been moments before.

Word had reached a Macon County deputy sheriff who lived in Oreana, which was just ahead of the fleeing bandits. He placed his car across the road to block the robbers' escape route. Deputy Miller had two advantages over his quarry. First, he had the wind at his back, giving him a clear view of the approaching truck long before Lefty saw him. The deputy also had a fixed position to keep his rifle steady.

With his Colt in his left hand, Lefty tried to make out what was ahead as the snow numbed his face. He might just be able to make it to the train station, which he knew wasn't too far. If he was lucky, he could hop a ride; otherwise, he would have to find another vehicle or a gas station. The truck was starting to sputter.

Brian Miller had been a soldier in World War I, and as a deputy he continued to practice shooting regularly, so his marksmanship was still just as proficient as the day he mustered out. Through his scoped rifle he spotted the pistol in front of the man's face as the truck grew closer. He was about to lower his rifle to disable the vehicle when he saw the gun being lowered in his direction.

Lefty finally spotted the car across the road. He thought that he might have enough room to get past it on the left side. He noticed the man leaning over the hood and started to level his pistol for a shot. Just as he bore left to attempt to go around the roadblock, he felt like he got punched in the chest.

If I only had my Stutz, I could outrun anybody, Lefty thought. He struggled to move, thinking about his stash and cursing himself for his greed and tempting fate one too many times.

Despite the near blinding whiteness, Lefty Webber's world grew dark as he passed into oblivion, taking his secrets with him.

CHAPTER TWO

Spring 2018—Wachau, North Carolina

IT WAS ANOTHER MILD day, signaling the transition from winter to spring. The trees unfolded their leaves as they awoke from their long winter nap. In the cloudless blue sky, birds chirped as they floated from tree to tree on the light breeze and alighted to outstretched limbs. The first flowers of spring dotted the landscape with a prelude of the bright, vibrant colors about to spill over the muted and dull tones dominating the palate of the lifeless winter season just passed.

"Well, Mrs. Gardner, that should just about do it," Miles said as his cordless DeWalt drill made quick work of the last deck screw in the newly refurbished front porch steps.

"My word, they look better than they ever did before," she replied.

Annabelle Gardner stood back and appraised the little white house donned with black shutters, where she had lived ever since marrying Dr. Thomas Gardner. The house had aged well over the decades. When her husband was alive, he was meticulous about keeping everything repaired and freshly painted; she had done her best to follow that example.

"Everything looks so even and precise, Miles. Doc would have approved of your craftsmanship and attention to detail."

Growing up on a local farm, Miles learned to do a little bit of everything. His dad's philosophy was often repeated. "You broke it, you fix it." Miles inevitably became a modern-day jack-of-all-trades.

In reality, most of his skills were a by-product of growing up on a farm, which nurtured a self-sufficient lifestyle. Some of his chores were challenging and others tiresome, like painting. He just didn't have the patience for dealing with drips, drops, and mucked-up paint brushes that leaked all over his hands and clothes. Unlike Tom Sawyer, he had not been able to talk his friends into doing that task for him. *Or was that Huck Finn?* he thought. *I'll have to read that book again sometime.* The only thing he disliked more than painting was chopping weeds, briars, and thistles along the property lines of their family farm.

In response to Mrs. Gardner's compliment, Miles blurted a phrase his mama always repeated: "If you're gonna do something, do it right."

"I swear, your mama said that at least once every time our bridge club met. I do miss her," she said, a bit misty eyed. "'T'ain't been the same 'round here without her. At any rate, I just baked some sweet potato jacks. I want ya to take 'em home. Take that sack of canned vegetables, too. They came fresh outta my garden, when I did my canning last summer and fall. I've still got way too much to use."

Miles looked over the white picket fence at the large garden plot. He had to hand it to the old gal. She was eighty-five, and each year she still tended an immaculate vegetable garden that had to be at least two acres. A neighbor with a tiller had already turned the soil for her. The freshly turned earth would be ready to plant when the temperature warmed up a bit more. *Good grief,* he thought. *She could probably feed the whole neighborhood.*

Thinking about it some more, he concluded that she probably kept the folks at her church stocked up too. He smiled to himself and turned to her.

"Are you trying to fatten me up, Mrs. Gardner?"

"Well, you could do with a little more meat on them bones. Being so thin makes you look like you're feelin' poorly."

At six feet and weighing just one-sixty, Miles wasn't exactly skin and bones, but his once-chiseled physique had gone soft. His closely cropped brown hair was a bit thinner and was definitely receding. It made his cowlick more pronounced. He had lost the bounce in his step and hunched a bit. His mental burdens appeared to weigh him down physically.

"Your mama would never forgive me for not makin' sure you're eatin' right." She was thinking about how sad it was to see him all alone. He was still so young. His beautiful wife had died more than three years ago.

Mrs. Gardner perked up. "Say, are you gonna go to the big auction tomorrow over at the Vogel estate? They say the Vogel sisters had some really unusual things. Nobody really knew 'em as they were so reclusive." Before he had a chance to respond, she said, "Would you take me over there?"

Miles thought for a moment. "I remember seeing the sisters drive around in that old '53 Ford pickup when I was growing up. I haven't seen them in years."

"Well, the youngest sister just died a couple of months back. She was 103 years old still living in that old place all by herself. Still driving that same old truck. In fact, she drove down to the mailbox at the end of her road and just pitched over dead after she got out to get her mail. Ya know, I don't think anybody would'a found her for a coon's age if she'd kicked the bucket in her old home."

Always in motion, Mrs. Gardner pruned some wayward branches on one of her rose bushes and looked over at him. "So, will ya take me over there?" she repeated in her slow Southern drawl. *There* had just the slightest trace of an audible *r* left, reminding him of his wife, who had spoken with that same accent and peculiar pronunciation. It almost disappeared when they moved to New York City. However, whenever they came home, she slipped back into her native tongue, complete with accent, colloquialisms, and idioms, just as if she were putting on a pair of comfortable old shoes.

While Miles enjoyed remembering her, he was still angry that she had been taken from him in such an unfair way. He floundered with the frustration of not being able to shove those annoying feelings in a mental strongbox and bury them forever.

Miles returned to the moment as he tried to discern what Mrs. Gardner was thinking. He knew she didn't give a flip about antiques, and, unlike many of her contemporaries, she wasn't a busybody nosing into everyone's business. She relished her independence and still drove herself everywhere.

"So, what's piqued your interest in the sale?"

She thought, *Well, I can't tell him there's a very fetching auctioneer I want him to bump into.* She quickly replied with a bit of a stammer.

"Ah . . . well . . . I haven't seen Hank Long in forever and an age. Thought it would be nice to say hello." She looked a bit sheepish, which Miles assumed was due to the mention of the octogenarian auctioneer and proprietor of the Long Auction Company.

"Okay," he replied. "What time do you want me to pick you up?"

"Come over round nine. If you come early, I can fix ya some fresh biscuits, eggs, and country ham with redeye gravy for breakfast."

He mulled over the breakfast menu and suspected the meal would exceed the recommended daily allowance of sodium by thirty-fold. It made him thirsty just thinking about it.

Better skip it, he thought.

"As tempting as that sounds, I'll just pick you up at nine."

CHAPTER THREE

MILES ROLLED UP PROMPTLY at nine the next morning in his 1974 Ford Bronco. It was light blue with a white top and a slightly worn luster, having been stored in his dad's barn for so many years.

Mrs. Gardner was just coming out of the front door with a picnic basket. He got out and walked around to open her door.

"How about we put that in the back? There is not much room in the front."

She opened the basket and pulled out a steaming cup of coffee and a biscuit wrapped in a paper towel. "Thanks for taking me over to the auction. I know ya didn't want breakfast, but here's a cup of coffee and a honey biscuit anyway."

Miles smiled. "Now I know you're serious about trying to fatten me up. Your honey biscuits are sweeter than most doughnuts. But since I didn't eat anything this morning, I do appreciate it."

The gigantic steaming biscuit smelled wonderful and made his mouth water. He balanced it on top of the oversized spill-proof coffee mug with one hand and closed the tailgate latch with the other hand. Following her around to the passenger side, he opened her door.

Mrs. Gardner bowed her head and batted her eyes. In a slow and playful Southern drawl she said, "Why, Miles, you *are* such a gentleman. If I were forty years younger, I'd marry you!"

"Well, Annabelle my dear, knowing how you cook, I might just have to propose anyway." They both laughed. His mood brightened.

As he climbed in she said, "I've been tryin' to git ya to call me Annabelle for years; that's the first time you've done it."

"Well, Mrs. Gardner, that's just the way I was raised. My folks always told me that it was important to show respect for your elders."

"I know, but when people say 'Mrs. Gardner' I still want to look 'round for Doc's mom. Guess I still don't see myself as an *elder*. Besides, not very many people pay much attention to old traditions these days."

"Well, chivalry and good manners are not dead just yet," Miles said as they rumbled slowly down the road.

"Speaking of not being dead yet, I see ya old truck hasn't given up the ghost just yet," she said, patting the dashboard.

"Windy is as faithful as they come."

"Windy?"

"Well, it's probably not very original, but I named her for her color. In 1974 Ford called this particular shade of blue 'Wind Blue,' so I named her Windy. Before you ask, 'Why do guys name their cars?' I have to admit, I don't really know. However, I read that about one in four of us do name our vehicles. In fact, what might really surprise you is that the same article stated that more women than men name their vehicles. So, I would infer from that bit of trivia that people see a vehicle as something that actually has a personality with which they can identify. Besides, if you stop and think about it, people have been naming their rides for years, whether it's a truck, car, horse or mule."

"Yeah, I suppose that's right," she said wistfully. "Doc had an ol' four-wheel-drive Jeep Wagoneer; said he needed it for making house calls and getting to the hospital regardless of the weather. Called it *Faith*, which was his shorthand for Old Faithful. He drove that thing for more years than I can remember."

They turned onto the old gravel road leading to the Vogel estate.

"Where does the estate begin?" Miles asked. Mrs. Gardner peered around.

"I'm not sure where the boundaries are now. Ova' the years they would sell off sections of the farm. I think 'riginally the whole parcel was over 12,000 acres stemming from a colonial land grant. By the time the Vogels immigrated from Germany and bought it in the early 1900s, 'twas down to just less than 2,000 acres. Believe Hank said it's only about 200 acres now."

In contrast to the mild, cheerful weather they enjoyed the previous day, the temperature was much cooler. The dreary overcast day matched the character of the weathered estate.

They drove through large iron gates that had faded from black to a dull gray strewn with rust. It almost looked like the redbrick columns were absorbing them. The estate had fallen into disrepair, and as the years passed, mother nature almost entirely reclaimed parts of it. As Miles motored up the red clay driveway, only faint remnants of gravel speckled the rutted, dusty path. On one side they saw an old structure that must have been a tenant house. Leafless trees and branches covered the sides and roof, and a twisted, mangled tree grew out of its two-story chimney, resembling a dried plant in a vase. When Miles squinted, the old structure looked vaguely like a balding head with a wisp of gray hairs sticking out in all directions.

The other side of the drive was thick with vines and weeds consuming old farm equipment. The carcass of a tractor looked like it had been picked clean.

As they moved closer to the main house, it was clear that someone had recently cut the dead grasses and weeds. Stalks and stems of various thicknesses and varieties protruded like stubble through the chopped, dried and matted vegetation. Tobacco barns had wooden sticks piled like cordwood under the adjacent lean-tos. The pond was full of lily pads and algae-ringed cattails. Huge trees with large, gnarled trunks lined the last fifty yards of the road leading up to the house.

At one time, the old house had been a stately plantation manor. Overgrown boxwoods hid much of the first floor. Behind those large clumps of greenery were towering round columns that supported a second-story veranda, which covered the front of the house. *A great place to enjoy a cold glass of lemonade and catch a fleeting summer breeze,* Miles thought as he scanned the dilapidated balcony. Four large chimneys stood as sentinels, two on each end of the old redbrick home. Black shutters sagged beside the windows; many of them had slats missing.

A couple of people in bright orange-and-yellow vests stood in the field and directed traffic, trying desperately to keep the parking organized.

Miles said, "I'll drive you up front and drop you off."

Mrs. Gardner replied, "Let's just park over there and I'll walk. I need the exercise." She was very agile for her age, although she did like to carry a walking stick. The rustic, handcrafted, deformed old walking stick was especially helpful on uneven ground. The roots of the trees lining her street pushed the sidewalks up, which made her daily stroll a bit of an obstacle course. Despite the irregular terrain, she moved with quite a bit of speed and persisted in letting everyone know that she didn't need assistance, "Thank ya very much."

"This is turning into quite a production. It almost looks like the county fair," she proclaimed.

As usual, auctioneer Hank Long had the big white tent with the blue stripes set up as the main pavilion. However, she was surprised to see three additional smaller tents. This was not his typical arrangement for an estate sale. Several food vendors had set up shop between the tents and the parking area. The smell of BBQ and fresh popcorn wafted through the air. More parking attendants in fluorescent vests waved colorful wands to guide the lines of incoming traffic into organized rows, while the odd assortment of automobiles disgorged their loads of passengers.

As they approached the main tent, they saw Hank giving out instructions. He told his men to hang the Long Auction Company sign with a level, because clearly it was askew. He boisterously pronounced that he didn't want any of his potential buyers to think that he was a crooked auctioneer. Hank was a very jolly and gregarious fellow, greeting Annabelle with a huge smile and a big hug.

"It's great to see you, Annabelle. Glad you came. We've got some unusual things in this auction."

"I can't wait to see what's so fascinatin'," Annabelle said. "By the way, didn't you say you had a new auctioneer with ya comp'ny?"

"Yup. Her name is Bramley Ann Fairchild. I snagged her from Christie's in New York. She moved back here to take care of her mom." He pointed left with his big outstretched hand and with a bit of flourish said, "Here she comes now."

Miles turned to look at the approaching auctioneer and did a doubletake; she was truly stunning. Then he glanced back, catching Mrs. Gardner's eye. He was onto her little setup. Mrs. Gardner just patted his arm as if to say, *It'll be all right.*

"Bramley, I want to introduce you to Annabelle Gardner and Miles West."

"A pleasure to make your acquaintance," Bramley said with just the barest hint of a Southern accent.

After exchanging the normal pleasantries all the way around, Mrs. Gardner turned to Bramley. "Hank promised me a private tour, so could you show Miles some things that might be of interest to him?"

Bramley replied coyly, "Why, I'd be delighted to give him a quick tour." Miles sheepishly acquiesced, though his gaze lingered on Bramley. Her eyes were a very rare shade of amber and very, very captivating. They gave her an air of elegance and mystery. Her shoulder-length brown hair framed a flawless face with features that seemed delicate on her five-foot, nine-inch frame. A sideways glance at Annabelle confirmed she was watching him with a mild curiosity.

As the older couple wandered off arm in arm, Miles returned his attention to Bramley. "How did you end up in the auction business?"

"Well, I have always loved antiques and art. I was actually an art history major in college, but I did have a lot of other interests. Between my junior and senior years, I interned at Christie's in New York. They hired me when I graduated. The next thing you know, I'd spent most of two decades at Christie's and loved every minute of it. Then, six months ago, Mama got sick and I needed to move back and take care of her. That's when I landed a job with Hank. It's not Christie's, but I get to keep a finger in the auction world. Until this particular auction, things had become fairly mundane and routine. The one part of the job I really miss is the research. I love finding the origins of the things that go up for auction."

"What's so unusual about this auction?"

"Well, the Vogel sisters had some unusual collections. For instance, they had twelve complete sets of silver." She spread her arms toward a glass cabinet flanked by two security guards and filled with sets of sterling silver flatware. He looked at the various labels that accompanied each silver set.

Buckingham 1910 by Gorham Sterling,
Brandon 1913 by International Sterling
Acanthus 1917 by Georg Jenson
William and Mary 1921 by Lunt Sterling
Suffolk 1911 by Whiting Sterling
Stratford 1911 by Whiting Sterling
Somerset 1913 by Wallace Sterling
Regent 1892 by Gorham Sterling
Princess Mary 1922 by Wallace Sterling
Pantheon 1920 by International Sterling
King Albert 1919 by Gorham Sterling
Fairfax 1910 by Durgin Sterling

Miles looked at the collection list. "That's interesting."

"What caught your attention, Miles?"

"The assorted collections barely span two decades."

"Hey, you're very observant," she responded. "The other odd thing I can tell you is that all the sets were purchased in different cities from 1920 to 1929. Is that mysterious or what?"

"I can see why that might pique your curiosity. Any conclusions?"

"No, just more curious anomalies. For instance, that collection of men's watches spans the same time frame, 1920 to 1929."

"There must be a hundred watches in that collection."

"There are 120 very expensive watches, to be precise," Bramley replied. "None of which appear to have been worn."

"Ah ha, the plot thickens. Next you're going to tell me that ten watches were purchased in each of the same cities as the sets of silver."

"How did you guess that?"

"Well you told me that 120 watches had been purchased over the same nine-year time frame, so the logical inference was that a set of ten watches was purchased at the same time a set of silver was purchased."

"Very intuitive observation, Miles."

He nodded. "Where did the money come from?"

"Well, they inherited a large estate from their father. Presumably they were flush with cash in the 1920s. I know from looking at deed records that they would sell off a large tract of land about every decade. The whole estate has barely 200 acres left." She added, "It appears that most of the furniture was shipped over from Germany when the family moved to America."

Bramley glanced down at her own much more contemporary wristwatch and said, "Let's go to the north tent."

She grabbed Miles's arm, guiding him in the direction of the smaller tent. As they made their way through the detritus of decades'-worth of farm equipment and automobiles, Miles stopped in his tracks.

"That's a 1928 Stutz BB Black Hawk Boattail!"

"Now how did you know that?" she said, standing hands on hips.

"It's a long story."

"Well, I'd like to hear it sometime."

Miles remembered going to the July 4th Independence Day parade in Winston-Salem with his mother. That was the first time he'd seen a true classic car. Miss North Carolina was perched above the backseat of a 1928 Stutz BB Black Hawk Boattail with arms outstretched, waving at the crowd.

"This was one of the other curiosities I was going to mention; it's being auctioned this afternoon. We'll have to get you a bidder's paddle."

"Uh hum," he mouthed, barely audible. Miles started his story.

"You know how you remember certain events in your life just like it was yesterday—all the sights and sounds, even the smells? Well, July 4, 1976, was like that for me. It fell on a Sunday. Church bells started ringing at two in the afternoon, the time the Declaration of Independence was signed. The weather was really nice. The high was seventy-six that day. Everyone remarked about how that seemed so appropriate; I guess that's why I remembered it—because it was also very unusual. It was always hot when I had to work in the fields in the middle of the summer, and this wonderful reprieve came on my day off.

"I had never in my life seen more American flags than I saw that day. It seemed like everyone had a flag. The parade was a huge event with fire trucks, bands, floats of all sizes and shapes and lots of antique cars. And it also seemed like everyone that was riding on a float or in an antique car had an endless supply of hard candies that they were tossing out."

"There were people dressed in period 1776 costumes. With the jugglers and acrobats and even a couple of clowns in the parade, you would've thought Ringling Brothers Circus had come to town. Then came the parade queen, and, as I am sure you already surmised, she was perched on the back of a red 1928 Stutz Boattail Speedster with the top down."

Miss North Carolina was regally seated on a blue pillow nestled on the trunk, in her long white dress with white gloves, waving at everyone. Her blond hair shimmered in the sunshine. She had a striking red scarf wrapped around her neck. Holding a red-white-and-blue bouquet of flowers across her lap, she waved to the crowds with the other hand.

"That was my first crush. I thought she was the most beautiful girl in the world. I named her Firecracker and I decided right then I would own a car like that one day."

"I suppose you named her Firecracker for her red scarf," Bramley said in a sassy voice.

"No, I named her Firecracker because she was painted red." *Two can play with a double entendre*, he thought. They looked at each other and burst into laughter.

When Bramley was once again composed, she explained the discovery of the old car.

"We found it just yesterday when we pulled some hay out of the barn to spread over the bare spots of ground around the auction area. It had been mothballed underneath the old hayloft. Fortunately, only the front of the hayloft had collapsed and, in doing so, hid the car. The old canvas tarp that covered it was still in pretty good condition considering its age. The canvas must've had oils or something that repelled rodents because the car was unusually clean—well, aside from the decades of dust. At the risk of sounding like a used car salesperson, I've got to say, it's very low mileage; less than one hundred miles recorded on the odometer. Given the way it was stored, we think that it's been sitting in the same spot since the late 1920s. The old Stutz was slightly raised on four wooden blocks so the wheels were a couple inches off the ground. I've seen some strange things in this business, but this was a rather bizarre sight; it almost looked like it was levitating."

She glanced down at her watch. "Wow! Look at the time. I'm sorry, but I really do have to get ready for the auction. Maybe we can catch up later?" she inquired with a coquettish grin.

"That would be great!" Miles stammered. He stared at her as she glided gracefully away, admiring her striking, lean yet muscular and lithe figure. She casually looked back over her shoulder with a radiant smile. All he could manage to do was throw an awkward wave and a giddy grin.

CHAPTER FOUR

AS PLANNED, MRS. GARDNER and Miles met up again and shared a picnic lunch under the trees.

"So, did you see anything interesting?" asked Mrs. Gardner.

Miles knew what she was really asking but decided to play with her. "Why, as a matter of fact I did. She's ninety and still looks great!"

That was definitely not what Mrs. Gardner expected him to say. *He's interested in some old bat rather than that attractive young auctioneer?*

Miles could barely keep a straight face and said, with a smirk that widened to a grin, "Yes indeed; she's a beautiful 1928 Stutz Black Hawk."

"You are so bad!" she exclaimed as she threw a biscuit at him, which he snagged out of the air.

"Thanks! I was just going to ask you to pass those over."

Although she wondered how Miles got along with Miss Bramley Ann Fairchild, she wasn't about to pry.

They enjoyed each other's company as well as a delectable lunch while they watched auction-goers move back and forth like ants on parade at a picnic. He appreciated that they didn't need to fill every second of their time together with banal small talk. It wasn't that he was anti-social, but he had never enjoyed abbreviated cocktail conversations. He thought about some of the things he did enjoy: good music and friendly banter over a great meal. His mind drifted, and he realized that he was curious about what Bramley Ann might enjoy. Her eyes were mesmerizing and alluring; he couldn't remember ever seeing such an unusual eye color. He contemplated inviting her out for a meal. He couldn't quite put his finger on what had changed, but he didn't feel as dull. No, that wasn't quite right. It was more like a mental fog had started to dissolve. He shook his head, not sure what felt different. Then he refocused on the old Stutz.

It was a unique find that appeared pretty well preserved, all things considered. He decided to restore it—one more thing off of his bucket list. Yes, the Stutz would be his next project, a complete restoration. He smiled at that thought as he reached for one of Mrs. Gardner's homemade pickles.

"Those are the best watermelon pickles you have ever made."

"Thanks. Flattery will definitely get you an extra jar to take home."

"You won't have to twist my arm. Let's go see what's happening under the tent where they're auctioning the old cars."

As they walked in Miles quipped, "It looks like this part of the auction is just picking up a full head of steam." Mrs. Gardner looked quizzical. Miles noticed her perplexed look, then pointed ahead.

"That rusted 1904 Case tractor up for auction was powered by steam."

"Normally I catch on to your witticisms and would reply with a chemistry joke, but I am sure I wouldn't get a reaction."

No one can say that old lady is losing her marbles, Miles thought. *She has a razor-sharp mind.*

The tent started to crowd with spectators; quite a few had paddles. Miles had been to some big auto auctions, like the Barrett-Jackson auction in Arizona. The Vogel sale was small by comparison—no long, red-carpeted runways for the automobiles or large screens projecting multiple camera shots of the vehicle up for bid. Thankfully, it also appeared he wouldn't have an auction assistant, or *barker*, yelling in his ear.

There was quite a mixed collection of old automobiles and farm equipment. A Ford Model A with a rumble seat sat on one side of the collection of machinery and paraphernalia, while a Farmall tractor anchored the other end of the gallery. With the exception of the Stutz, all the vehicles and equipment showed considerable wear.

Bramley stood centered in the back of the tent on an elevated platform with a boxy podium in front of her. She had a gavel in one hand and microphone in the other. She called out bids and quickly encouraged bidders to up the ante, without the rapid-fire repetitive chanting most auctioneers used. Her conversational bid style matched the cadence of her gaveled arm swinging back and forth across the crowd like the pendulum on a metronome. It was hypnotic.

Miles moved closer to the crowd of bidders as the Stutz came up. He glanced across the small gathering, wondering how many people would be bidding against him. It would all sort itself out in short order.

"Next up for auction we have a 1928 Stutz Black Hawk Boattail with less than one hundred miles on the odometer. Who would like to start the bidding at $15,000? Make that twenty. I have $20,000 from a phone bidder. Who will give me thirty?" Miles held up his paddle. She pointed her gavel in his direction—"I have thirty"—then two paddles to the left went up simultaneously as she jumped from thirty-five to forty. The phone bidder chimed back in at forty-five; then a guy that looked like Andy Warhol poked his paddle up, trying to snag it for fifty. He was quickly outbid by the absentee phone bidder at fifty-five. Miles pitched his paddle up for sixty as the bidding ground to a stop. With a final pronouncement of "Going once, going twice," and a quick swing of the gavel—"Sold! To bidder 127"—Miles had his Stutz.

With the commission, Miles paid $66,000. It seemed a little on the high side, but he shrugged it off. *Economics 101: supply and demand,* he reasoned. *They aren't making any more of them.*

He would have been even more surprised to learn that in New York a lawyer had been ranting in the phone for the last few minutes, complaining that he had not finished bidding. He said his assistant had interrupted him mid-bid to ask him an urgent question for one of his clients, to which he had responded, "No! Definitely not!" never realizing he had failed to mute his phone call with the auction company. The interruption occurred at the exact moment the auction assistant asked Howe if he would like to up his bid. A recording by the auction company had captured the entire exchange. The lawyer slammed the phone down in frustration. One nefarious client, Mr. Carlo Bello, was not going to be happy. Howe had been instructed to acquire the car for Bello "regardless of the cost."

CHAPTER FIVE

AS WAS HIS REGULAR habit at this time of day, Carlo was sitting in his New York City office reading the newspaper when he received the highly anticipated call from his lawyer.

"We missed the purchase," said Mr. Howe in a soft, squeaky voice. He had been Carlo's legal counsel for many years and had noticed that Carlo was becoming increasingly volatile and bitter. Recently, whenever he needed to talk to Carlo he preferred to converse via phone rather than visit the temperamental old man in his lair.

"How did you miss the purchase? I gave you explicit instructions to purchase the Stutz no matter what it cost," Carlo roared in a thick Italian accent. Despite having been born in the US, Carlo clung to his family roots. He secretly idolized the *Cosa Nostra* of old Sicily and held a lifelong ambition of lording over the entire Italian organized crime empire in the US. He never gave voice to that particular dream.

His lawyer was being evasive, which he hated. *You'd think they would learn to just say what needs to be said.* Of course, he was not thinking about the times he shot the messenger, quite literally.

Howe finally replied. "Sorry, Mr. Bello, but there was a glitch in the communications with the auction company."

"What kind of a glitch?"

Howe was sweating and happy to be halfway across the city. He grabbed at his neck tie and tugged to loosen its stranglehold around his neck. As he waited for the mob boss to explode, he stewed in a mix of fear and dread and could almost taste the acids churning in his stomach. Quickly he popped open the bottle of Tums he kept in his desk drawer. He chewed the chalky pills and screwed up his face at the taste. The bottle was almost empty. It dawned on him that he had started to consume them like candy. He wondered if he should be worried about any side effects from overdosing on antacids. While he listened to the bellicose old man on the other end of the phone, he glanced down at his scuffed, black leather Allen Edmonds shoes. The antacids might be the least of his problems if he ended up being fitted with a pair of concrete shoes.

"You know I have been looking for a Stutz like that for more than sixty-five years," Carlo continued in his staccato Italian accent. "That one could be Lefty's missing Stutz. And you just let it get away."

Over the decades, Carlo had purchased or stolen five Stutz vehicles, only to discover that none of them held the secret he had long sought—because none of them were ever in the possession of Max "Lefty" Webber, the notorious bank robber. With each find, he was confident that he would finally unlock a secret treasure that would help him fulfill his lifelong dream of becoming the head of all the crime families. With each disappointment, Carlo became volatile and unpredictable. Everyone steered well clear of him until the dust and ash of his fury had settled.

Carlo's grandfather discovered many years earlier that mechanic Clarence Lieder had customized a 1928 Stutz for Lefty Webber. Lieder had worked at the Oakley Auto Company of Chicago and revealed—under duress—that they had indeed modified a Stutz for the infamous bank robber. The modifications included bulletproof windows, armor in the doors and trunk, a smoke screen device, spray nozzles and a special oil tank to make oil slicks, as well as a container with a remote release to cast roofing nails on the road to disable pursuing vehicles. But the most important modification was the secret compartment: the perfect place to stash a stolen journal. Otherwise the journal's hidden location went with

Lefty to his grave after he was killed in a shoot-out following a botched bank robbery.

The elderly Bello was convinced that Lefty had stashed Bello's stolen journal in the same place the robber had stashed his stolen fortune. Over the years he had convinced himself the Stutz and its hidden compartments were the key to recovering his lost fortune. He had a clerk who received email alerts every time a Stutz was listed for sale. When the Vogel estate sale items were advertised in various newspapers and by the auctioneer, he was immediately alerted to the latest Stutz find.

"Do you know who bought it?" the annoyed kingpin demanded.

"I'm looking into that right now." The lawyer's voice cracked as his throat tightened. "I should have an answer shortly."

"Let me know when you do. I'll have to send someone down there to investigate in person and see if that's the car I've been looking for all this time." Then, as an afterthought he said, "I think you should be the one to go down. We will need to make the buyer an offer he can't refuse. Find out how much he paid for it. Perhaps we can just buy it for a premium and avoid other complications that might draw unwanted attention to our activities."

Carlo had not been this excited about a Stutz coming on the market since the 1996 find in East Orange, Vermont. A guy by the name of A. K. Miller had a secret car collection that was discovered in old fallen-down barns and lean-to sheds. Millions in gold, silver, and stock certificates found in the owner's home were seized, along with the man's Stutz car collection. Carlo was sure that, at last, he had found Lefty's missing Stutz and his family's missing fortune. It had cost Carlo a small fortune to bribe the police to let his lawyer and his ace mechanic examine the cars before they went up for auction. It turned out that there were no hidden compartments and no journal. And the stock and gold certificates were part of an inheritance that Miller never reported.

CHAPTER SIX

DRIVING BACK TO HIS farm, Miles noticed that his own homestead had fallen into disrepair. His home was in an open field, part of a 1,400-acre farm that successive generations of his family collected over many decades. With the acquisitions of parcels from adjacent landowners who had died, retired or moved away, his family had cobbled together an efficient crop farm.

The main house had a big wraparound porch with white clapboard siding and a red roof. Chips of white paint were peeled back, some flecked off, which made the place look a little dingy. The chimneys on each end of the house had cracks in the mortar and needed to be repointed. On one side of the front porch sat an old wooden swing glider that would comfortably hold four people facing each other as they rocked back and forth. It too could use a fresh coat of paint. The shades of reds on the roof had blended over time with the rust, mutating into a rouge, camouflage-type pattern.

Behind the main farmhouse sat a series of outbuildings, each similarly covered with peeling white paint and matching weathered red roofs. The odd collection of old farm buildings included a chicken coop, machine shop, tobacco barn with stacks of tobacco sticks, as well as a smokehouse and, of course, an old outhouse listing to the right, unused since the farmhouse plumbing had been installed.

It's funny how you see something every day, but your senses get dulled and you don't really take it all in, Miles observed. Seeing the Vogel home in such a state of disrepair heightened his senses. *I really need to get this place painted and spruced up a little bit.*

There weren't piles of rusting equipment in disrepair lying around. He had kept the yard tamed and the weeds pulled, but the flower beds needed new plants and mulch.

Miles was the fifth generation of his family to live on this farm. His ancestor Joseph Thomas West migrated from England to escape a cholera outbreak. Every generation until Miles had added size and scope to the farm. Miles appreciated the hard work, sweat, blood, and tears that were invested in the family enterprise, but he had also wanted to do more than just work the land and grow crops. That was why he worked so hard in school, first to earn his admittance to college, then to obtain his MBA as well as his spot at Morgan Stanley. He thrived at the investment brokerage company, crafting buyouts and facilitating merger negotiations. Miles felt challenged and stimulated and earned millions. He and his wife had an active social life. Along with their friends, they stayed busy helping nonprofits and various charities. It seemed that he had become a poster boy for the American dream. He was high on life, right up to the night his wife was murdered in a botched robbery three years earlier.

At first, he threw himself into his work. However, well-intentioned colleagues and friends and the ever-present reminders in his home, *their* home, ate away at him, sucking the life from everything he did. He became depressed, wry and beleaguered. Every day was a challenge. He decided to take a leave of absence from his investment banking firm and change his venue.

Shortly after he returned home, his parents perished in an airplane crash. That second calamitous event ripped another huge hole in his heart. That additional loss left him without any family connection, which was one of the foundational elements of his life. He was also in the midst of a crisis of faith, having heard no response from God as to why this had to happen to him.

It took him more than two years to settle his father's estate. Some of the land parcels had to be surveyed, and timber stands had to be appraised;

a gas pipeline demanded a right-of-way through a corner of one of the parcels, which further complicated matters. He used all these distractions as excuses to stay on just a little longer and put off going back to his old life.

Since that dreadful point in time, he wandered through life in a haze. For the first time in his life, he didn't have a plan; he just bobbed about, like a ship on the ocean without a rudder. If a neighbor needed help, he would lend a hand, but he didn't have the energy to do much more than what was required to get by.

He had inherited the family farm with a small note, which he immediately paid off. Most of his land was leased out to local farmers. It was a practice his dad had started after stepping away from farming to enjoy traveling with his wife. The leases more than paid the property taxes and kept the fields from becoming overgrown and unruly. He enjoyed seeing the tobacco, soybeans, corn, sorghum, and cotton progress through growth cycles each season.

Miles's mom had cut out pictures of exotic places while they dreamed and planned their worldwide adventure and pinned them to the bulletin board in the kitchen, creating a collage that he still kept mounted on the wall—a memorial tribute to their bucket list. His parents left with a plan to cover one more leg of that dream trip around the world, but a terrorist with a shoe bomb blew their plane out of the sky.

Aside from some meager living expenses, he didn't need to work. Somehow, the basics of housekeeping, a little lawn mowing and some assorted odd jobs now filled his days.

Miles had *always* maintained a vigorous exercise regimen, but after the loss of his family, his life morphed into a slow, plodding and very sedentary routine. He spent most of his time lost in reflections of the past, wondering what might have been, yearning for what could have been and speculating on how differently his life might have turned out if his world had not been so abruptly torn asunder. It wasn't that he had never been tested by adversity before; he had overcome lots of obstacles over the years. He thrived on challenges and was known for his dogmatic persistence. However, these cataclysmic events sent him reeling. All of his dreams and ambitions had been intertwined with his family. He felt, at times, no reason to live.

Many people had advised him to let go of the past and move on. But moving on meant having something to move toward, and Miles just couldn't find the right thing to invigorate him, engage him and reignite his zest for life. Each time he started an endeavor, he found some excuse to let it wither on the vine. Refurbishing the Stutz would provide at least a temporary reprieve from this banality.

CHAPTER SEVEN

MILES FELT EXCITED ABOUT the arrival of his Stutz. It was delivered on a flatbed tilt truck and rolled off the sloped truck bed into the machine shop.

"Can't say as I ever heard of a Stutz," the driver said.

"They're pretty rare," Miles said. "They stopped producing them back in the 1930s."

Miles was already thinking that the disassembly would be the easy part. Putting it back together would be more of a challenge. Replacing parts, especially for rare old cars, could be problematic. Undoubtedly some of the parts would have to be hand forged or custom made. Miles knew someone who could help.

William Carr, better known as "Wic," worked out of his dad's barn. He could fix just about anything. A few years earlier, when Miles needed help with his old Bronco, Wic came to his rescue. At the time the kid was a lanky fifteen-year-old and already an automotive boy wonder. He could weld, grind, create needed parts, and seamlessly patch and replace rusted metal. Rebuilding an engine was child's play for the boy.

Miles had called Wic earlier to see if he could get the kid interested in this project. "I'll be there in a flash," Wic replied without hesitation. Miles never even got the chance to inquire about what he was working on now.

Last time he saw the young man, Wic was restoring an old Farmall tractor, a 1929 Ford Model AA truck, and an old motorcycle all at the same time.

Since the old workshop was a bit dark, Miles pulled out a couple of work lamps and plugged them in, positioning them around the shop. He wanted to be able to take lots of pictures with his digital camera and avoid flash reflections. He worked methodically, capturing every detail of the old car from a variety of vantage points. When he finished with the exterior he moved to the interior, then took photos of the engine compartment and trunk. He raised the car on the lift and started taking snapshots when he noticed a few things that looked very peculiar. He traced several surplus cables and wires back to the firewall in front of the driver. He was just lowering the lift when Wic arrived.

"Wow! This is a beauty," the kid said. "They didn't make too many of these. Never seen one, but I read that in 1927 this was the fastest production car manufactured." He walked around the car, waving a screwdriver around like a pointer.

"Look at the way the frame is slung down in the center of the car. It gave it a much lower center of gravity, which made it much safer and improved the performance."

Miles smiled as he watched the young man push his ball cap back, taking stock of the old car. Wic continued circling the car like a cheetah stalking its prey. Excitedly he pronounced, "We have a couple of options for restoring the old girl. And once we do, you may want to consider showing it in one of the classic car shows. Given its prominence, it might even qualify for the Pebble Beach Concourse de Elegance. We might be able to get it running without doing a significant restoration or a major overhaul. You just never know until you get into it. If that's the case, you could enter it in a class for unrestored cars; people show them pretty much in their original condition."

He poked at a couple of minor spots of rust on the frame, then continued. "Or the other possibility is that we could go to the other extreme and do a complete frame-off restoration, where we take everything apart, repair and replace as necessary in order to bring it back to a pristine original condition. We would remove the trim, glass, interior, hood, trunk, doors, engine bay parts, label all the wires, drain fluids, remove exhaust, engine, transmission, cables and wires, as well as body panels. Then we make repairs as necessary, repaint and start putting it all back together."

Without even pausing he threw out a third option. "You could do both. I've got to tell you, though, I think it would be really cool to enter it in Pebble Beach as an authentic un-refurbished antique. You just don't see something like this every day; it's very unusual for something this old to be in such good shape."

They heard the familiar sound of gravel crunching in the driveway. It was Bramley pulling up in an old beat-up pickup truck.

"Hey, y'all," she said in the finest Southern tradition.

"What brings you out to these parts?" Miles said, smiling.

"Well, I have a couple of days off after the big sale, and I started doing some research on your car last night. I was curious about the old Stutz. I thought I'd come by and share my findings with you."

She was toting a handful of printouts with colorful stick-on labels protruding around the edges like multi-hued flower petals. The stack was bound with a huge binder clip.

Miles turned toward Wic. "Bramley Ann Fairchild, let me introduce you to William Carr."

"Pleased to meet you, ma'am, and call me Wic; most people do."

"I've never heard that nickname before."

"Well my mama put my initials, *W-I-C,* on all my stuff— shirts, coats, books, notebooks and pencils. Before long, everyone at school started calling me Wic, and it just sort of stuck. And I already know what you're going to ask. What does the *I* stand for? Don't laugh; it's Ignatius."

"Come here, you two. I want to show you something," Miles said, raising the car on the lift to expose its underbelly. "Wic, what do you make of these extra cables and wires?"

Wic traced the lines, cables and wires back and forth. Abruptly, he moved out from under the car and stated, "It sorta looks like you've got a rumrunner, but this car is not really configured very well for that purpose."

Miles and Bramley looked at each other, then peered at Wic and said in stereo, "What's a rumrunner?"

Wic explained. "During Prohibition, people would modify cars for bootleggers to ship alcohol. Traditionally, they were set up with secret compartments, and on occasion they would have modifications like some of these to evade the police." He pointed with a screwdriver like he was giving an anatomy lesson.

"You have a device that is attached to this extra oil tank. I am guessing that's to create a smoke screen. You have an extra switch to manually cut the brake lights off. Another switch, that's on this cable, goes to the auxiliary oil tank and feeds into these tubes, which dump liquid out of these spray nozzles behind the back tires. My guess is that this creates an oil slick. Not sure what this one does . . . let's see." He pulled the cable and a bunch of rusty roofing nails dropped out behind the rear fender. "Oh, wow. That would slow down anyone in hot pursuit."

Miles looked at the car. "What in the world?"

Wic was puzzled. "I don't get it; there's not really a lot of room to haul alcohol, so why have all these countermeasures?"

Miles asked Bramley, "Did anyone own the car before the Vogel sisters bought it?"

"We never found any records indicating they purchased it—not to say they didn't. There was a lot of stuff that didn't have a receipt or bill of sale. But that's not unusual in many of these old estates; receipts get lost, sometimes filed and misplaced or even destroyed over the decades." She added, "Nothing they owned appeared to have been stolen. The really odd and expensive things like the collections of silver and watches and jewelry all had receipts."

"I wonder if they could have been related to or affiliated with a gangster?" Miles mused.

"According to the notes we found in their family Bible, Otto and Christianne Vogel immigrated from Germany. They only had two girls, and neither of them ever got married. Otto was the only son of Fredrick Vogel. Doubtful they could have had a relative that was a gangster," Bramley said.

She retrieved her backpack from her car and pulled out her iPad to search the web for clues. "This could take a while. It appears that most of the notable Prohibition and Depression-era gangsters were located in the Midwest. It will take some digging to see if any of these characters ever came east."

"Maybe the car will give us some more clues," Wic said. "I'll check it out."

Under the driver's seat, Wic found the original build sheet—a blue tag created out of heavy card stock with the corresponding numbers of the chassis, engine and other parts. He held it up and announced, "This is a rare and unusual find that confirms the originality and authentic condition of car. You almost never see a build sheet on a car this old."

Underneath the floor lining in the trunk, Miles found a 1928 Illinois license plate. "Well, this could add some credence to the theory of gangsters or bandits coming east. Wait a minute. Not bandits—bank robbers," he exclaimed emphatically. "If the car was not modified for bootleggers, then maybe it was customized for bank robbers."

Bramley shook her head in disagreement. "From what I'm reading, they usually stole a big, fast car, large enough to hold the team that was robbing the bank."

"What about Bonnie and Clyde?" Miles said. She looked at him and just shrugged.

The only other thing they found was a torn scrap of paper that had parts of words printed on it. They could barely make out *Oakley Aut* on one line, and what appeared to be *Divisi* on the second line. Bramley added those to her search terms list.

In fairly short order she said, "Hey, this is interesting. There was a company called Oakley Auto Construction Company and it was located at 2300 West Division Street in Chicago . . . I found it under an article titled 'Dillinger: The Untold Story.' That gives us one more gangster connection. According to this article, Oakley went out of business back in the 1930s."

Wic continued surveying the car inch by inch with his flashlight. After about an hour, he discovered a hidden compartment under a mat covering the floor panel. He was convinced that the floor just didn't look right.

"This has to be an access panel, but I can't see any way to open it."

"What do you see?" inquired Miles.

"Well, you can just barely make out a seam right here; it's almost indistinguishable from the floor. Someone did an excellent job of matching the contours of the floor, but at these spots you can make out the edge pretty clearly. Guess the metal has flexed a bit over time. What I can't see is how it latches."

They all peered at it; he was right. It resembled one of those perfect optical illusions that registered with the brain as normal until the viewer knew what to look for, and then the truth magically appeared.

Wic studied it for another twenty minutes trying to figure out how the latch released.

"Ah ha! I think I found it." He discovered a small hole just large enough to stick a miniature screwdriver into. "Miles, hand me a small standard screwdriver and that little can of lubricant."

First, he sprayed the mechanism liberally with PB B'Laster penetrant, plunging the straw deep into the locking mechanism. Gingerly, he turned slightly left and it didn't budge. Then, with a quarter turn to the right, the latched released with a dull metallic click.

"That is ingenious."

Opening it up, Wic pulled out a small leather bag that must have been well oiled because it was remarkably well preserved. He handed it to Miles, who turned it over in his hand and examined it as he moved to the workbench. Miles opened the leather satchel slowly and removed a small journal and several smaller pouches. When he dumped the contents of the pouches on the worktable, he found that one had been filled with gold coins while the other was filled with diamonds. They each looked at one another, dumbfounded.

Miles laughed. "Most people are waiting for their ship to come in. Whoever heard of waiting for your car to come in?"

"Well, I sure could use a new best friend, if you care to pass me some of those diamonds," Bramley said with a wink. "Looks like you got the deal of the century, Miles."

"I guess I don't have to worry about your restoration budget," Wic chuckled.

Miles looked at them both. "I can't keep this stuff. Most likely it's stolen."

"It looks like 'finders, keepers' to me," Wic said.

"Seriously, let me get a couple of those diamonds. I might be able to track down some information on them," Bramley said. "I have a friend in that line of business. I used her when I worked at Christie's. I would like to get a couple of pictures of those gold coins, too."

"I can't help much on that front, but I can help with the car. It appears that the fluids were drained before it was stored, or at least the gas and water were drained. Which is really good news, because that has helped preserve the inside of the radiator and gas tank, both of which look to be in great shape. I will still need to flush them out, but I think they will be good to go. Normally, they have to be replaced. However, I will need to replace a couple of those lines, belts, and wires that have dry-rotted, but other than that it looks remarkably well preserved. I'll take the spark plug wires with me and make a new set that replicates the original ones. We might be able to try and start it tomorrow!" He took a picture of the wires once he had added labels, then removed them. "I am going to head out to the store before it closes and get a few things. I'll see you tomorrow, first thing." Turning toward Bramley and tipping his hat, he said, "Bramley, it was nice to meet you."

"Hey, Wic, please don't say anything to anyone about the coins and diamonds. I'd rather not attract the wrong kind of attention, if you know what I mean."

"Not a problem, Miles. All I care about anyway is the restoration. This is gonna be fun."

Miles lowered the car and said, "Well, I think I will at least get this layer of dust off of her."

Bramley rolled up her sleeves and pitched right in, grabbing some of the extra rags from the bin where they were stored. While they worked, she tossed out tidbits of information she gleaned from her internet research. They spent the rest of the day scrubbing, rubbing, and dusting off each piece of the old car, cleaning the windows, mirrors, chrome and headlamps until they sparkled again. The leather started to come back to life after generous amounts of conditioner was carefully kneaded into every square inch that was exposed. He had to admit that the car was starting to look pretty good in its original state.

Bramley also looked at it with a growing appreciation. "You have quite the barn find. I have to say that this is turning out to be a real catch, a true hidden gem." She reflected on her remark. "Ah, no pun intended. She's quite the beauty," Bramley remarked as she rubbed one last spot.

Miles stood behind her and gazed at her silhouette. "Yes indeed. I really appreciate all your research, as well as your elbow grease." Tentatively he asked, "To show my appreciation, may I take you to dinner?"

She beamed. "I would love that, but I can't go this evening. I need to check in on my mom. I have a new caregiver today and she doesn't know the ropes. Can I get a rain check?" she asked.

"Absolutely!"

Around five thirty in the evening, Miles decided it was time to take a break and grab a bite to eat. He picked up the old leather pouch with all of its mysterious contents replaced, and then headed to the house. While his dinner was in the microwave, he made copies of a couple of the journal pages on his home office printer—the journal seemed to be written in code. He stashed the contents of their find in his gun safe. He took the copies of the coded pages from the journal, grabbed his microwaved lasagna, a dinner roll and a glass of Chianti and headed out to the glider on his front porch to eat.

Just as he was finishing up, a man in a generic mid-sized car pulled into the driveway. As the car rolled to a stop in front of the porch, Miles thought he saw a rental car sticker affixed to the front windshield. A frumpy, wiry little man in a gray pinstriped three-piece suit slowly emerged from the car carrying a leather briefcase.

"Good evening," he said with a bit of a Brooklyn accent. "I am looking for Mr. West."

Miles looked over the man suspiciously. "I'm Miles West. How can I help you?"

"I'm Herbert Howe, glad to meet you." They shook hands and the lawyer presented his business card. "I understand you purchased a car at auction the other day—a Stutz, I believe."

Miles just stared at him with the stone-cold expression of a sphinx.

"Well," the man said uncomfortably as he tugged at his collar with one finger, "I have a really good proposition for you."

Miles responded flatly, "Not interested."

"But you haven't even heard what I'm offering. I have a client that is very interested in this car and he would like to offer you $100,000 in cash for the Stutz."

Howe opened his briefcase to show Miles its contents. Stacked inside were ten stacks of crisp new $100 bills bound with paper bank wrappers; *$10,000* was printed on each of them.

Miles raised his eyebrows. "Is that so?"

"We know you paid $66,000 for it, so we thought this would be a fair premium."

"Who's your client?"

Howe replied, "I really can't say; attorney-client confidentiality. Needless to say, my client values his privacy."

Miles's mind was firing. "You were making that phone bid the other day, weren't you?"

"Ah yes, that was me."

"Well," Miles retorted, "you should have bid for it then. The auction's over, and I am not selling."

"What if my client paid you twice what you paid for it?"

"Why are you so interested in this car? There are other Stutzes that could surely be bought for that kind of money."

"Sentimental reasons," Howe said. "My client thinks this car was owned by a family member at one time. May I see the car? Maybe then I could tell if it is the car he's trying to find."

Miles stood erect with his arms crossed. "Just how could you tell whether it's 'the one' he's hoping to find?"

Beads of perspiration rolled off of Howe's forehead as he grabbed his handkerchief.

"Since you don't have any good way to identify it, I guess there is no reason to go look at it. Even if it is the car your client wants, it's not for sale. So, you can be on your way," Miles said tersely. "I'm sorry for your inconvenience."

Howe snapped his briefcase closed and stomped off like a petulant child. He slammed the door and spun his tires, throwing up gravel and dust.

Miles flashed back to his days as an investment banker and one of the deals that he passed over because the opposing counsel was cagey, aloof and devious. Howe gave that same vibe.

On the way back to the private airstrip, the hapless, miserable lawyer called Carlo Bello and left a short message. He climbed aboard eager to get one or two of those miniature bottles of vodka to settle his nerves. Carlo was going to be livid. *Why in the world did I go to work for Bello in the first place?*

At the time, Howe was going through his second divorce and was almost broke. The devil Bello had offered a large cash retainer. There was no going back. If Bello didn't get him, his ulcers or a heart attack would surely take him. *Where is the flight attendant with my drink?*

Just after the plane touched down in New York, Howe's phone rang.

"So, what happened?" asked Carlo.

"He turned down the $100,000 cash offer for the car. I doubled the price, but he wouldn't budge. I asked to at least see the car, but he wouldn't even let me get a look at it."

"I guess I will have to make other arrangements," the mobster replied in his cold, soulless voice. "You're worthless."

Carlo knew who to use—a fixer named Rocky who ran a salvage yard and chop shop. Rocky had the equipment to haul the car back to his warehouse and owed Carlo a few favors.

"Matteo," Carlo called to his driver. "I need to pay someone a visit. Bring the car around."

Carlo climbed into his customized stretch Cadillac SUV. It was outfitted with armor plating and bullet-resistant glass as well as the latest electronic gear to interfere with surveillance equipment. He often used it as his mobile office to make sure his conversations could not be overheard. The sleek black SUV was not only elongated but also had a slightly raised roof, making the interior feel very spacious despite the televisions, mini refrigerator and wet bar incorporated into the luxurious leather interior.

The SUV turned into the cavernous driveway bordered on both sides by chain-link fences covered with dark green privacy cloth and topped with concertino wire. As the big, black vehicle rolled to a stop in front of the salvage yard office, Rocky emerged. Carlo rolled down his window.

"Rocky, get in."

Rocky climbed in and wiped his dirty hands on his pants, then grabbed a rag in his pocket and tried in vain to clean the smudges of grease.

"Rocky, 'ow you doing?"

"Ah, we're fine, Mr. Bello. I hope you are too. What brings you to my little corner of New Yawk?"

Carlo grabbed a piece of paper and handed it to him. "I want you to go down to North Carolina and get this car for me and bring it back here. The owner has refused my most generous offer, so he will just have to settle for the insurance coverage. Do whatever you need to do to get the car back to my warehouse at the docks."

"Uh, when do you need this done? I can send Sal to get it, but my lawyer says I gotta appear in court tomorrow or they're gonna put me away."

"For what this time?" Carlo inquired.

"One of the vehicles I salvaged had some parts that were identified from another vehicle that was stolen. Can you believe it? Someone selling me a vehicle with stolen parts?" Rocky laughed.

"Okay, send Sal, but tell him not to come back without the Stutz. I don't care what he has to do to get the car back here, but whatever he does, he don't come back without the car. *Capisci?*"

CHAPTER EIGHT

BRAMLEY HAD CONTACTED HER friend Jane Smithson, a renowned gemologist who did estate appraisals and consulted with auction houses. Bramley felt confident that with over three decades of experience in the diamond trade, there was no one better to help her assess these diamonds. She packaged them up and sent them via courier to Smithson's New York–based consulting practice.

Bramley felt reinvigorated. She was in her zone once again. She absolutely loved doing antiquities research for the auction companies for whom she worked, but what got her really excited was a research assignment on an antique piece that didn't have any background information. It was detective work without blood, challenging and often surprising.

She smiled and hummed a little tune as she contemplated this self-nominated assignment. Then she thought about Miles.

"Admit it—the other reason you're really doing it is that you get to spend time with him," she said aloud. She hadn't dated anyone seriously since her fiancé left her at the altar. *Maybe it's time to get back in the game.*

Before she went to sleep, Bramley called her mother's evening caregiver, Ms. Elsee.

"Miss Bramley, your momma is doing fine. She fell off to sleep a while ago, just after you left. I meant to tell ya earlier, the other caregivers said she wouldn't eat much today either, just wanted to rest."

Somedays her mother's dementia was so bad that her mom couldn't put two words together into a single coherent thought. She might blurt out a string of words, but none of them could be connected in any sensible fashion. At those times she would be very irritable and lash out at everyone, hitting, kicking and screaming. Bramley remembered the first time that her mom hit her, she was shocked and flabbergasted. This was not the same loving, caring person that had nurtured her through her childhood, cheered her on through each of her sporting events and comforted her when she got hurt. This demented person was some alien imposter.

The tipping point finally came when her mom started leaving the stovetop burners and toaster oven on and forgetting to eat. Bramley's stress level quickly ratcheted up, and she knew she needed help. Her work became her only respite. Bramley was grateful that her father had the foresight to set up a health trust for his wife. She wished her dad was still alive; he could always make her mom smile. Bramley hadn't smiled enough herself lately.

Perhaps that would change with Miles West and the intriguing Stutz that brought them together.

Bramley had performed a cursory web search to dig up a little information on the Stutz. Of the thousands of hits the web search yielded, only a few provided information about the particular automobile that Miles had purchased, but there were loads of articles about the Stutz auto company.

Bramley awoke at two in the morning churning with ideas for researching the history of the Stutz. She knew from experience that the best thing to do was to get up and process her thoughts; otherwise, she would never get back to sleep.

Finding out who initially purchased the car would be difficult because vehicles often were not registered back in the early twentieth century. The Stutz Motor Car Company went out of business in 1935. She mulled over the idea of trying to see if any of the executives or key personnel at the company were still alive and might have retained ledgers or something of significance. She concluded that the best path was to search for news stories about robbers or bootleggers known to have driven Stutzes.

Another way to get ownership information might be to go back through the remaining boxes of Vogel estate records, paperwork and memorabilia.

She reviewed the backgrounds of famous gangsters and ran across an article about Al Capon's 1928 Cadillac and the modifications that had been made on the vehicle, which included armor plating, special gunports and one-inch-thick glass. She thought it might be fruitful to dig into the history of the companies that made modifications to the cars used by various iconic felons.

She knew Miles's car had been manufactured in 1927. Additionally, it had been an expensive automobile at the time, so the original buyer—villain or otherwise—had to be pretty successful. She also discovered where the car was produced and where it was stored. The odometer only had 100 miles on it. Since those geographical locations were more than 100 miles apart, it must have been shipped by rail.

Bramley researched gangsters of the 1920s, developing quite a list of suspects. After a couple of hours, three had jumped to the top of the list: "Fuzzy" Dean, Dan "Happy" McGraw, and Maximilian "Lefty" Webber.

About seven that morning, Jane called Bramley.

"I hope I didn't wake you up."

Bramley replied breathlessly. "No, I just got back from my morning jog. Gotta tell you, Central Park is much more conducive to jogging than rural North Carolina."

"So, Bramley, what's the story? Where did you find these diamonds?"

"They were found hidden in one of our auction items. I can't really go into detail yet. The buyer asked for confidentiality. Did you find out anything interesting?"

"Yes, they were a bit of a surprise. They are a combination of old European-cut diamonds and one old mine-cut diamond. We don't run across these particular types of diamonds very much anymore. The European-cuts were essentially stopped by the early 1920s, while the old mines-cuts go all the way back to the 1800s. Old European-cut diamonds can be more valuable than modern diamonds—first because they are rare, and second because they generally have a higher carat weight compared to modern diamonds. However, as always, it still depends heavily on the quality of the diamond."

"What does the quality look like based on the samples I sent you?" Bramley asked.

"I would have to say those are a very high quality. They are just slightly darker, which suggests they came from either Brazil or possibly Venezuela. All the white stones we have today come from South Africa, Angola, Botswana, or Sierra Leone. None of them were producing diamonds at that time. The one mine-cut diamond is not as valuable."

"What's the difference?"

"Old mine-cuts were produced much earlier, the tools available at the time were much less sophisticated, and a lot of it was done by eye, so there were significantly more imperfections. They tend to be either square or rectangular, with corners that were rounded. European-cuts were more rounded, although somewhat lumpy or imperfectly round. Also, the cutlet, the point at the bottom of the stone, was usually large and flat. Today they are almost always pointed."

"What's the bottom line?"

"Of the four diamonds you sent, the three old-world cuts are worth from $9,500 for the 1.75-carat diamond to $23,500 for the 3-carat diamond; the other one is about 2.5 carats. The old mine-cut diamond is only worth a couple thousand."

Bramley whistled. "Wow, that's a lot more than I thought. Is there anything else you can tell me about them?"

"Not really. While many of today's diamonds are catalogued or marked, that practice just didn't exist at the time these diamonds were produced. Sorry I can't be of more assistance."

CHAPTER NINE

MILES SCROLLED THROUGH HIS iPhone address book while sipping his second cup of decaf. He was looking for his old college buddy Trevor Martin, who had gone on to Washington and Lee University for law school before moving to New York City. Trevor was an extrovert who seemed to know someone everywhere he went.

Miles speed-dialed his old friend.

"If it isn't Miles West!"

"It's me," responded Miles.

"Miles, you back in New York?"

"No, I'm still in down in Carolina."

"Well, you need to get back up here; it's just not the same without you!"

Miles smiled, he was suddenly nostalgic for the old days with "Mr. T," as everyone used to call Trevor.

"Hey, I've got a quick question for you. I bought an antique car, and the next thing I know, this lawyer from New York is on my doorstep with a suitcase full of cash offering me more than double what I paid. Said he was buying it for a client. The guy's name is Herbert Howe. I was wondering if you knew anything about him."

Trevor thought for a minute. "No, I can't say that name rings a bell. But I can ask around if you want me to."

"That would be great. But keep it very low-key. I have an uneasy feeling about this guy. I think he is bad news, and I'm concerned his client may not be what you call a law-abiding citizen."

"I can make discreet inquiries and see what I find. What have you gotten yourself into?"

"I'm not sure, but it's definitely mysterious and a lot more perplexing than I bargained for when I acquired an antique car in need of a little restoration."

Trevor joked, "I guess you fell for the used car salesman's oldest ploy, believing you were buying a car belonging to a little old lady who never drove it, but when you get it you find you've been sold something altogether different instead."

"You may not be far from the truth," replied Miles, thinking about the reclusive Vogel sisters and his car sitting on blocks.

"Gotta run, Miles, but I'll call you when I have some information. Keep your head down man. This car deal sounds sketchy."

Miles wandered to the kitchen and spotted Wic's truck coming down the driveway. It was only seven thirty. Wic was up and going early this morning. Miles grabbed an extra cup, filled it with coffee, then headed out the door toward the machine shop.

"Good morning!" hollered Wic as he bounded out of his truck, circled to the back and dropped the tailgate. He pulled out a couple of plastic crates that had coolant, oil, a flush kit and a bunch of spark plug wires. Miles figured that there were probably another half dozen things that weren't visible packed in there as well.

"Good morning, Wic. Coffee?"

"Thanks, Miles, but I'm already wired. On my second Red Bull. Wanted to get an early start. We're gonna get the old girl running today! Hey, man. The Stutz is lookin' pretty sweet; you got a lot of clean up done yesterday after I left."

"It wasn't too bad. At any rate, I think you're right. At first, I wanted to take it all apart, repaint it and make it look like it was when it was brand new. But after getting all the dust and dirt off, I think I have decided I actually like the old-patina look." Miles inquired, "Is there some way to seal it so it won't rust?"

"For sure," Wic grinned, "but I'll need to take it over to my place and put it in the paint booth to do that procedure. I went ahead and brought replacement spark plugs, even though the original ones don't look too bad after I cleaned them. Give me a couple hours to see what we can do to get it running."

Miles left him to it, heading back to his home office to see if he could make heads or tails out of any of the coded journal pages.

After spending a little more time examining the journal for additional clues, Miles scoured the internet, consulting notes and web searches on cryptography. Looking down at his watch, he realized that he had been at the task for a couple of hours and had made scant progress. He was so immersed in his efforts that he didn't notice another vehicle in his driveway until the car door shut with a *thunk*.

Bramley adjusted her backpack on her shoulder and ambled toward the house. She scanned the front porch, absorbing and cataloging every detail like she always did, anywhere she went. She didn't have a photographic memory, but she trained herself to notice details. Over the years she had honed the ability to capture a moment, taking it all in; all the sights, sounds, smells merged into a mental snapshot that she could revisit at any time. It was one of the things that made her really good at her job. She noted the color of the porch floor, various images of the house and swing, the creak in the wooden step, the smell of fresh-cut grass, the muted sounds from the workshop, and the classic shape of the balusters.

Miles pushed the screen door open, the spring groaning as it stretched, then ushered her in. "Would you like some coffee? I was just going to brew a fresh pot."

"That would be great," she replied. "I found several, shall we say, nefarious individuals who could have potentially owned your car."

Miles smiled. "I take it you're not into pleasantries."

She looked up at him with an odd expression. Then her eyes widened as she landed in the moment.

"Well, I have been thinking about the mystery surrounding your car last night and most of this morning, I guess sometimes I get a little caught up in my research. Sorry about that. Nice weather we're having. Very *pleasant*, wouldn't you agree?"

"Okay," he responded slowly. "So, what did you discover?"

"I narrowed the time frame of my search to the 1920s, given the manufacture date of the Stutz and the mysterious purchases by the Vogels of watches and silver. My working hypothesis is that we are looking for a bank robber who was using either one or both of the Vogel sisters to launder his stolen money. I further assumed that since no purchases were made after 1928, our bandit was either killed or captured. This narrowed the list of outlaws considerably.

"We have about a half dozen candidates on my short list. However, one nefarious fellow in particular rises to the top of our little docket. His name is Maximilian 'Lefty' Webber. The thing that makes him so interesting is that he was arrested in Winston-Salem on April 15, 1927, along with two other men at the Robert E. Lee Hotel. When Webber was captured he pretended to be someone named Robert Freeman from New York. He and a couple of his friends got into a brawl at a local pool hall. They took off in a hurry after one of the old boys broke a bottle over a local's head. Then someone got tossed through a window, which attracted the attention of an off-duty policeman. According to this account, several other things were busted up pretty bad.

"When they were finally apprehended, at the Lee Hotel, one of the trio was positively identified as the notorious bank robber 'Wild Bill' Wilder. A big-shot attorney from Chicago hired the local law firm of Smith and Wellington to represent all three men at a hearing. The lawyers posted bond for all three men. Freeman, who was later identified as Lefty, skipped town and was never seen again in Winston-Salem."

"That is interesting," Miles said as he leafed through her notes and listened to her findings.

"I found out that Lefty was killed three years later on December 5, 1930, after robbing a bank in Decatur, Illinois. That also fits pretty well with the time frame in my hypothesis."

Miles started thinking out loud. "The paper we found in the car referenced a garage in Chicago, and you also have a lawyer from Chicago arranging for representation for the guy arrested in North Carolina . . . Interesting." Miles turned to Bramley and asked, "You said this Lefty guy, or his alias, was a notorious bank robber arrested in Winston-Salem. Did he rob a bank there, or anywhere else in North Carolina?"

"Well, that was another rather odd thing. I couldn't find any bank robberies reported around that time anywhere in the state. The only reason he was picked up in Winston-Salem was that two deputies spotted a car with Ohio plates suspiciously parked on a road near the pool hall. The two guys in the car took off and cops found the car abandoned at a local garage in town. The garage attendant told the deputies that the men driving the vehicle were staying at the Lee Hotel, which is where all three men were arrested for their part in the brawl. However, no one ever determined what else they might have been involved in."

Bramley shuffled her notes and resumed. "There is not a huge amount of information on Webber. However, we do have his basic background and a brief biographical sketch. Webber was a very methodical bank robber who mostly worked in the Midwest. His technique was to case a job, plan it out in meticulous detail, and pull off the heist with three or four other men. Typically, they would steal a sedan with a big engine for a speedy getaway. Most of the time he stocked them with roofing nails and extra gas cans. While no one has been able to identify all the robberies Webber was involved in, he was thought to have stolen more than two million dollars from various banks. You may not be surprised, but I estimated that given historical inflation rates, that haul would total about fifteen to twenty-five million today!"

Miles whistled. "That's not chump change."

"That kind of money would definitely have been able to be converted into diamonds and gold as well as jewelry, watches and silver. Speaking of diamonds . . ." Bramley told Miles about the type and value of the diamonds her friend appraised.

"The current value of those four diamonds is around $50,000. How many of them did you have in that pouch?"

Miles scratched his head. "I didn't count them, but I would guess between fifty to sixty diamonds." He did some quick math in his head and whistled. "That would make that little pouch worth between half and three quarters of a million dollars."

Bramley pointed out, "That doesn't even include the value of the gold coins that were there too. Some of those are extremely rare and worth much more than either their face value or their gold value." She mused, "I wonder what happened to the rest of it."

"Well, I suspect that this coded journal may give some indications about its disposition. But so far, I have not been able to make heads or tails out of it." Switching subjects, he inquired, "Did you discover anything else noteworthy about Webber?"

She paused to consult her notes. "He was in the German Army but was forced out of his regiment when he was caught stealing supplies and then reselling them. He then immigrated to the United States just before World War I, and he was apprehended once for a failed bank robbery and served time in a Missouri prison. Other than that, background information on him is pretty sparse."

"He spoke German? Maybe the codes and ciphers in his journal are based on German rather than the English language," Miles said. "I would also like to see if we can cross-reference any of the dates of the silver and watch purchases. We need to catalogue the dates and locations where those items were purchased as well as each item's original cost. Perhaps that information can be used as reference points and assist my efforts to decode the journal. Can you get me copies of those purchase records?"

"Sure. Those records were digitized so we could include them in the sales brochures next to the pictures of each item being auctioned. It's an extra perk for buyers to get the original sales receipt. I have a PDF copy of the sales catalogue on my iPad; I'll send it to your email."

Miles wondered if there was other vital information that the Vogel sisters might have retained. "What happened to all of the old pictures, letters, receipts and papers that came out of the Vogel house?"

"I thought about that too and made a note to follow up on it." Bramley started pacing around the room, thinking over the various activities involved in cleaning up the affairs of an estate when no descendants or heirs existed. She started reciting the steps involved.

"We do an inventory of all the things that are not sold at the auction and then we generally parse some of them out on consignment. We will go through old papers, and if there is anything of historical significance, those things we will often donate to one of the historical museums or societies. You would be amazed at some of the historical finds we run across in stacks of old papers. At any rate, there may be a couple of boxes of things still at the house, but most of it was taken back to the auction company and is being sorted in the warehouse."

"Can we go look through it?"

"Sure, but what will we be hoping to find?"

Miles started to gather up his notes and papers, stuffing various items in his own backpack.

"Well, I'm not sure. Maybe a picture of one of the sisters with our mysterious bandit, perhaps some letters, telegrams or other communication. It could be some other artifact or clue linking our find to that era. We need to look for anything that may validate some of these assumptions we're making or perhaps even connect some of these people."

A short time later, they pulled up to the offices of the Long Auction Company. The business was located in an old tobacco warehouse, once the home office of the Star Tobacco Company, which was bought out as the tobacco industry consolidated. The brick facade had the remnants of a faded sign—translucent white letters that read *Star Warehouse* on a muted black background. To the left of the entrance was a massive door that was clearly designed to admit large trucks and trailers. The main pedestrian entrance was through a much smaller door leading to office space. This door appeared to have been recently replaced, as its new finish contrasted with the dulled paint covering the rest of the trim work.

They wound through the maze of office cubicles toward the center of the warehouse.

Trucks with tents and trailers were parked at the far end of the building. Massive steel shelves adorned half of the warehouse between the offices and the interior parking spaces on the other end. The translucent skylights allowed a significant amount of ambient light to shower onto a series of rectangular tables arranged in two semi-circles around one large, round work table. On cloudy days they were supplemented with the big round halogen lights hanging on the rafters between the skylights, providing even more illumination to the workspace.

"We generally take the boxes and unload them onto this large central table. Then we will sort out the stuff and stack it in piles on these other tables. For example, we might put all the pictures that might be of interest to a museum in one pile, while historical memorabilia like this San Francisco World's Fair brochure would be gathered in another stack. We have tried to presort some of the boxes based on content, so that table has boxes with mostly photographs, while the table next to it is full of boxes with books. Files with financial records and letters are on the middle table."

Miles looked toward the dumpster.

"That is a recycle bin. It's mostly full of *National Geographic* magazines," Bramley said. "You wouldn't believe the number of these magazines we find when we do estate sales."

Miles walked to the table with the boxes of pictures and grabbed one at random. "Let's start sorting and see if we can find things from the 1920s that might provide some clues. If it's something questionable, include it. We can always toss it back on a second sorting."

Bramley grabbed a box of memorabilia and dumped the contents on the table and started sifting through dusty layers of the sort of history that every family accumulated in their attic and storage spaces. She thought about her own full closets and made a mental note to have a spring-cleaning purge. The items smelled musty as sunrays illuminated particles of dust floating in the air.

After several hours of sorting, they had found a couple of pictures and some memorabilia that seemed relevant. Several of the pictures appeared to have been taken in the cities where the watches and silver were purchased. Miles was interested in one picture in particular and studied it closely.

"Does this look like either one of the Vogel sisters? There is some guy standing with her in front of this building in San Francisco. I wonder if this could be our mystery man."

"Here, let me compare it to the images I saved from the internet search of the known felons on our short list." Bramley pulled up the pictures. "Take a look at this! Tell me what you think," she said excitedly.

Miles studied the faded photograph. "I think there is a pretty strong resemblance here. What did you find out about this character?"

"That's Lefty Webber, one of the three notorious bank robbers at the top of my short list. He was known for doing everything left-handed. I think he was the guy arrested in Winston-Salem using an alias, the one the Chicago lawyers arranged to get out on bail."

"So, we have a possible Chicago-connected bank robber linked to the Vogel sisters," Miles said.

"Looks that way, doesn't it?" said Bramley, who was pleased with herself.

Miles leafed through the pile of memorabilia and grabbed a telegram originating from San Francisco and posted to the other Vogel sister. Holding it up he exclaimed, "This gives us a date and general time frame for this trip and picture. That might be another useful data point for decoding the journal. We need to dig a little more and see if we can find any other pieces of information that may provide additional dates."

"Let me pull up the receipts for the silver sets we auctioned. Here we go. Well, what do you know? Look at this one, Miles; it was purchased just two days before the telegram."

"Indeed, it appears that she was laundering his robbery proceeds by purchasing silver, gold and probably diamonds too. The other thing that might be useful would be to plot the dates and locations on a map and see if that geographical view might provide any additional clues." He found a couple of rail passes and took snapshots of them with his iPhone. They didn't have specific dates on them, but they did at least provide date ranges.

"I wonder if she knew or was an unwitting accomplice?" Bramley said. "We don't have anything that really implicates her in this scheme."

"You mean aside from the fact that she and her sister had twelve sets of silver and 120 expensive watches, as well as the fact they were storing a car with hidden diamonds and rare coins," Miles responded.

Bramley slowly turned and looked up at Miles while flipping over another brochure.

"I'll concede that point, but they or she never did anything with it. Perhaps she was waiting for him to come back. Or maybe they were supposed to meet but she never found out what happened to him. She might have known him only under the alias of an entirely different man."

They methodically captured images of all the scraps of information they had compiled and collected it into a banker file box. "I will save this stuff for a while, just in case we need to reference it again," Bramley said. "We can stash it in my office cubical on our way out."

Both were lost in their own thoughts as they headed back to Miles's farm. His phone chirped. It was Wic.

"We're just turning onto the old mill road and should be there in less than five minutes."

Wic was pleased with his efforts. He worked to clean the grease and grime off of his hands with some Orange Goop and old rags. It took longer than he had expected to flush out the cooling system and replace the dry-rotted hoses. Now, at last, he had the old car running like a top. It was surprisingly quiet as it idled in the cavernous garage, once again ready to hit the road after its ninety-year slumber. He climbed in and put it into gear and slowly backed it out of the old machine shop. Just as he was turning it around, he saw Miles and Bramley coming down the driveway.

"He got the old girl running!" Miles said with excitement. Bramley leaned forward in her seat to get a better view.

"It's a beautiful old car," she remarked.

Miles agreed, "They just don't make them like that anymore."

As he hopped out of the truck, he turned to Wic and said, "You are a miracle worker. She sounds great!"

Wic beamed with pride. "You can take her for a spin, but I wouldn't go far or fast. We need to get those tires replaced. I ordered a new set, but they won't get here until next week. Also, I replaced all the fluids and brought some fuel that doesn't have any ethanol. That mixed stuff just eats up the old lines in these cars and creates all sorts of problems. There are only a couple of places around here where we can still get it. I'll send you a list."

Miles patted Wic on the shoulder. "Why don't you take it for the first spin?"

"You don't have to ask me twice." Wic put it into first gear and was puttering down the old farm road in no time flat, swinging left, then right as he tested the steering.

"He sure loves what he does."

Bramley agreed. "You would have thought you just gave him the best Christmas present ever."

Bramley's face was bathed in a soft glow from the streaks of sun showering down through a break in the clouds. Her amber eyes looked like liquid pools of honey. She was radiant and energized as her eyes darted back and forth tracking the progress of the Stutz making its way down the driveway. Miles was happy to have her company. He was tired of being alone.

When Wic returned, Miles turned to Bramley. "Would you like to go for a ride?"

"Of course I would!" She opened the door, and reverently placed her hand on the seat as she slipped in. She felt the coarse texture of the reconditioned leather seat, while her eye caught the gleaming chrome as she gently pulled the passenger door closed.

"It's like stepping back in time," she uttered softly. She closed her eyes and imagined Lefty Webber behind the wheel.

"You're not getting a sudden urge to rob a bank, are you?" Miles joked.

"I was just envisioning Lefty and his dame, driving down some dusty road."

They reached the end of the road and slowly turned around. On their return Miles declared, "This has been a full day. How would you like to go out and grab a bite to eat?"

"I'm famished. I just realized we didn't take a break for lunch . . . Actually, that happens quite often when I get caught up in one of my research projects. I just forget to eat. What did you have in mind?"

"Let's go over to Winston-Salem. There's this great restaurant in an old house, a very charming place with both indoor and outdoor seating and great food."

CHAPTER TEN

BRAMLEY SOAKED IN THE warm ambiance of the restaurant. "Looking at this menu reminds me of the one thing I really miss about New York City—all the great restaurants," she said to Miles.

"I know what you mean. There was such a diverse array of restaurants, you could try something different every night of the year. Just reading about that pan roasted curried grouper with grilled eggplant, jasmine rice, curried tomato and mint chutney is making my mouth water."

Miles handed the bread basket to Bramley. "Shall we *roll* ahead with dinner?"

Without missing a beat, she grabbed one, held it like a microphone and replied in song.

"Oh, don't go bacon my heart!"

They both broke into wide smiles with barely subdued chuckles. Miles was surprised; most people thought his sense of humor was just a bit too corny, but she just went with it. Her easy-going charm and wit made him more comfortable with her than he had been with anyone for a long time. It was nice to not be on guard for a change.

"I understand you moved back to take care of your mom. How's she doing?"

Bramley said, "She has her good days and her bad days; that's just how it goes as the dementia progresses. She can't do much for herself anymore and that's frustrating for her, so she sometimes lashes out. I noticed the onset of the dementia a few years ago, and for a while she was able to live on her own. For a short time it was fine. I had people deliver food to her. When she left the stove on, I had to draw the line. Then, finally, I just had to move back, because trying to juggle caregiving at a distance was not working. But now I have a great group of people to help me out. Honestly, the other thing that helps is my work. It has been a great diversion and I hate to admit it, but it's also therapeutic. Do you know what I mean?"

"I think I do."

"I know she wouldn't want me to give up my life for her, but I want to take care of her and make sure she is as comfortable as possible."

"That's very admirable and quite a selfless commitment, Bramley."

"It doesn't leave time for much else, but it's important to me. We talked about looking at retirement communities after Dad died. She remained pretty adamant that she didn't want to move to a retirement home. She just wanted to be in her own home. She has always been a private person, very attached to her home. At any rate, I wanted to honor that request."

"I lost both my parents at the same time in a plane crash," Miles said. "That seemed pretty tough at the time, but I can't imagine the pain and difficulty of losing someone through such a long, slow decline."

"Well, it's an emotional roller coaster, that's for sure. I wish you could have known her in her prime. She was just so loving and caring. I don't think she ever said a cross word to anyone. She had a quiet grace, style and sophistication. My dad always bragged that he married way up."

"She sounds a bit like you."

Bramley blushed. "Oh, I'm not that soft spoken. On that trait, I admit I take after my dad."

"With your appreciation for antiques, art, and fine dining, I'd say you've got sophisticated taste, and you definitely have style."

She blushed again, cocked one eyebrow and just replied, "Thank you. For a farmer you seem pretty sophisticated yourself."

"I have to admit I am not much of a farmer anymore. I lease all the land out to neighboring farmers. Honestly, I had my fill of it growing up. Until a few years ago, I worked on Wall Street as an investment banker. I really liked taking all of the disparate pieces of information for a merger or acquisition, then figuring out how to put together a successful deal. Often, we had to structure deals and make them work in a very short period, so we all worked together in an environment of loosely organized, high-stress chaos."

"I can't see you getting stressed about anything."

"Well, that's the thing. I didn't get wound up like everyone else—almost the opposite. The more frantic the situation, the more centered I would become. It helped me see what everyone else was overlooking and focus on the few key things that were most important. I liked the challenge of solving problems. While all the deals had similarities, each of them was also very different, so you always had something flying in from left field."

"Speaking of challenges, your Stutz looks like it's turning out to have one of those bizarre twists, as it came with a rather, shall we say, *unique* payload."

"Yes, it's definitely not what I expected. I thought it would be a real challenge to restore it and get it running. Wic made short work of that part. Although, at some point, I may want to do an entire frame-off restoration. What I didn't expect was to get a mystery thrown in as part of the deal." He took a sip of his pinot noir. "Now it gets even more interesting. Some wiry, high-priced New York lawyer with a Brooklyn accent paid me a visit last evening and tried to buy it for $100,000 in cash."

"I take it you are not going to sell."

"No, but I will wager that whoever he represents is trying to find what was hidden in that Stutz. When I turned him down, he raised the offer to twice what I paid for it, which I also refused. Maybe the guy who wants it knows about the diamonds and coins. Or maybe it's the journal."

Bramley rubbed her chin. "Sounds like the same guy who got into an argument with one of our phone-auction representatives. He claimed he wasn't finished bidding, but we had it recorded, and he couldn't refute it when it was replayed, although he tried to blame it on a response to his secretary's inquiry. He was very upset."

"It was the same guy, a lawyer named Herbert Howe," Miles confirmed. "I called a buddy who is a lawyer back in the Big Apple to ask around and see if he can find out who he represents. I suspect his client could be on the unsavory side. I don't want to be an alarmist, but I am concerned this could get unfriendly before all the dust settles. I appreciate all the help you—"

"Wait just a minute, buster. You're not going to sort through all this stuff and solve this mystery without me! Besides, you might need me to protect you." Bramley lifted a Walther PPK pistol from her purse, showing only the grip. "I know how to take care of myself and I am pretty darn proficient with this thing too."

Miles couldn't have been more surprised if the Publishers Clearing House people had just popped out from behind the corner. "Look," he explained, "it's just that I don't want anything to happen to you." His voice cracked.

"Miles, there are no guarantees in life. I could always get hit by the proverbial bus." She saw him wince. "I love to live every day to the fullest. I try not to take any of them for granted. After September 11th, some people decided not to fly; that wasn't me. I was on a plane the next week. Granted, I was a bit uneasy being on a plane with so few passengers, and I admit I was checking out every passenger that got on that plane with me. But I decided back then I was never going to let anyone make me afraid to go about my life. I don't take lots of risks and don't try to put myself in bad situations."

Miles saw the resolve on her face and a glint in her eyes. Knowing he was not going to dissuade her, he said, "Glad to have you covering my six."

She raised her wine glass, clinked his and said, "Cheers! Here's to a great adventure!"

CHAPTER ELEVEN

SAL ROLLED UP TO the edge of Miles's farm with a flatbed car hauler. He had been sent on these types of retrieval projects before and knew they could get dicey quick, so he decided to do a little recon first. He pulled out his binoculars and scanned all the buildings but didn't see any activity. In his experience, that did not necessarily mean that no one was around.

Since he was as big as a refrigerator, no one usually messed with Sal. He could just glare at people and they'd go in the other direction. From his scarred face and broken nose, anyone could tell he did not mind getting into fights.

He put down his binoculars and reached across the seat for his most recent purchase. It was a miniature drone; he had blacked out all the lights on the thing. For kicks, he and one of his associates would race them around the salvage yard. The little machine quickly rose to 400 feet and hovered in one spot as he fixed on his target location. In the next instant he had the thing zipping over the fields, then stopping above the collection of buildings on the farm. He turned the lens toward the house and zoomed in. No one appeared to be home.

Sal quickly retrieved his drone and returned it to the box, then drove down the gravel road toward the farmhouse and its collection of outbuildings. Most of the tractors and other farm implements were stored under an attached open-sided metal storage building. One building seemed large enough to store farm vehicles and equipment; it had a big door on a track secured by a padlock, so he backed his truck up to that door and got out.

A small plasma cutter was built into the truck frame under the bed. Sal used it to cut everything from wheel boots to those padlocks that couldn't be easily severed with bolt cutters. In less than sixty seconds the lock was on the ground with a glowing molten gap in one side of it. With one big yank on the handle, he pulled the big door across the rolling track to reveal the darkened interior of the old machine shop.

Miles had dropped Bramley back at her house and was just turning onto the road leading to his farm when he saw a light flick on in the machine shop. He doused the headlights on his dark-blue Ford Expedition, pulled over and called 911 to report a burglary in process. Miles hopped out and removed a tire iron from under the rear seat. In short order he had circled around to the back of the machine shed through an adjacent soybean field.

Sal found the Stutz, just as described, perched on a lift. A large green John Deere zero-turn riding mower was parked beneath it.

Damn, this job is taking too long, Sal thought. *Okay, how do you start this thing?* He turned the key, but nothing happened. He folded the levers across his lap, but it still wouldn't start. After a few more cranks, Sal pulled up on the choke, and with fuel flowing, the mower finally sparked to life.

Miles heard the mower starting and sprinted toward the barn, figuring the intruder wouldn't hear him over the mower's clatter. He stopped short at the corner of the building and caught his breath, thinking, *I really need to get back to jogging on a regular basis.* He ducked low and took a turkey peek around the corner. Seeing only one person, he decided to try to get a little closer, and glided silently into the shadows of a line of farm tractors and other equipment.

I'll put him in the dark, then lock the door and let the police handle him.

Miles quickly dashed out of his hiding spot, reached the switch to kill the lights and simultaneously flipped another switch to start the air compressor right behind the intruder. *That'll throw him off.*

When the lights went off the big man moved with surprising speed, grabbing a Glock pistol from under the folds of his jacket. He spun toward the compressor and let loose a volley of shots, some of which pinged off steel girders. Others bored through the thin aluminum siding like exploding firecrackers.

Miles rushed the intruder like a linebacker, shoulders down. The jolt knocked the Glock from the larcenist, who cursed and started flailing. Miles swung wildly with the tire iron, hitting the man's head. The behemoth dropped to the floor like falling timber, knocking over a large rolling tool chest on his way down. The wrenches clattered, while sockets shot off in every direction.

An eerie silence fell on the room, interrupted by an occasional *zip zap* of the bug light. Miles turned on the lights and from his workbench he quickly snatched some oversized zip ties used for tying down ventilation ductwork on an air handler.

"That should hold you," he said to the unconscious man. Minutes later he heard the gravel in his driveway crunching. Miles stepped from the machine shop, raised his hands above his head and called out to the sheriff's deputies, who had weapons drawn.

"I called 911. This is my place. The intruder is inside," he said, gasping for air.

An ambulance hauled the thief off to the hospital, and, a bit ironically, his tow truck was towed off to the city impound lot.

Detective Miller went over the whole story one more time and asked Miles, "So, what were you thinking? Why didn't you just wait for the deputies to arrive?"

"I didn't want him getting away." Miles shrugged. "Wasn't sure when you guys would get here."

"You sure found the wrong guy to pick a fight with. We ran his identity through the NCIC database and discovered he has quite a rap sheet in New Jersey and New York. With this stunt and his prints on that Glock, I think he is going to have a nice long vacation in a small room with no sunshine when he wakes up."

"Did you find out anything about the company he was working for? The sign on the door says Rocky's Salvage."

"We probably won't get anything on that until the morning. We will try and link up with local law enforcement first thing and follow up on it."

After the police left, the reality of what had just occurred settled in. Miles started shaking.

"I need a drink and a shower," he said. "What the hell was I thinking?"

CHAPTER TWELVE

DETECTIVE MILLER CALLED MILES bright and early. With little preamble he dove right in.

"Rocky's Salvage claims they never heard of the guy in a coma at the hospital. They also claim that their truck was stolen—they just hadn't had the time to file the report with authorities yet. I don't believe that fairy tale for one minute. I mean, seriously, the guy had the keys to the truck. We've got a little more legwork to pin them down, but we will get to the bottom of it. My counterparts up there are doing a little investigating and should have some answers for us later today."

"I appreciate the call, Detective. Thanks."

"The guy who attacked you got his skull fractured. You clubbed him pretty good. He is in an induced coma. Good thing we have proof he fired shots. This little caper could take a while to unravel, so don't expect any immediate breakthroughs."

Miles was already moving through his mental to-do list and was not too surprised at the status of the investigation.

"Thanks again for the update, Detective Miller. Hopefully something will break loose for you."

Miles spotted Wic's truck lumbering down the driveway with an enclosed car trailer in tow. Bramley slowly followed at a considerable distance, letting the gentle breeze clear the dust out of her path. She drove a light-blue 1957 Thunderbird convertible. Miles ambled across the front yard to greet them.

"Morning, Wic. I forgot you were coming today." They both turned to look at Bramley coasting to a stop in front of the shed. Wic and Miles walked over as she slid out. Wic grinned from ear to ear.

"This is a true classic—the last year of the first generation of T-Birds." Placing his hand reverently on the retractable white soft top he asked, "Do you have the matching hard top too?"

"Good morning to you too," Bramley grinned, "and yes I do. This was my daddy's car. I very rarely drive it, but considering your passion for old cars, I thought I might find you over here this morning and figured you might like to check it out."

Wic said, "She's a beauty. Do you mind if I look under the hood?"

"Please do," she responded.

"Wic, I should have called to let you know you didn't need to pick up the Stutz."

Wic looked puzzled. "Did you change your mind about getting the sealant put on?"

"No, but I had a purloining prowler visit last night who tried to steal it. I am very concerned that someone else may try to steal it again and I don't want you getting hurt. The guy pulled a gun on me last night."

"Hold on! A gun? You hurt?" Bramley gushed.

"I'm okay. I cracked the guy in the head with a tire iron. Snuck up on him. The police came and arrested him, then hauled him off to the hospital. He's in an induced coma."

"My God, Miles. You could'a been—"

"I know. Better to be a live coward than dead hero."

"Miles, don't you think the car would be safer at my place?" Wic asked. "No one even knows I'm working on it, except you and Bramley."

"That's a really good question. I am not sure how to answer, but let me show you the results of last night's visit," he stated as he pulled his machine shop door open. They saw tools strewn about and the holes in the metal siding. "Are you really sure you want to take it?"

"Look, I understand your concern, but I don't know how someone will find out that I have your car. Besides, it will definitely be safer in an 'undisclosed location.' Right?" He emphasized the point with air quotes. "I think you should definitely let me take it for safekeeping. This thing is a one of a kind. You just don't find one this old in a condition this good. It will be in good hands. I won't let anyone know I'm working on it. Besides, the tires should be here in a couple of days."

Miles looked at the immovable young man with his stained ball cap and cheerful, self-confident grin, then after a bit more self-deliberation announced, "Okay, then let's load it up and get you on the road as quickly as possible. Just slide the tools out of the way so we can get the lift down and the car off. I'll pick them up later."

In less than fifteen minutes they had the old Stutz loaded into the trailer and Wic was on his way.

Bramley was still in disbelief. "I still can't believe you attacked a guy with a gun. Are you crazy? No car is worth dying for."

Miles shrugged. "I really didn't expect him have a weapon, much less start shooting at everything in sight. Trust me, I won't make that mistake a second time. Someone really wants that car, or I suspect they want what they think is in it. The guy who was here was a real gorilla. The police said he's from New York or New Jersey. I'm wondering if the mysterious guy who sent that lawyer down here is behind this little caper. There must be something really significant in the journal. I want to go take another look at those journal pages, and I'd like more information on that Webber guy."

"I'll be glad to dig into it. Knowing more about his background may help explain the gold coins."

"What do you mean?"

"I didn't get a chance to tell you earlier, but I dug up additional information on some of those gold coins. A few of the coins you have are actually 20 mark Prussian coins, minted between 1871 and 1913. The older ones from 1888 had the image of Frederich III on them and are worth about $430. He was the emperor of Germany and king of Prussia for only ninety-nine days, so they are pretty rare. Others have various dates up to 1913 and are only worth about $320 apiece."

"You said some of the coins. What about the other ones?"

"Well, that's the thing. I only took a couple of pictures of them and didn't get all of them, but we will need to inventory every single one of them to establish the value of the collection. It appears that you may have some very rare coins in your collection. You are not going to believe this, but a couple of the 1920s $20 Saint-Gaudens coins appear to be uncirculated and could have a value between $100,000 to $300,000 per coin."

"Now you're just pulling my leg." Miles grinned. "No coin can be worth that much."

"No, I am not kidding! Most of the original ones produced were melted down in the 1930s gold recall, so very few even exist. I can show you the results of an auction in July of 2002 held by Sotheby and Stack, where a 1933 gem brilliant uncirculated Saint-Gaudens double eagle sold for a record seven and a half million dollars. They were all supposed to have been melted by the mint; however, it is rumored that thirteen survived, and the one that was auctioned is the only one that ever went on the market. So, yes, a single coin can be worth a fortune. I am not saying you have any that are nearly that valuable, but you definitely have some very rare double eagle coins."

Miles looked at her and said with his silly lopsided grin, "I'm starting to think you just might be worth your weight in gold!"

"Don't you know you should *never* reference a girl's weight?" She punched him playfully in the arm.

"All right, let's go up to the house. I'll get them out of the safe and you can start doing an inventory, taking pictures and cataloging them. Then we will stop off at the bank and put them in my safe deposit box. This find just gets more and more intriguing the further we delve into it."

Miles opened up his gun safe to retrieve the leather pouch with all the diamonds, coins and the journal.

"Oh my; you have a well-stocked arsenal in there," Bramley said.

For the most part, Miles used his safe to store his firearms and ammunition, but he did have space for some files, hard disk backups, as well as a few other valuables

"A couple of the shotguns belonged to my dad. When I was ten years old he gave me that .22 Ruger rifle for Christmas. Over the years I added the pistols to my collection."

"Well, well, well, Mr. West, I think you've been holding out on me. I believe we will have to go out to the shooting range and have a little competition," Bramley said with a grin. "Now I just need to decide what the stakes should be."

She was well practiced and felt very confident of her skills. She often medaled in her skeet and trap competitions in college. She and her father had bonded over their shared passion for the sport. The first time she beat her dad, she was in her late teens. She was always stumped about why she couldn't do the same thing in tennis.

"Hey, I'll concede before we start, I am a little rusty," Miles said. In truth, he was more proficient today than he had ever been in his life. Sometimes he liked to go out and target practice to relax or vent frustrations. In fact, he had become quite proficient at tactical shooting as well and could nail his targets with either his left or right hand while on the move.

She took another glance at the stockpile.

"Sure, I believe that, and by the way, I have some great swamp land I'll sell you."

Miles and Bramley laid everything out on the dining room table. Making a grid framework with tape and string, they assigned each item a specific number. After that, Bramley started taking pictures and compiling an inventory of the coins. Next, she counted the diamonds as she placed them in rows on a large piece of black fabric, then matched a number to each one and placed them into the pre-numbered plastic pouches she had brought for just that purpose.

"When Jane gets back, I'll get her to fly down and do an appraisal for you. I am not sure who I can find to evaluate the coin collection, but I will touch base with one of my former coworkers at Sotheby's who can point us in the right direction."

They had just finished packing all the coins and diamonds into a small leather satchel that would fit easily into Miles safe deposit box when his phone rang. Looking at the caller ID, he recognized his lawyer buddy.

"Thanks for getting back to me, Trevor."

"Hey, I just wanted to let you know that lawyer represents some mob types. One of the big fish is Carlo Bello. Old CB has a very nasty reputation up here, so I would recommend you be very careful and steer clear of him."

"I think I met one of his thugs last night. The guy showed up with a car hauler trying to steal my antique car."

"What happened?"

Miles gave him the short version. "At any rate, he is in a coma and can't provide us with any information."

Trevor said, "I know you like to tackle things head-on, but on this thing, I think you should consider taking a little vacation and get lost—let the authorities sort it all out."

"Well, I am definitely not planning to wait around here for another one of his goons to show up. You're right. I think a little trip is definitely in order. Maybe I'll try my hand at code breaking."

"Not sure that sounds like much of a vacation; be careful."

"I will. Thanks again for the information."

With Trevor's booming voice Bramley easily overheard both sides of the conversation. Her eyebrows lifted at the mention of "mob types." She had several prior run-ins with some unsavory characters in the auction world. They could definitely be difficult to avoid and problematic to deal with as one could easily find oneself inadvertently drawn into some shady deal.

After he got off the phone, she turned to him and asked, "Do you remember that I said Lefty Webber reportedly stole $1.5 million to $2 million? Well, the total value of all these coins and diamonds you have in these pouches, in 1929 values, might add up to less than a tenth of that sum. It looks like there are about 200 coins in this collection." She paused to consult her notes. "The face value of these twenty-dollar gold coins is only about 4,000 dollars. At any rate, my point is that the coins, like the diamonds, would have had a smaller relative value back in the late 1920s. Today the value of gold is significantly higher, without factoring in the appreciation due to the collectability of the rare coins."

Miles thought for a few minutes. "I still think there has to be something else to this mysterious find. I'm not sure what, but it seems like we are missing something even more significant. I can't see why some mob boss has so much interest in this find. Even if the total value of everything stolen is a couple million or so, that's still peanuts for a big-time mobster."

"It could be a lot more than that, Miles. Millions of dollars is big money to anyone."

She noticed he was making some notes of his own in a little black book.

"Let's finish up."

Miles collected a couple things from his desk to stow in his backpack. A plan was taking shape in his mind. He was getting back into his working modus operandi: solving problems, sorting out hidden agendas, bringing open-ended plans to resolution. When he had been in the middle of big brokerage deals, people would be frantic, stressed and in a state of panic. But for Miles things seemed to slow down. He could filter out the white noise created by the myriad of trivial details, while concurrently zeroing in on key issues with a laser-like precision. It was second nature for him to size up a problem or opportunity, weigh the options, then 'slice 'em and dice 'em' in short order. Like a grand chess master, he saw several moves ahead and planned his countermoves well in advance.

Miles turned to Bramley. "I'm headed to Baltimore."

"What's in Baltimore?"

"The National Cryptologic Museum. I'm hoping that the types of codes in this journal we copied have been solved. I figure that if we are correct and this is Lefty Webber's little book, and considering he was in the German military in the early 1900s, he might have used a cryptographic method of the time period. From what I have read, most of those codes were rendered useless with the advent of increased computing power. I bet that somewhere in their archives is a methodology for decoding this journal. I need you to learn as much as you can about Webber and get me that information. The more we can learn, the better we can understand what his plan might have been. It seems to me that he was setting something into motion. You mentioned that he was very meticulous about his bank robberies; he had this car stashed in a barn, he was converting his loot into gold coins and diamonds, and additionally the Vogel sisters had sets of silver and watches. Then we have a coded journal. All of these disparate pieces of information seem to add up to some sort of master plan."

"I can work on it going up the road," Bramley offered.

"I need to leave right now."

"No problem. I'll just grab my backpack and get a duffel bag out of my car."

He looked at her with amazement and admiration.

"What?" she said, feeling his stare. "I always keep a packed duffel in my trunk. Being spontaneous does require some preparation!" She was actually one step ahead of him, as he still had to add a few more things to his own duffel bag. He hadn't planned on including her in this little side trip, but after their conversation last night, he knew it would be fruitless to argue the point with her. If her mind was made up, she would be immovable.

Miles searched for the business card that Mr. Howe had left behind. While a lot of people had given up their landlines, Miles was still holding onto the same phone number his parents had used, although the phone company changed the area code a decade or so ago. One of phones in the old home was a rotary dial no one had ever bothered to replace. This was not the case for his office phone, which had been updated to a high-frequency cordless handset model. It even had an earbud he could use for hands-free conference calls. He found the earbud worked much better than the speakerphone.

After the second ring, a receptionist answered and directed his call to Howe.

Almost immediately the lawyer picked up. "Mr. West, good to hear from you. You've reconsidered my offer, I take it."

"Counselor, you might want to ask your client why he sent someone to steal my Stutz and shoot up my garage."

"Ah, I . . . I'm sure there must be some misunderstanding."

"Tell Carlo Bello to give me a call at this number in the next ten minutes."

Howe was shaken. *How does he know? What does he know?*

"Oh, and tell him his guy is in the hospital in a coma. With his arrest record and his use of a firearm in the commission of a felony, he's going away for a long time. The Stutz is gone, too. You've got less than ten minutes."

After the phone went dead Howe immediately called Bello.

"What?" Carlo bellowed.

"He knew it was you. I don't know how, but he specifically asked me to have you call him. He said the guy you sent to steal the car is in a coma. He said the Stutz is gone, too. He said you had ten minutes to call him. This is his number."

"Did he say why he wanted me to call?"

"No, he just gave me the message to pass along to you, then hung up."

Carlo was reeling. *How can Sal be in a coma? Sal is tougher than an ox. Who does this ass think he is, anyway? He doesn't know who he is dealing with. I will just have to educate him,* he thought as he dialed.

Miles noticed the New York area code on the caller ID and quickly jotted down the phone number. "This is Miles West."

"You asked me to call you, Mr. West, and according to my attorney you are making some pretty wild accusations. Perhaps you don't know who I am. You should be careful about making slanderous comments. That could land you in a lot of hot water . . ." Carlo continued with his threats, and when he stopped talking the line was dead.

"That idiot just hung up on me. No one hangs up on me!" He quickly redialed the number, but it just rang and rang with no response. He sat, his old wrinkled face contorted and red. He picked up a ceramic paperweight and flung it across the room, putting a hole in the very center of a huge picture window and setting off his alarm system as soon as the glass shattered.

His security guys came running in with guns drawn. "Cut that damn alarm off!" he yelled. His face was beet red.

"That was a short conversation," Bramley said.

"He was apparently not ready to negotiate," Miles said. "But now I am convinced he was behind the attempted theft. Actually, I knew it as soon as I talked to his lawyer. Up to that point I was just guessing." Picking up the notepad and waving it like a flag he continued, "Now we also have his phone number."

A few minutes later his office phone rang again. Miles looked at the caller ID.

"Well, he's persistent for someone who has nothing to do with it."

"You're not going to answer it?" Bramley inquired.

"Nope. He will continue his denials and try and browbeat me. I've negotiated with his type before. They like to be in control. They think in terms of 'my way or the highway.' We're just going to leave him and hit the highway. However, it now raises the question of how Carlo Bello is connected to a 1920s bank robber. This mystery takes a different tack every time we turn around. That will be one more thing to run down. Do you think you can find anything on Bello?"

She looked contemplatively at her computer. "I'll give it a try. It just depends on how much public information is available."

Miles stood. "I have to head upstairs and get my duffel bag. I'll meet you at the car. Here, take this too." He handed her the leather satchel to put in his safe deposit box.

They decided to drop Bramley's car at her office. She could leave the T-Bird parked inside the Long Auction Company building, which was not too far away from Miles's bank. As they were driving, he kept one eye on the rearview mirror while intermittently speeding up and slowing down then taking several extra exits and turns until he was confident they were not being followed. They made a quick stop at his bank then headed for the interstates that would take them east toward Durham then north to Baltimore.

The skies were filled with gray clouds, it looked like it was going to rain any minute. An early-season tropical storm that had formed out in the Atlantic had strengthened to a category one hurricane and was just reaching the Outer Banks of North Carolina. The revised track was going to take it directly into their path when they merged onto Interstate 95 around Petersburg, Virginia.

Traffic was surprisingly heavy as they jockeyed down I-40 East. While Miles drove, Bramley was busy on her computer. She was a little surprised at how speedy her phone's hot spot operated given the increasingly bad weather.

CHAPTER THIRTEEN

CARLO BELLO WAS IN his eighties and still ruled his kingdom with an iron fist. He called his cadre together and started barking orders.

"Antonio, I want you to get down to North Carolina and go through Miles West's house—and life. See if you can find some clue to where he has stashed the Stutz. Also, see if you can find a picture of this guy and get it out to all our boys. I will pay a hundred grand to anyone who brings him in—unharmed. I will teach him some manners personally. No one disrespects me. Roman, get hold of Rocky and find out what happened to Sal. Howe said that Sal is in a coma. Okay, boys, get a move on; find me some answers."

The whereabouts of the Stutz had vexed both Carlo and his grandfather for almost ninety years. Carlo picked up the quest from his grandfather, Giovanni Bello. His father, Mario Bello, had been killed in a mob war when Carlo was only seven, so Giovanni was a surrogate father to him for most of his life. Eventually the old family patriarch passed away on a trip back to his beloved Sicily.

Giovanni had immigrated to New York and settled in Little Italy. There he became a small-time operator until Prohibition, when he built wealth and power selling and transporting black market booze. After Prohibition, he expanded into drug trafficking, illegal gambling and labor unions in the concrete and construction trades.

Giovanni encouraged quite a few associates to migrate from Italy. The criminals came hidden in the vast waves of immigrants entering the United States in the early part of the century. In New York City the number of Italians soared from about 20,000 in 1880 to over 500,000 by 1910. While most of the immigrants were law-abiding citizens, a few Mafia transplants helped build and secure the Bellos as one of the handful of crime families dominating the New York City underworld.

Giovanni's plan suffered a significant setback when a journal he acquired, and a small fortune, were stolen in the midst of a Prohibition raid. An opportunistic thief who had once worked for Bello cracked his safe. At the same time, the warehouse was raided by both the police and another crime family. During the ensuing melee, which quickly turned into a shoot-out, the thief escaped both the bloodbath and the raging fire that burned down a city block.

Eventually Giovanni tracked down the thief and discovered that the items stolen from him had been stashed in a bank in Indiana, which had subsequently been robbed by Lefty Webber. It had taken Giovanni over three years to track all of these ensuing events. Then, just before he located Lefty Webber, the bandit was gunned down on a snowy, rural Illinois road. He tried in vain to discover where Lefty had stored his ill-gotten gains but only turned up a few thousand dollars at his home. Giovanni's hunt appeared to have been permanently quashed, until a couple of years later when he learned about the Stutz that had been modified for Lefty. Thus began the lifelong quest for the elusive, mythical Stutz, which would lead him back to a secret that would help finance his plan to dominate the American mafia syndicate.

The secret Giovanni discovered was that the journal contained the location of a large shipment of gold bound for Russia, which had been lost during transit. He set out to track down the lost gold shipment and add it to his war chest.

Giovanni's thirst for power and dominance was passed to his grandson like a baton. Along with that Machiavellian bequest, the legend of the tsar's treasure and the lost journal containing the information necessary to recover it transitioned from grandfather to grandson. Carlo Bello accepted the mantle of responsibility and kept the dream alive for the Bello family. Over the years the Bello empire continued to expand. But so did that of competing New York mob families, who, like the Bello clan, wanted to control all mafia activity in the city. Carlo knew he needed a huge war chest to facilitate his master plan. He also knew in general terms where those spoils were located.

Like a modern-day Captain Ahab, Carlo Bello had spent a lifetime chasing his whale. He was confident that the missing journal would lead him to the tsar's missing treasure. He implicitly trusted his grandfather's legend purporting that the tsar's gold shipment had been transferred to a fishing trawler before the *Republic* finally sank. In private, Giovanni often recounted the story about the overloaded fishing trawler that capsized before reaching port. The only information about its final location had been transmitted in code on a Marconi radio device broadcast by Edward Stallings, who was recovered from the water a short distance from where the fishing vessel was swamped by a rogue wave. As he broadcast the coded information, he recorded it in his personal journal so that it would be preserved for the government salvage operations that were sure to follow. However, before he could pass the journal to the United States Treasury Department, he died from pneumonia in a Newport hospital. Giovanni purchased the personal journal of Edward Stallings from an undertaker well-known for liberating effects from the dearly departed. In an ironic twist of fate, the same journal was quickly liberated from Giovanni's own safe.

Shortly after Carlo began his own search, he had his first Hatteras sportfishing boat equipped with diving gear and even recruited several divers to work for his organization. He suspected the trawler sank somewhere offshore between the last known position of the RMS *Republic* and the City of Newport. Every summer he made trips to the waters off Nantucket, exploring the ocean along a very specific corridor. Between Newport and a spot in the Atlantic at 40°26'0"N 69°46'0"W, he created a search grid that covered 175 nautical miles. Assuming he had the path correct, the width of his search still had to take navigation error, drift, and unknown sinking patterns into account. Finding the lost fishing trawler was truly like hunting for the proverbial needle in a haystack.

Regardless of the odds, he cast off in pursuit of this elusive catch each and every year. He fished while his men dove on any wrecks they found. They had actually discovered a couple of shipwrecks, but none of them contained anything of consequence.

He didn't have the type of equipment needed to explore the wreck of the *Republic*. But he was confident the gold wasn't there anyway. He was nervous and amused when a professional recovery team found the wreck in 1981. It had sunk in 270 feet of water. No one found any of the rumored gold. That bolstered his sagging confidence that the old stories were true and continued to fuel his quest. From 2015 to 2017, another attempt was made to recover the tsar's gold. Each new revelation seemed to confirm Carlo's suspicions: the gold had indeed been off-loaded and sent to Newport.

His grandfather had paid a small fortune for that original encoded journal. Carlo just needed to recover the journal and learn the coordinates of the sunken fishing trawler, and he would have all the gold he needed to expand his empire.

CHAPTER FOURTEEN

ANTONIO RACED TO NORTH Carolina from New York, arriving late in the day. He drove past West's farm and parked his car in a copse of trees. Once the car was sufficiently hidden, he scoped the farm out with his binoculars and didn't see any activity or sign of life. He had been told that no one would be there; however, he was cautious about his craft. Burglarizing a house during daylight hours was trickier than a similar pursuit under the cover of darkness.

After about fifteen minutes, he noted the traffic pattern along the rural road was very intermittent, so he decided to make a dash for the house. His plan was to work his way along the tree line to the back of the farm where he wouldn't be so easily spotted.

Thirty minutes after he arrived, he was testing windows and doors. Finally, after verifying that there was no alarm system, he gave up and kicked the front door in with his boot. The long deadbolt splintered the doorjamb. He quickly ventured from room to room getting the lay of the land, then circled back to the office. The desk file drawer was locked, so he pried it open with the crowbar strung across his back.

Miles was very meticulous about his paperwork and organization habits. Antonio couldn't believe his luck. "Finally, I get someone who is OCD and organizes their records."

He went straight to the vehicle registrations and found the most recent record was for a dark-blue Ford Expedition; he snapped a picture of the license and registration information. He looked at a couple of other file jackets. They were for an old Ford pickup, which he had seen in the driveway, and an old Ford Bronco, which was under the open-sided barn next to the machine shed. He didn't see any calendars or computers; in fact, the desktop was devoid of any paper. He spotted the gun safe but decided to save that challenge for last. He went back to the file cabinet and found some credit card statements. Again, he captured images on his phone and just left the open files and statements scattered on the desktop. He planned to contact the credit card company and figure out where the most recent purchases were made. That might put him on West's trail.

He was just turning his attention to the safe when he glimpsed a reflective glare from a picture frame on the wall. He jerked his head around, peeking out the window, and immediately spotted a four-door sedan that looked like a ubiquitous unmarked police car turning into the driveway. With no time to waste, he made a mad dash out the back door and took off for the woods.

"Shit!" He crouched in the woods and caught his breath. "All right, let's see who is crashing my party," he said as he reached for his binoculars.

Detective Miller returned to the scene of the crime for one more look around and to update West on his findings. He was pulling up to the front of the house when he noticed the door was ajar and quickly spotted the damaged doorjamb. He radioed in another burglary at this location, then quietly got out of his car, drawing his sidearm. He didn't see any movement but stepped slowly and cautiously around the perimeter of the house. When he made it to the rear of the house, he noticed the back door was wide open as well. Cautiously, he inspected the scene, spotting footprints in the dust leading away from the house. The stride was long—looked like someone had been running. He continued to move with stealth and caution; he was pretty certain the intruder had been there minutes before and escaped toward the woods. His quick inspection revealed that the footprints continued into the field toward the woods. He scoured the tree line but didn't see anyone.

Antonio watched through his binoculars. "Well, I won't be able to get back in there anytime soon."

After easing his car out on the road, he headed away from the scene of the crime, maintaining his pace just under the posted speed limit. "Shit," he said aloud. "I should have changed license plates." His New York tags would stick out here like a sore thumb. "I need to find a place to hide until dark," he muttered. In the meantime, he would send the information he had collected back to Carlo.

Detective Miller called Miles and left a message. He surveyed the files strewn all over Miles's office and quickly surmised that this was not a typical home invasion. *This was no robbery*, he thought. *Someone was looking for information.* He called Miles again, but there was no answer.

Nervous, the detective issued an APB on Miles to see if someone could find him and get him to call back. He had come to tell Miles that the police discovered that Rocky's Salvage Yard was reportedly linked to the mob. *If the mob is involved, this whole mess could take a really bad turn*, the detective thought.

Antonio pulled into an abandoned warehouse and reported his findings to Carlo. The mob boss told his soldier to stay hidden until dark.

"What did you find?"

"A bunch of car registrations, but nothing on the Stutz. Somebody came to the house while I was there. I think it was a cop."

"Did you grab a picture of the guy?" Carlo asked.

"Sorry, boss. I had to get out of there fast."

"Okay. Stay hidden until dark. Don't do anything stupid. I have a couple of contacts on the inside. When this West guy uses his credit card, they'll let me know his location. I'll call you, so keep your phone charged, and stay awake."

CHAPTER FIFTEEN

ON THE WAY TO Baltimore, Bramley noticed her hot spot connection slowing as the rain picked up. The wipers flipped across the front window like a pair of synchronized metronomes on steroids.

"This is becoming quite a storm," she said.

"Yeah, I had to slow down considerably, and the wind is picking up too," Miles responded as another gust buffeted the side of the big vehicle. "What have you come up with? I didn't want to break your concentration by asking. I don't think you have looked away from that computer for the last one hundred miles, although I have to tell you there was not much to look at on this stretch of interstate—at least not any scenic vistas."

She put her hands behind her neck and stretched, twisting her head from side to side. With each sideways movement, he heard her neck pop.

"Sorry, I tend to be very focused at times." She adjusted the seat, trying to get a little more comfortable. "At any rate, let me give you the highlights of my findings. With regard to Carlo Bello, he is in charge of one of the more stable New York crime families. The other major crime families of New York resemble a revolving soap opera with all the infighting and backstabbing. In contrast, the Bello family has only been run by Giovanni and then his grandson Carlo since the 1920s. They're purportedly into drugs, the construction trades . . . all the typical stuff, including labor unions."

"One of my deals was hamstrung by problems with labor unions on the docks," Miles said. "Essentially, the mob controlled the docks and wouldn't let people load or unload products they were shipping through there without paying a bribe. That created quite a few challenges for getting the corruption eradicated, so we could consummate the deal. I am not sure if the authorities managed to keep it clean or whether it reverted back to corrupt practices after we finished our transaction."

She nodded. "I saw where some members of his gang were indicted on racketeering and extortion charges, although they have never been able to make any charges stick on Carlo himself. It seems very surprising that he has eluded prosecution. According to online news accounts, at one point they almost nailed him, but he managed to get off on a technicality. The only other indictment was sidetracked when prosecutors had a witness disappear, while the other witness's statements proved to be unreliable. So far, I have not been able to link Lefty Webber in any way to the Bello—WHOA!" Bramley grabbed her laptop and braced her feet on the floorboard as Miles slammed on the brakes and attempted to avoid the unfolding disaster.

In front of them, a tractor trailer had locked up its brakes and started to jackknife. Still braking, Miles steered for the median. The big Expedition mired down in the sodden grass. Miles felt like he was riding a bouncing bobsled as they careened down the embankment. In the blink of an eye they reached the bottom and started sliding up the other side and into oncoming traffic. Miles deftly steered between two oncoming cars that blew their horns and swerved. He yanked the wheel hard to the right and hit the accelerator, making a fast U-turn. He then pulled off to the side of the road.

"Are you okay?" he asked. To Bramley's credit, she had not spewed any bloodcurdling screams during their impromptu roller coaster ride.

"You sure have a funny way of showing a girl an exciting time! Yes, I am fine, although I think I will soon need a rest stop."

They looked across the median at the dozen or so vehicles that were piled up.

"Glad you made a hasty exit, otherwise it looks like we would have been sandwiched between the trailer and that red truck that now has a huge speed boat on top of it."

Miles said, "I have a first aid kit in the back. I'm going to grab it and see what I can do to help anyone who's been injured."

Bramley leaned forward and peered in the mirror on her door, then looked over her shoulder, opened the door and followed him to the scene of vehicular mayhem not typically seen outside of a demolition derby. Fortunately, there were only minor injuries, which was quite miraculous given the number of vehicles involved and the way they had careened into one massive interlocked pile. It would take a while to get the northbound side of the interstate open again.

After their hasty exit they were now headed south. "Let's find a restaurant. We need to get some food and dry clothes," Miles said. "There are food signs for the next exit. Hopefully we can plot a detour around that mess."

They pulled into a retro dinner just off the highway. It looked like it hadn't been updated since the 1970s. The linoleum was well-worn, and the red imitation-leather seats in the booths were cracked and stiff. The stools at the counter didn't look much more comfortable. The cook, adorned in a grease-stained apron, stood behind the grill flipping sausages and burgers on the griddle. At least the old diner was clean, warm and dry. They were both coming off of their adrenaline high, and they sank into the booth like deflating balloons. A plump waitress with a hair bonnet appeared out of nowhere to take their order.

"Hey folks, what'll ya have?" she asked with a pleasant smile and a lipstick-stained grin, as she pulled her pen from behind her ear.

Miles deferred to Bramley with a wave of his hand. "I'll have whatever she's having."

"Are you serving breakfast?"

"Yep, we serve breakfast all day. What'll ya have?"

Bramley ordered coffee, pancakes, sausage, and eggs scrambled with cheddar cheese.

"When you've been cold and wet, and nearly killed, a hearty meal will revive your spirits," Miles opined.

"Hey, I am celebrating not being a pancake."

She looked up at him with her penetrating amber eyes, her thin lips curled slightly in a smile. Then, for some reason she couldn't fathom, she realized she was blushing. She cleared her throat.

"Ah, um . . . with regard to Lefty, I couldn't find out much about him prior to his arrival in the United States. However, I think I have pinned down the general location he came from in Germany. With a little more digging I may be able to find some other relevant information. The translations on these websites leave a lot to be desired.

"Maybe if we can break the code in the journal it will help fill in some connection between Lefty Webber and the Bello family."

She added, "As I run across other criminals Webber was associated with, I'm adding them to a list of his known associates. It's a possibility that Webber was connected to Carlo somehow; however, other than the fact they were both criminals, there is no obvious connection. Criminals very often used aliases, which makes this path more difficult to track and validate."

The waitress returned with their steaming coffee cups, which were more like oversized mugs. Bramley grabbed hers with both hands. Reveling in the warmth radiating from the cup to her fingers, she sipped it slowly. "Now that's a great cup of coffee."

She continued. "I also tried to catalogue each of the dates and locations that we found in the Vogel memorabilia. I took your suggestion and started putting each of those locations on a map, although I didn't finish that project before we took our little rocking roller coaster detour."

Their oblong plates arrived, and they ate in a comfortable silence, both enjoying the other's company, both lost within their own thoughts.

Feeling refreshed and calmer, the two returned to the northbound interstate via a rather circuitous route. The rain had eased only slightly with intermittent downpours. A radio news weather station reported that the hurricane heading up the coast had been downgraded to a tropical storm but was still dumping lots of rain. Hardest hit would be the Virginia-Maryland corridor.

"Sounds like the worst is over, but it's still gonna be nasty," Bramley said. "No sense in driving through this all night. Let's see if we can find a room."

Antonio was roused from his nap by his chiming cell phone. "Yes?"

"West used his credit card a few hours ago at a diner, then a gas station just off of Intestate 85. I am sending you the information."

The line went dead and a text message chimed. Antonio brought up the location on his map and set off. He thought, *This might be easier than I thought.* His new destination was only a couple of hours away. *The guy is headed north; I wonder what he's after.*

By the time they stopped at a hotel it was almost one in the morning. Bramley went to the front desk to register while Miles made a detour to the restroom. As he emerged, he heard the receptionist say they only had one room left with two double beds. She looked at him questioningly, and he shrugged.

"We'll take it."

When they opened the door, the air was still and a little bit stuffy and stale, but neither of them cared. They dropped their bags on the floor and flopped onto their beds.

Bramley woke up in the middle of the night, grabbed her bag and went into the bathroom. Digging through her duffel, she pulled out her favorite pair of sweatpants and a sweatshirt. After donning more comfortable sleeping attire, she removed all of her makeup and washed her face, then brushed her hair and her teeth. She rubbed her shoulder, which was sore, so she grabbed some Advil. It was close to three. With the pain reliever she could hopefully get a few more hours of sleep.

Miles heard Bramley stir and got up and propped the desk chair under the door latch. Then he changed into a pair of gym shorts and a T-shirt. As he completed his lap around the room, he stopped at the thermostat, dropping the temperature down, then climbed back under his covers, but he left the light on so Bramley could find her way back into her bed.

When Bramley came out, she had her hair pulled back in a ponytail. As she slid under her covers she said, "I'm sorry I woke you up."

"Don't worry about it. I was hot, and I like to sleep in a cold room, so I turned the temperature down to sixty-eight degrees; hope you don't mind." He said it with a muffled voice as he was laying on his stomach with his head in his elbow.

"No, that's perfect for me too. Thanks." She paused; then, as she reached for the light switch, she said, "Good night, John Boy." He looked up with a crooked grin, rolled his eyes and responded, "Good night, Mary Ellen," referencing the closing scene in the TV show *The Waltons* as she turned the light out.

He awoke refreshed at seven and grabbed his bag and went to the bathroom to shave and shower. He emerged dressed and ready for the day. Bramley was standing over the single-cup coffee maker, brewing a second cup of coffee. She turned and handed him one.

"Good morning," she said. She had taken her hair out of the ponytail and brushed all the knots out. Her baggy sweatshirt and sweatpants contrasted with her silky hair, china-doll face, and fair complexion.

"Good morning. Thanks," he said as he lifted his coffee cup for a swallow. "While you're getting ready, I thought I would run out and fuel up. We were almost empty when we pulled in last night. Need me to pick anything up?"

"No," she replied as she grabbed her bag and headed for the bathroom. "I'll be ready to roll in thirty minutes or less."

"Great, I'll see you in a half hour," he said as he headed out the door. "There's a 7-Eleven a few blocks down the street."

The rain was still coming down in sheets. He pulled under the overhang, filled up, and then went inside to buy some more coffee and donuts for the ride. Just as he approached the cashier, a couple of guys came through the door wearing long trench coats.

"Everybody freeze!" yelled one. The other waved a short-barreled shotgun around. "Show me your hands." The first one howled at the cashier to open the register. Miles had his hands raised slightly in front of him. The guy looked at him and said, "What's in your other hand? You gotta knife?"

"No, just my keys."

"Slide 'em over here, across the floor." The guy looked like he was high; his eyes were wide and wild, and he was jittery. Miles tossed the keys. The other guy grabbed the plastic sack full of money, then yelled, "Let's get outta here!" The second guy grabbed the keys and toggled the unlock button on the key fob to figure out which vehicle went with the keys. The guys backed out of the store and piled into the SUV, then peeled out of the parking lot.

The girl behind the register was crying and shaking. Between sobs she said, "I thought they were gonna kill me!"

"You're going to be fine. Let's just call the police."

The girl stammered and said between sobs and gasps, "I did. I pressed the alarm button with my foot."

A couple of minutes later a cruiser pulled up with lights flashing. In due course, everyone was interviewed and gave their statements to the police.

A young officer dressed in a new, freshly creased uniform collected information about Miles's stolen car. After putting his name and vehicle in the system, a message popped up. The officer said, "Hey, buddy, a Detective Miller has been trying to track you down. Apparently, your house was burglarized. He wants you to give him a call. Do you need the number?"

"No, I've got it. Thanks for the info."

"Sorry to be the bearer of bad news, I guess you're not having a very good week, are you?"

"You don't know the half of it. Do you guys need anything else?"

"No. We'll let you know if we find your car. I'll call you a cab."

A taxi arrived within a few minutes and took Miles back to the hotel.

"Do you know where the National Cryptologic Museum is located?" Miles asked the driver.

"Yes, I take you there too!"

"I don't have a car anymore, so I may need to hire you for the next couple of hours."

"No problem. I will keep the meter running," the cabbie responded.

"Antonio, where are you?" came the garbled voice over the phone. "I have been trying to reach you for the last half hour."

"The storm is making the cell service sporadic," Antonio replied.

"West just used his card again at a service station. I'll send you the location. I have put the word out to our union boys to be on the lookout for his car and to call you. Find him and bring him to me."

Miles walked through the hotel's front sliding door into the lobby to find Bramley sitting in a chair, reading the newspaper with all of their bags next to her feet. She looked at her watch, then at him.

"I was beginning to think you ditched me, except for the fact that you left your duffel and backpack. Why are you riding in a taxi?"

"It's a long story, but the short version is that my car was stolen."

"Do you always have this much trouble hanging onto cars?" she quipped.

"Let's just go get some breakfast before we go to the crypto museum. At some point I need to call Detective Miller to find out what happened at my house; apparently my home was burgled last night too."

"You have got to be kidding."

The thieves that had stolen Miles's car rode around aimlessly, calling various people, trying to figure out how they could sell the car for some quick cash. They needed another fix and the 7-Eleven heist had only bagged them a couple hundred bucks, hardly enough to sustain their expensive habit for very long. They had to find a quick buyer for the car, before the police had a chance to catch them with the stolen vehicle.

Antonio found the service station where Miles had fueled up. From there, he started a methodical search pattern, going up and down the road trying to see any obvious places that Miles might have stopped to eat breakfast, but he didn't see the dark-blue Expedition anywhere. Then, about four blocks ahead, he thought he saw it pass across his path, headed toward the docks. He quickly sped up, streaking through a yellow, then a red light. An angry motorist laid on his horn as Antonio cut him off and sped past.

He drove up to the cross street, and then, seeing a break in the traffic, blew right through another red light in pursuit of the dark-blue SUV.

The guy driving the SUV was creeping along when he noticed a pair of lights speeding in his direction. He mashed his foot down on the accelerator. The big old car roared as all eight cylinders sucked in fuel and spilled out a gray cloud of exhaust.

"Oh shit! Oh man, it must be the popo." He turned right and accelerated again. They were moving into an area that had lots of warehouses.

"Lose him!" his partner screamed.

The residual drugs in the driver's system, combined with the slick roads, made his driving even more erratic. He took a quick left, slid sideways and bounced off the side of the warehouse like a pinball hitting the bumpers in a pinball machine. Flooring the gas, he thought he could make another quick left and lose his tail.

Antonio couldn't believe his good luck. His quarry was right in front of him. "Damn, he must have spotted me." He cursed as he slammed the pedal to the floor in an effort to close the two-block distance. He turned in hot pursuit of the vehicle but didn't see it, so he slowed, glancing left and right for anywhere that he might have sought to escape. An instant later, he caught sight of a taillight as the vehicle made another right on a parallel street. He thought, *I will just continue parallel for one block, then take a left and cut him off.*

The plan almost worked, except the SUV made a left on the same street he was now on. He sped up, closing the distance.

"He found us again. He's gaining on us. Open up with that shotgun." The two vehicles were now speeding down the allies at speeds in excess of seventy-five. Sparks flew from the undercarriage as the vehicles launched over bumps and then landed with bone-jarring crunches.

Kaboom! The shotgun sounded thunderous as it exploded in the confines of the SUV, blasting the back window to shards.

"What the—"

Antonio reflexively slammed on the brakes as the front windshield was instantly filled with spiderweb cracks. He overcame his surprise, then floored it; he could hardly see a thing between the rain falling in sheets and all the cracks in the window.

The driver of the SUV was so focused on the vehicle behind him that he didn't realized until too late he was running out of road. He slammed on the brakes and jerked the wheel hard to the right and rolled into the cold, dark waters of the harbor below. Antonio tried to stop but had too much momentum. He hydroplaned across the pier right behind the SUV and plunged into the water too. He pushed the door open in an effort to escape the car before it plunged over the edge of the dock. However, his reactions were just a bit too slow as he only managed to get one limb partially through the opening. The pressure of the water on the open door clamped down on his leg, momentarily pulling him under and sending a searing pain through his leg and spine. He screamed in agony as he was dragged under, taking in a mouthful of oily, salty, muddy water. He grabbed at the door with both hands, freeing his trapped leg; then, gagging and retching, he popped up to the surface, gasping for breath.

Antonio looked around and didn't see anyone else. The cold water was already numbing him as he started swimming along the edge of the pier's concrete wall. It was flat with no handholds, the top edge out of reach. He flailed in the water, his waterlogged clothes threatening to pull him under. As his energy waned, he spotted a boat that was tied up just a short distance away. Using the rope from the boat, he hauled his soaked and nearly frozen body up and over the bulkhead. He was shivering and numb and close to the point of passing out. In the midst of his dazed state, he realized that if he didn't get warm soon, he might die of hypothermia. Then he thought, *Bello might just kill me anyway for not bringing back West alive.*

CHAPTER SIXTEEN

THE NATIONAL CRYPTOLOGIC MUSEUM was a one-story brick building. The soft, muted tones of the exterior brickwork blended with the gray sky above. The museum parking lot was packed.

"Who would think a specialized museum like this would attract so much attention?" Miles said.

They entered the museum and spotted clusters of uniformed armed forces servicemen and women mingling and socializing. The museum was in close proximity to both the National Security Agency and Fort Mead, which obviously made it a very convenient location for meetings. It appeared from all the people milling about that some conference was about to convene in one of the large rooms located in the back of the building.

The reception desk was located just inside the front door on the left. The cheerful greeter welcomed Miles and Bramley, bidding them good morning and launching into her standard introduction, letting them know they were welcome to take a self-guided tour through the various parts of the museum. She explained that each of the displays had a thorough explanation posted nearby. Without seeming to take a breath, she also informed them they could use their smartphones to hear about each of the displays with a narrated tour.

"We may take a tour a little later, but we have a couple of coded pages that we found in an old 1920s car and really want to see if we can figure out how to decrypt the notations," Miles said. "We are hoping that your archives might help shed some light on methods we can use to decode the messages on these pages. Would it be possible to get some assistance?"

"We will be glad to help if we can. Let's see. You think your pages might date to WWI or earlier." After a few moments of scanning her computer screen the greeter said, "We have several people that specialize in codes across several different time periods." Her finger stopped on one of the entries and she tapped it a couple of times.

She picked up her phone, dialed an extension in the museum's library and inquired, "Dr. Matthews, do you have a couple of minutes? I have a couple out here with some coded pages they found in a 1920s car."

"Certainly, I'll be right there." They heard his voice echo from a room just down the hall on the right. Momentarily, he popped around the corner and they made introductions all around.

Dr. Matthews was a tall, tanned and lean fellow, with a lanky build. His glasses and beard make him look like a stereotypical college professor. He invited them to follow him. "Come on back to the library. We can grab a couple of seats and you can fill me in with the background of these mysterious pages you've found."

They followed him into the research room, which was filled with bookcases and shelves of countless books lined up neatly, as well as assorted thick volumes stacked on worktables. Miles launched into his story with Bramley adding nuggets of information to fill in the occasional gap.

Wrapping up, Miles summarized, "That has led us to your doorstep, to see if you might be able to help us unravel this mystery."

"Let's take a look at what you have there. Humm. Yes. Your instincts appear to be correct. This looks like it is a six-by-six cipher common to the time period." He explained, "Ciphers have actually been used for thousands of years. Ciphers such as this have their origins in Medieval and Renaissance cryptography. If you get a chance, go over to the other end of the building and look at the displays we have set up. One of them has a cipher wheel from the Revolutionary War."

After he made a few notes, Dr. Matthews wandered around the room, grabbed a couple of books off the shelf along with several pieces of paper and returned to the work table. With little preamble, he drew out a grid and launched into his explanation.

"Let me show you how this works."

Over the next thirty minutes, he explained the process of manually creating and decoding a six-by-six cipher.

"Those are the general principles of the process. You can always make it more sophisticated by increasing the reference table to, say, seven by seven or eight by eight. If you had the key, it would be a snap to decode it. However, as you have seen, it would take you quite some time to decode it manually. Fortunately, we now have laptop computers which make solving these types of problems relatively easy."

He went to a file cabinet, then rifled through various file folders until he found what he was looking for, a reference sheet with instructions for downloading a program to help automate the code-breaking process. He perused it through the reading glasses perched on the end of his nose as he wandered back to the table where they were sitting.

He mumbled something and chuckled, then said, "These are the instructions for locating our web page link where you can download a program with the algorithms necessary to solve your mysterious message. I have to warn you, it's not as pretty as the app store, but it's functional nonetheless. After you have downloaded the program on your computer, you open it up and enter the information in the queue. Essentially, you should type in as much of the code as you can, tap the start icon and then your computer will start cranking through various permutations to arrive at a solution. In most cases, the more code you put in, the faster it will arrive at a solution. It's difficult to estimate how long it will take to crack the code. If you run into trouble, go back and use a smaller portion of the code. While it's unlikely, it's possible that someone shifted cipher codes. In other words, you might actually have multiple messages with different cipher keys."

He placed the page on the table between them, and they both leaned forward to scan the instructions. Surprisingly, it looked straightforward.

"May we call you, if we have any trouble working through this process?" Miles asked.

"Certainly." Then he peered over his spectacles and asked, "I don't suppose you would tell me what it says."

Miles smiled. "Given its age, I am sure it's nothing earth-shattering, but we will be happy to share our findings. After all, without your assistance we might never get to the bottom of this mystery. We really appreciate your time. Thanks so much for letting us barge in like this, especially without making an appointment."

Dr. Matthews removed a business card from a brown leather card holder he carried in his coat pocket, flipped it over and scribbled his private cell phone number on the back. As he handed it to Miles he added, "Happy to help. If you get stuck, give me a call anytime."

After concluding a few hours of code research, the couple was hungry and still needed a rental car for the trek home. An Uber driver awaited as they stepped outside into the damp air. The weather had improved, but it was still dark with intermittent rain clouds and gusty winds.

A local gourmet deli recommended by one of the museum workers offered a colorful menu with a wide variety of soups, sandwiches and salads, but the house specialty appeared to be the crepes. The right half of the menu had been evenly split between sweet crepes at the top and the savory crepes on the bottom. They had finished their meal and were just departing when a dark-clad figure raced around the corner, missing them by mere inches.

Bramley shrieked and launched herself back against the wall, extending her arm out and away as the top of her coffee cup sprang off and floated to the ground.

"Wow, that was a close call."

"Yeah, did you see that guy? He must have been late for something. He was flying around that corner like he was running with the bulls, or rather running from a bull while avoiding being skewered by one of its massive horns." As an afterthought he said, "I have never understood why anybody in their right mind does that run."

"I have to find a trash can for this coffee cup," she responded as she poured the rest of the contents into a flower bed along the street. "It would have been very unpleasant wearing coffee for the rest of the day." Then she added, "I think you hit on the most salient point: anybody running with the bulls is most definitely NOT in their right mind."

He looked off into the distance and declared with a circumspect air, "They started keeping records of that run around 1910. Since then, fifteen people have been killed, most of them gored. The origins of the event go back to the fourteenth century, when they would run the bulls from the fields to the market. Boys would jump in front of them to show their bravery; thus, a tradition was started and evolved over time to its current ceremonial incarnation."

"You are just a fount of interesting facts and information," she replied with true amazement. "I definitely want you on my team when we play a game of Trivial Pursuit."

"You can thank the Discovery Channel for that little tidbit. They were doing a segment on Pamplona, Spain, and that nugget of information was a sidenote."

Bramley pointed at an approaching car and said, "I think that's our Uber." They climbed into the back of a Mercedes GL350. The driver had dirty blond hair and yellow-tinted Maui Jim glasses, which he removed as they got in. He had a twinkle in his blue eyes.

"You folks are headed for the car rental agency I believe?" he asked as he looked at them for confirmation. Miles West admired the SUV and its cargo space.

"Thinking about trading into one of these?" Bramley quipped.

It was spooky how she knew what he was thinking. He looked out the window and said in a somewhat prosaic tone, "Somehow I doubt I'm going to have a car to trade in. My bet is those drug-crazed car thieves sold it to some chop shop, and I bet it's in a million pieces by now. I hadn't planned on getting a new vehicle, so I'm not sure what I'll get next."

Antonio called Carlo from the hospital where he had his broken leg set and put in a rigid cast. He started to relay what had happened, but before he could finish, Carlo went into an apoplectic rant. Antonio covered up the earpiece as well as he could, afraid that people around him would overhear part of this obscene tirade.

Carlo went from furious when he heard that Miles West had driven off the end of a pier and died, to outright demented when he discovered that West's credit card had been used at the National Cryptologic Museum several hours later. Everyone in Carlo's inner circle knew to stay as far away from him as possible when he was in one of these explosive moods.

At first, they speculated that Miles West had actually used the card before the "accident" and that the charge was delayed before it registered in the system. Then another charge appeared a short time later for a car rental agency. That fact seemed to confirm he had survived the plunge into the icy harbor.

"Get some guys down to that museum and find out what the hell he was doing there," Carlo yelled to one of his soldiers.

"Yes sir."

Carlo's squad of ruffians arrived at the National Cryptologic Museum shortly before five that evening. They thought they would quietly corner someone and get the information they needed. However, they discovered no one was around; the museum had closed at four o'clock. Consequently, they wouldn't be able to interrogate anyone until tomorrow. With no one to pressure, they also had no additional clues where Miles was headed next.

Miles finally connected with Detective Miller. Only then did he learn about the activity of the thief who broke into his home. It appeared that the stranger had not actually stolen anything; however, he had ransacked the office. His filing cabinet had been forced open and its wooden drawer face was split and splintered. Vehicle files and credit card files were removed and strewn about the desktop. Miles was a little startled and surprised, but mostly very annoyed.

"I think they're trying to track you down," Miller declared. "We should probably get you into some sort of protective custody."

"How can they track me down? No one knows where I am. Have they penetrated law enforcement too?"

"I hate to tell you this, Mr. West, but there are people on the dark web who specialize in this type of thing," the detective said. "Once they have your credit card and financial information, they can follow your purchase records and zero in on your location. Sometimes these guys can even track you through your cell phone."

Miles looked at his phone. "How can I tell if I've been hacked?"

"We have equipment in the lab we can use," Miller said. "When are you going to be back here?"

"Not sure. I'll get back with you." After hanging up, he said to Bramley, "Well, it looks like they were tracking us, or rather me. I don't think they know about you yet. We need to get rid of this car and I need a new phone as well as some new credit cards."

He mulled the problem and quickly declared, "No, maybe I'll get some prepaid debit cards and more cash."

They were on I-95 headed south in their rental, twenty miles from Fredericksburg, Virginia. Miles decided an airport would be a good place to drop a rental car.

"We need to find someplace we can rest and decode the journal. Somehow, we need to figure out why this journal is so important and just what we got caught up in," he said.

In Fredericksburg, they stopped at a branch of his bank where he took out several thousand dollars in cash and also purchased a couple of prepaid Visa cards with $5,000 on each of them. Next, they headed to the electronics store to purchase a couple of prepaid cell phones and a tablet computer. About an hour or so later, they arrived at the Richmond International Airport.

After they turned in their rental car, they lugged their bags onto the bus headed to the terminal. They were unceremoniously deposited at the arrivals curb, where they scanned the scant crowd for unfriendly faces. Miles walked up to the counter and asked for a ticket for the next direct flight to Miami, Florida. He was informed that he was "just in time" to catch the next flight. After purchasing a ticket, he thanked the agent for her help, then walked back downstairs where Bramley was waiting with their bags. As they passed a FedEx drop box, he sent his phone, wrapped in several layers of aluminum foil and packed in an overnight envelope, to Detective Miller. Miles hoped Miller's lab would be able to determine if it had been hacked, and if so, who was behind it.

Bramley looked up from her phone and announced, "Our Uber should be pulling up outside in a minute or so."

Miles smiled at Bramley and noticed she too looked a little less stressed. He was confident no one was following them, at least at the moment. With a little luck, this diversion would throw their pursuers off track for a while.

"Thanks for booking the suite at the Jefferson Hotel. I'll take care of the charges with one of my prepaid cards," Miles said. "They have a great restaurant called Lemaire; the food is outstanding. At least we can get a great meal and a good night's rest. This will give us a chance to regroup and try to figure out what is going on."

"I take it you've stayed here before."

He squinted, trying to remember exactly when, then shook his head and replied, "Back in my former life, one of my merger deals brought me to Richmond and I actually lived out of this hotel for a short period of time. There are a wide variety of great restaurants in this city. Many with their own unique character and flavor profiles. We'll have to come back when we have more time for a tasting tour."

They arrived at the hotel's cobblestoned courtyard in their Uber with duffels in tow, looking a little road weary and a bit like a couple of vagabonds. She whispered, "I'm not sure I've packed the right attire for this place."

"Don't worry. I'm sure we can find something for you to wear."

They got out under the portico, with water from a nearby fountain splashing in the background. As they wandered in through the main entrance, Bramley reached out and touched the large white columns with reverence and noted the statue of Thomas Jefferson on display under a colorful rotunda resembling a kaleidoscope. The sounds of a harp filled the air, giving the lobby a very elegant and relaxed ambiance.

The suite was equally as gorgeous, with a beautiful seating area. Bramley was absorbed by all the decorative details, especially the ornate wooden mantel and panels. The French doors opened to their own private marbled balcony with a picturesque view of Franklin Street. Both of their king bedrooms were attached to the suite.

"I love the classic look of the furniture and the beautiful architecture."

"Given your love of antiques and history, I thought you might enjoy this place." Miles was delighted to see her smile as she soaked in all of the intricate details. She picked up a brochure on the way in and read excerpts about the history of the grand old hotel as they checked in and made their way to the suite.

As the porter put their bags in their respective rooms, Bramley spied the luxurious tub. "I don't suppose I have time for a long, hot, soaking bath before dinner."

"I think you'll have plenty of time. I will make a late dinner reservation. I need to go down to the gym and get a good workout. Hopefully it will help clear my head a little bit."

"You sure know how to spoil a girl," she said as she wandered over to the grand piano. She sat down and started softy striking the keys, tentatively at first, then adding her second hand to the melody. The song was simple but beautiful.

"You're a woman of many talents," he said, applauding her mini recital.

"I can't play very many songs. My mama made me learn how to play it and I dabbled with it, but I didn't spend as much time practicing as I should have to be really proficient. In retrospect, I wish I had."

Later, seated at the dinner table and enjoying the quiet ambiance of the restaurant, they sipped a superb pinot noir while waiting for their appetizers to arrive. Bramley had ordered the fresh strawberry and beet salad, while Miles was looking forward to the braised Shenandoah Valley rabbit.

"I appreciate the late dinner. It was refreshing to have a long, relaxing soak in that bathtub. I think I could swim laps in that thing," she added with gleeful exaggeration.

"I found my treadmill run to be therapeutic too. It's been a while since I have been in perpetual motion for extended periods of time. The last couple of days have been an adrenaline junkie's adventure, which I have to admit is a pretty rare experience for me, at least for the last couple of years."

"What's keeping you from bailing on this crazy quest?" she asked.

"I guess it's a combination of things. First, I have never liked bullies." He got a faraway look. "When I was in the fifth or sixth grade there was this boy picking on this girl; he was being pretty rude. I told him to back off and leave her alone. He was a lot bigger than she was and everyone was tired of being bullied by him. He punched me in the arm and I decked him in the side of the head and he hit the ground. He never bothered anyone after that fight. My dad had always told me not to start a fight, but don't walk away from one either. I was amazed I didn't get into trouble. Later I figured out the teachers turned a blind eye because the kid had it coming in spades."

He paused, lost in his reflections of other such battles, then resumed.

"In some form or fashion, I have been fighting for the downtrodden or underdogs ever since," he said. "In my merger and acquisition deals, it was the people that would be getting downsized. When the hurricanes hit, I would spend a week helping people rebuild in Florida, Louisiana, or South Carolina. I have always tried to lend a hand when I had the opportunity. I can't really explain why. It's just the way I'm wired, I guess."

Bramley watched Miles as he swirled his wineglass, savoring the various distinct fruit aromas nuanced in this particular vintage. He was thoughtful, polite and sophisticated, different from other men she had known.

"At the moment, I am not sure who I'm trying to help," Miles continued. "But Bello is another bully, albeit in an altogether different class. I guess I'm also pursuing this because I like to solve problems and puzzles."

Bramley thought about it for a minute. "I can relate to that. I suppose it's why I'm so hooked on the research projects I have taken on. One of the most challenging pieces I researched was a late-Jacobean Welsh hunt board handcrafted out of oak. I started out going backward through ownership records, then got stuck. It looked very similar to a couple of other pieces I found that had originated from Wales. Long story short, through carbon dating, examination of wood fibers, construction techniques and a couple of tests on the metal square-cut nails used in its construction, I was able to tie it to a specific cabinetmaker in a specific town in Wales. It took about eight months to get it all pieced together. It was a challenging assignment, but very rewarding."

"That sounds like a pretty extensive project."

"Most of them are not nearly that involved, but every once in a while, one comes along with a bit of a different twist. Those are the projects I really enjoy."

"I applaud all your research efforts on my behalf, Bramley. I'm not sure I would have learned more than a fraction of what you have discovered about my Stutz, its previous owner and its mysterious cargo. The gold coins, diamonds and coded journal, modern gangsters . . . I am concerned about your safety. I would never forgive myself if anything happened to you."

She crossed her arms. "Miles, I think we already covered that ground."

Miles's elbows rested on the arms of his chair, his forearms pitched up with his hands steepled together. He looked down at them. In a voice that was almost inaudible he said, "Just over three years ago, my wife was murdered on the streets of New York City. The police said it was a botched robbery; no one was ever caught. A lot of things didn't add up, so I was never convinced the case was as cut and dry as they wanted to portray it. I guess I'm still haunted a bit by the lack of resolution and the fact that her killer has not been brought to justice. When I lost her, then my parents, my entire family was gone. A huge part of my life was suddenly just a big void."

He paused, picked up his water glass, sipped, then continued. "I . . . I have really enjoyed being with you over the last few days. It feels like I've known you forever. You are easy to be around. It seems like, almost instantly, you have become a long, lost friend. I am not sure if you understand—"

She interrupted. "I get it. I feel the same way too. In fact, I consider you a friend that I would go to the mat for, which is why I'm here. I can help you, even at the cost of everything. That's what good friends really do."

"This is not some schoolyard brawl. I am moving in uncharted territory," he said.

"What would you do if you got into a deal and found yourself up against a fellow like Bello on the other side of the table? Throw in the towel, cut your losses and run to the next deal?"

"No, I most definitely would not throw in the towel." Miles's demeanor changed a bit; his posture was straighter, and he projected a look of more ferocity, which softened as he noticed the waiter coming their way with their entrees. "It will be interesting to see what insights the coded journal gives us."

"Indeed it will. There is no doubt that this has turned into one very complicated mystery," Bramley added. "By the way, I have found someone in New York who can give us some more background on the collection of gold coins."

"We now have a couple of different threads to follow." Miles glanced at his new friend and, with a twinkle in his eye, asked a personal question steering the conversation in a whole separate direction. "So, where did the name Bramley Ann come from? Was it an old family name?"

"It's a long story."

"Well, we have all evening," he prompted.

She smiled. "You asked for it. But I'll try and give you the short version." She sipped her wine and set the glass down and told the story of her grandfather, who was killed in WWII. Her grandmother Grace, who everyone called GG, was left at home with their two-year-old daughter, so she became a postmistress in the next county. She was hardworking and very industrious, and conveniently, the post office was located in the front part of their home. They had a chicken coop out back, and when people came to get their mail, they would buy a dozen eggs or so. She also sold stamps or shipping parcels and was a seamstress who did repairs and made clothes and curtains from scratch.

Bramley's mother helped sort mail and did other chores. "Mom told me that she loved it because she would sneak a peek at everyone's magazines and dream about the places she might go one day and the beautiful clothes she might wear. She read the names on all the mail as she sorted each piece into the postboxes. One of the return addresses had the name Bramley Ann written over the sender's address. My mom thought it was very unusual and really liked it. Fast-forward a couple of years, her mom sends her over to the Fairchild Mills to buy some bolts of cloth out of their seconds room. That was the place they put all the bolts with defects and sold them for a discount.

"I'm not sure about all of the details, but in the course of buying fabric, my mother met my father that day in the seconds room. He was there inspecting the milling defects. To make a long story short, they fell in love and got married. When they found out Mama was pregnant, they started to consider names that they would use if I was a girl or a boy. Mama suggested that they both write down their favorite names and they could try them all out. To their surprise, they both had Bramley Ann written at the top of their respective lists of girls. Those two lists are actually taped into my baby scrapbook. It turned out that Dad's great-aunt, who was a spinster, had that name, and he always remembered her fondly. As the story goes, they decided that meant I was destined to be called Bramley Ann."

"That's a pretty amazing story," Miles said as he gazed at her mysterious, sparkling amber eyes. "Did your mom make it to all those places she read about?"

"She and my dad traveled quite extensively. With his milling operations, he would travel the globe looking at other milling operations, checking out different materials from different countries. When they weren't traveling for work, they enjoyed visiting other places for the simple pleasure of going somewhere they had never been. She loved the different cultures and traditions. She was quite the lady, a real disciple of Emily Post. In her mind there was no reason to be ill-mannered. Regardless of who she encountered, she could make them feel special, whether the person was a waitress or a duchess. Dad always said she was a class act and that he married up. That seemed ironic to me because she came from meager means and he was wealthy and successful. He was self-made and had a few rough edges. My mama loved him just the way he way he was; she never tried to change him. On the other hand, she was relentless with me. I would ask, 'Can I go to Jenny's house?' Then she would reply, 'I don't know, are you able to go over to Jenny's house?' I would groan, then ask, '*May* I go over to Jenny's house?' She was a stickler about grammar and manners."

"So, did you go over to Jenny's house?"

She shot him a glare, then smirked and in a sassy little voice said, "Why yes, I did, but I had to be home before dinner. She always wanted us to have dinner together."

Finishing his meal, he placed his silverware on his plate. "Sounds like she loved you a lot and wanted the best for you."

"I wish you could have known her like she was back then," she lamented.

"Well, I am getting to know her through you, and these wonderful stories."

CHAPTER SEVENTEEN

THE NEXT MORNING, ANOTHER of Carlo Bello's men, Luco, showed up at the National Cryptologic Museum. This brute was one of the more polished of Carlo's collection of ruffians, but he still gave off a menacing air.

He asked the receptionist, "Have you seen my friend, Miles West? I was supposed to meet him here this morning, and we were going to do a little research together."

The receptionist brightened up. "No, he's not here today. He stopped in here yesterday."

"You're kidding. Don't tell me I put the wrong date on my calendar. Don't suppose you know who he finally ended up meeting with, do you? I mean, I came all this way. Maybe I could just meet with him or her and introduce myself. After all, we are working on this project together."

"Oh, I am sorry. Dr. Matthews was already scheduled to be off today."

"When will he be back?"

"Next Monday. I will be happy to take your card and have him call you."

"I don't have any cards with me. Do you have any of his cards? Perhaps I could take one and call him on Monday."

The ever-efficient receptionist had little stacks of cards for each of the staff members placed neatly in little clear plastic card holders behind her credenza wall. She plucked out a card and dropped it on top of the wall, then pointed to the phone number.

"The second number goes directly to his desk, so you can bypass the switchboard. If he is not there, it will go to his voicemail. He is very good about returning calls, unlike some of the other members on staff," she whispered.

"Thank you, you've been very helpful. I just can't believe I messed up the date of our meeting."

"Mr. West didn't mention he was looking for you."

"Oh, he can be the absent-minded professor type, but don't tell him I said that. He's sensitive about it."

"He didn't strike me as an absent-minded professor at all." But before she could probe any further, the mysterious visitor had turned and was striding out the door.

"Hey, I didn't catch your name," she yelled after him. He just kept barreling toward the parking lot.

Online resources had made finding people significantly easier. Carlo's organization had a guy that specialized in doing just that. The guy was downright weird and had more tattoos and metal piercings than anyone Luco knew. Luco never cared to meet the guy in person; fortunately, they didn't often have to meet face-to-face.

He dialed the number. "Pass phrase," said the voice on the other end.

Luco rolled his eyes, then blurted with annoyance and disdain, "The knight of the goths is at hand." After a pause the web hacker asked, "What do you need?" The voice was distorted and synthesized, undoubtedly going through some voice-altering machine. This guy was absolutely paranoid about his security.

Luco held his phone up and gave it the middle finger salute. "I need you to track down a guy named Dr. Arthur J. Matthews, goes by 'Arty,' and he works at the National Cryptologic Museum in Annapolis. Bello wants us to get some information out of him. Also, can you take a peek inside his computers? He has been working on something for a guy named Miles West who we are trying to track down."

"Okay, I'll get back to you when I've got something." The call was immediately disconnected.

Less than five minutes later he had a call back.

"According to a Facebook post, Dr. Matthews planned on taking his sailboat, called *Cypher*, out for a cruise today on the Chesapeake Bay. I hacked his phone and found a reservation for the Robert Morris Inn in Oxford, Maryland. I would infer from this that his plans are to sail over there for the weekend."

"Can you tell me where he is right now?" asked Luco.

"It looks like he is still in the marina near Annapolis," announced the synthesized voice. Luco swore under his breath. It would be just his luck that if he left now, the guy would have already set sail by the time he arrived at the marina. He checked his location on his phone. It would take him a little less than two hours to get to Oxford. Then he would just have to wait. He decided to go ahead and try for the marina anyway.

"Give me the address," he barked. *Who knows? I might get lucky.*

The marina was closer than Luco expected. As the marina was a modest size, it didn't take him too long to find the *Cypher* and its owner.

Luco didn't know much about sailing, but he knew one thing about sailboats—they always needed repair. And he suspected, given the current weather outlook, the conditions were undoubtedly too bad for sailing. He figured he'd find Matthews at the dock doing what boat owners do. Ropes got worn, blocks failed to work smoothly, sails tore, winches needed lubricating and decks needed to be cleaned.

Matthews had taken the day off to check the boat and get things in order. He was oblivious to all the foot traffic coming and going along the pier, so he never even noticed the oddly dressed man standing on the dock leaning against a pylon.

Luco tried to decide how to corner this guy and where he could interrogate him. The boat would be an obvious place if he could sail it somewhere remote, but he didn't know anything about boats, especially sailboats. There were too many people around to interrogate Matthews here. Luco didn't like all the people popping up. He doubted he could even get the man below deck and keep his interrogation quiet. Luco's windbreaker and sunglasses only made him slightly less conspicuous. To any observant seaman, the pressed, black wool pants and polished leather Allen Edmonds shoes gave him away as an interloper among the sailing class. An older couple with gray hair stepped off of their fifty-four-foot Hatteras Sportfish onto the dock. Although he was quite a distance away, he could tell they were keeping an eye on him. He decided to retreat to the little shop he passed on the way in. He had located his quarry; now he just needed to develop a plan to lure him in and catch him.

When he entered the shop, he scanned the place for cameras and was pleasantly surprised to not see any. Then he scouted out various vantage points. When he had a lay of the land, he started taking stock of the various items for sale. He could always use more duct tape; he grabbed a roll and tossed it in his plastic basket. He noticed a pair of deck shoes on a display and then looked down at his own attire. He thought, *They are the ugliest shoes ever manufactured*, but decided to buy them anyway. As he passed a large cooler, he opened the glass door and retrieved a couple of bottles of water and added them to his basket. The clerk noticed him making his third lap around the store and asked, "Can I help you find something?"

"No. I know I came in to pick up something else, but I forgot what it was, so I am just wandering around looking at things to see if it will jog my memory."

The old shopkeeper laughed. "I do that all the time. Don't worry, it will come to you."

Out of the corner of his eye he noticed Matthews had gotten off his boat and was walking up the pier toward the parking lot with some boat part in his hand.

Luco looked down at all the various rope options and picked up a small roll of nylon rope. Quickly he took his stuff over to the register to tally it all up. "I changed my mind about the shoes, so don't ring those up."

"No problem," replied the elderly shopkeeper as he picked them up and put them on a counter behind the register.

Luco casually watched Matthews continue his slow trek to the parking lot.

"Did you remember what else you needed?"

"No, but I'll come back when I do."

Luco paid in cash. "Keep the change," he said as he quickly scooped up his bag and made for the door.

As he crested the gangway leading from the pier to the parking area, he saw Matthews over in the far corner of the parking lot with his tailgate down working on his boat part. He looked around the parking lot and didn't see anyone else.

He slid into his sedan and drove around behind Matthews. As he emerged from his car, he glanced around again to make sure he would not be interrupted. Matthews was so focused on fixing his winch that he never noticed the guy walking up behind him. Luco hit him on the head with the butt of his pistol, knocking him out cold. As he collapsed, Luco caught him, then returned the pistol to his shoulder holster. He had the back door open and the unconscious man stuffed inside in mere seconds. After he closed the door, he went back to the tailgate of the truck and used the sleeve of his right arm to tip it up and shoved it closed. He peered in the truck window and, spying the man's briefcase, grabbed that too. Behind his ball cap and his Ray Ban sunglasses, he made another furtive glance around, reassuring himself that his snatch and grab had gone unnoticed.

Luco was unfamiliar with Annapolis, Maryland, so he just headed for the more rundown parts of town. Finally, he stumbled on an industrial site that was fenced off but appeared to have some old, deserted warehouses. He stopped and, making sure he was alone, used two shots from the silenced weapon to open the lock.

Luco looked around nervously. When he had the gate unchained, he opened it and drove his car inside. He had not hit Matthews very hard, so the man was already starting to stir when he opened the back door. Quickly he grabbed part of the man's shirt and ripped it. Then he tied it around Matthews's head, covering his eyes. Next, he opened one of the water bottles and splashed some water across Matthews's face.

Matthews groaned and in a raspy voice asked, "What do you want?" He reached up to feel a lump forming on the back of his head. Then he made the mistake of reaching for the blindfold.

"If you want to live, you'll leave that on," Luco said with a menacing tone. "Now, I want you to tell me everything about your visit with Miles West yesterday. Don't leave out any details."

"Miles who?"

"The guy you met with yesterday."

"Oh, him. There's really not much to tell," Matthews sputtered.

Luco, pulled out his pistol, racked the slide, and placed it next to Matthew's face.

Matthews recoiled. "Whoa, hold on." He stammered, "The receptionist called me and told me someone needed some help decoding an old, World War I–era message they found in an old car. That's one of my areas of specialty. I invited him to come back to the conference room, and I took a look at a couple of pages of code that he had on hand.

"He wanted to know if there was an algorithm that could decrypt it. It appeared that the code was using a pretty common cipher technique for that period of time, and we do have algorithms to solve it. I showed them how to decrypt it; all the information is in the public domain. He didn't actually decode it in front of me, so I don't know what it said or anything else about it. The only other thing I know is that they found it in an old car. I promise that's all I know."

The guy was shaking in his shoes. Luco swung his arm back to hit him again in the head; then he stopped mid-swing. "You said *them*. You said 'I showed *them* how to decrypt it. They found it in an old car.' Who else was with him?"

Matthews froze. Luco's barrel was pressed firmly on his sweaty forehead. He quickly blurted out, "Bramley Fairchild, her name was. She's an auctioneer from North Carolina."

"What's the password to your computer?"

"Numeral *9, cyclops* backwards, then *1*," he replied.

"How can I contact West?"

"His home phone number is back in my office."

Luco brought the butt of the gun down on Matthews head. The man crumpled to the ground; he would have two large welts and a screaming headache, but at least he would be alive.

Now Luco had another lead to follow. *Even better than that,* he thought. *When I find them, I will also have the leverage I need to bring this problem to a quick conclusion.* He smiled at the thought of all the things he could do to the woman.

Luco reported to Carlo. "West is traveling with a woman named Bramley Fairchild. They met with Dr. Arty Matthews at the Cryptologic Museum, and he instructed them on how to use a computer program to decrypt several coded pages. They didn't run the program while they were there, so he didn't know what information was contained in the old journal."

Carlo gasped and whispered, "He found it." He faltered, then sank into a seat. "You have got to find them quickly and bring me that journal!"

"We can probably use her as leverage and get him to turn it over to us when we find him," Luco replied while checking out his surroundings.

Carlo's anticipation spiked. He thought, *At last, I have found Lefty Webber's Stutz.*

"Did he say where West was headed next?"

"No. He didn't have anything but West's home phone number, but I did grab his laptop."

"Damn it!" snapped Carlo.

"Studs got another hit on his credit card from an airport in Richmond, Virginia. I'm headed there next."

"Find him and bring me that journal!"

CHAPTER EIGHTEEN

AFTER A FEW HOURS of sleep, Miles was wide awake running through various scenarios on how to handle Carlo. He also wondered about the journal and its secrets. Before going to bed, he had started typing pages of coded information into his computer to be run through the various decryption algorithm cycles. He played Matthews's instructions in his head. *The more coded passages we put into the program, the faster it will be able to run the various permutations and decrypt the mysterious codes.*

With a myriad of different thoughts zipping around his brain, Miles gave up on trying to sleep. As he sat at a writing desk in the hotel suite to resume typing, he heard the adjacent door squeak as it slowly swung open. Bramley emerged wrapped up in a luxurious hotel robe that swallowed her.

"I guess I'm not the only one who couldn't sleep."

He shifted the laptop and attached the power cord, noting the time: *3:32*. "I got a couple of hours of rest, but then my subconscious must have kicked into high gear because I found myself thinking about a thousand different things and unable to sleep. I hope I didn't wake you."

"No, I pretty much had the same experience," Bramley said. "I thought I might as well pull out my computer and dive back into our mysterious research project. I was kicking over a couple of other angles to get at some of the information and decided to test those approaches. Do you want coffee? I was just going to brew some."

"Thanks, that would be great," he replied as he retrieved his photocopy of the journal. He was thinking there must be a program that could transcribe the handwritten pages, but he didn't have a clue where to find it. He would just plow through it the old-fashioned way and transcribe it one keystroke at a time. It was a painstaking endeavor, because he was constantly checking to be sure he had typed the lines correctly. Since each line was written in a mysterious code, it appeared as just a jumble of letters and numbers.

After a while he got up and stretched to loosen up his back and get some life back into his numb wrist. Bramley was on the couch with her feet curled under her legs. Her hair was pulled back, with loose strands hanging down the side of her face. Her face was a mask of concentration, and those mesmerizing amber eyes sparked with the reflected light of the computer screen. Cocooned in the white fluffy robe, she looked very angelic. He was still astounded that he had crossed paths with this charming, fearless and ambitious woman.

Not wanting to get caught staring at her, he refilled his coffee cup and returned to the desk to continue typing in the codes, double and triple-checking that every single digit was accurately recorded. He had been tempted several times to let the computer start cranking through its myriad of permutations. But he remembered Matthews's advice and pressed forward.

Faint sounds of the city stirring to life drifted up from the street below as the morning sky lightened. A trash truck banged a metal dumpster, followed by the incessant backup *beep, beep, beep* warning. Vehicles passed by, each making their own distinct sounds. Birds started their predawn chorus with their cheerful chirps, whistles and trills.

The pair had been diligently working their respective tasks for a couple of hours when Bramley broke the quiet clicking of keystrokes.

"Carlo Bello has two sons, one from a first wife and one from his second wife. The oldest son appears to be quite the philanthropist. He has worked diligently on behalf of a variety of different organizations over the past several decades. The business leaders seem to be enamored with his earnestness as well, because Benito was even recognized as Businessman of the Year. From what I have been able to glean so far, it appears he is just a normal guy.

"His younger brother, Armani, on the other hand, runs a construction company that gets slammed mercilessly on social media. You would not believe the number of citations he has accumulated. I am not talking about the good kind. He has racked up quite a few fines for poor building construction practices. Given his awful reputation, Armani doesn't sound like a very upstanding citizen. I would not be surprised to discover that he is part of his father's mob empire."

"I would put both in the bad guys column until proven otherwise. I think we need to play on the cautious side, given what has transpired so far."

"I can't disagree with you." She flipped over her notepad and continued. "The other interesting thing that I found is an article concerning an FBI agent named Stanley Carter. He was investigating the contracting practices of one of the companies owned by Armani Bello, the younger son I just mentioned. It doesn't appear that anything more developed."

Miles looked at the ceiling. "I thought about trying to see if there were any law enforcement officials interested in our bad apples. I wonder if this FBI Carter guy got bought off, or whether he is just still building his case."

Bramley responded, "Ouch! That's pretty cynical."

Miles swiveled the chair toward her. "I could never prove the allegation, but given what I experienced with the dockworker bribery and extortion scheme that I mentioned the other day, I am positive the agent handling that matter was being paid to look the other way. The only thing I'm trying to point out is that it's not always easy to tell which team the 'good guys' really play on."

Bramley put all of her things in her backpack. Miles had noticed that she liked to keep things organized and tidy.

She interrupted his musings. "I've got a lot of other stuff, but I need to mull it over and decide how to put it together. I'm going down to the gym to workout. Want to join me?"

"I should, but I'm not back in shape yet. I just recently started running again, and I am a bit sore from my run last night."

"Come on down; you can soak in the big jacuzzi tub and loosen up your sore muscles."

He thought about it for a minute. He felt tight, sore, and he needed to stretch and give his wrist a break. "Actually, that might not be a bad idea."

"You should really do some stretching too," she suggested. "It might help you loosen up."

"Oh, so now you think I'm as stiff as a starched shirt?"

"No, that's not what I said. But if the starched collar fits, wear it." She smiled and ducked back into her room.

After the trip down to the gym, they returned to their rooms, showered, dressed, and met again in their joint living room to order a room service breakfast. They decided to keep working and eat in their suite.

Miles was nearing the end of the journal notes when he suddenly stopped. He looked again at the text strings he had been transcribing, then back to the page. That's when he realized the next entry was not like the previous lines he entered from the other coded pages. The shapes of the handwritten letters were different. And, more importantly, the code was different. The letter groupings weren't the same, and the spacing was also different.

This has to be a different code. But why on earth would you switch codes? He leafed through the last remaining pages. Whatever the next message, it appeared to be short.

He decided to stop transcribing, certain the code was different. He didn't want to slow the decryption algorithm with bad data. He would come back to it later. Looking down at the computer and flexing his aching fingers, he decided that he needed a backup copy as he didn't want to repeat this painstaking process again. He rummaged through his backpack for a flash drive. After he plugged it in and saved it, he returned it to the front pocket of his backpack for safekeeping. He rubbed his eyes. They were tired and dry and itchy. He would have to find some eyedrops. He glanced around his makeshift workspace, then swiveled his chair to find the printed instruction sheet he had set on the coffee table. Before running the algorithm, he reviewed the instructions Matthews had provided.

There was a knock and Bramley opened the door to find a chipper young lady pushing a cart loaded with covered platters, juice carafes, and a couple of coffee carafes, one decaffeinated, and one regular.

Miles finished and set the instruction page down. A draft from the open door sent it to the floor under his computer.

"Good morning! Where would you like me to set it up?"

"Just put it on the table."

She scurried across the room to set the breakfast service on the table. She was carrying a tray in her left hand as she passed the desk. She didn't see the computer power cord hanging over the end and caught it with her foot, throwing her off balance. The computer slid off the desk and crashed on the floor as Miles watched in horror. The juice carafe teetered on the tray for just a moment before it too fell to the floor. A shard of glass from the carafe impaled the computer screen as juice splashed everywhere.

"I am so sorry," the woman sobbed.

Miles went over to help her clean up the mess. "Don't worry about it; it's nothing that can't be replaced." He thought, *I just dodged that glass bullet.*

The girl, who was certainly a college student, had tears streaming down her cheeks.

"I'm sorry I ruined your computer and your breakfast." She soaked a towel with water trying to get all the sticky residue from the juice off the floor. "I will bring you some more beverages in just a minute. Let me know how much the computer cost. I promise I will pay for it."

Miles tried to calm her. "It was an accident. Don't worry about it." Miles looked at Bramley. "Shall we eat while it's hot?"

Bramley lifted the aluminum covers to find two breakfast plates as well as saucers and cups ready to be filled with fresh coffee.

Before they had finished their meal, the young girl had returned with a large carafe of juice, more coffee and her manager. "Lori explained what happened. Just let me know what kind of computer we destroyed. We will replace it, and of course breakfast is on the house."

Miles said, "Look, it was an accident."

"No! I insist we will take care of it."

Miles opened his wallet and pulled out the receipt. "I just bought the thing yesterday. It's not a big deal; I'll just get another one."

The manager looked at the receipt. "We will be happy to apply a credit to your hotel bill for the cost of a replacement."

"Thank you," said Miles.

Miles picked up the disposable phone he had purchased and glanced down at the business card for Detective Miller. Then he dialed the number for his mobile phone.

"Miller," came the gruff reply.

"This is Miles West. Did you get the phone I shipped you?"

"Yes, I did. Where are you?"

"In a hotel in Richmond, Virginia, at the moment. What did you find on the phone?"

"It has definitely been hacked. Someone was trying to track you. I think we should get you into protective custody. What I really want to know is why they are trying to find you."

"I suspect all this has something to do with the old Stutz I bought at an auction a couple of days ago. It had been hidden in a barn for about nine decades. We learned that a mob boss who lives in New York City wants it. His name is Carlo Bello."

"That fits with what my counterpart investigating Rocky's Salvage Yard said. He told me that Rocky was a known associate of Carlo Bello."

"We read online that an FBI agent by the name of Stanley Carter was working on a case involving one of the Bellos. I would like to try and meet with him and swap stories."

Miller said, "I can try and reach out to him. Let me call you back in a few minutes."

Miles picked up the business card for Dr. Matthews and dialed the number written on the back.

"Hello?" a dazed voice murmured.

"This is Miles West. I'm trying to reach Arty Matthews"

"Oh, thank God you called! You're in danger. I told them about your code book. He had a gun to my head!"

"Wait, what? Back up, slow down and tell me what happened and take it from the beginning," Miles urged.

Matthews composed himself and proceeded to tell Miles what had transpired.

"I didn't mean to tell him about her. It just came out. I'm sorry."

"Hey, Doc, it's not your fault. At any rate, I need another copy of the algorithm. Can you upload it to a drop box account?"

"I will have to find another computer to use. They stole my password and my computer has been wiped clean. I am getting all new accounts and emails set up."

"Thanks, Doc. I am sorry to have pulled you into this mysterious, surreal and very bizarre saga."

"Just let me know how it all turns out, and be careful. These guys play rough."

Miles looked at Bramley. "They know about you now. Where's your phone? We need to power it off."

She took out her phone and powered it down, then asked, "What happened?"

Miles thought about it for a second. "I used my credit card at the Cryptologic Museum. That's the only way they could have tracked us down."

"Let me have that other disposable phone. I need to text a couple of people and let them know how to get in touch with me at an alternative number."

Miles was about to put the phone down when Detective Miller called back. "I reached Agent Carter with the FBI. He is in the New York field office and is very interested in what's happening to you. He wants to hear about your encounters with the Bello family. He has been investigating the family for the last couple of years trying to build two cases, one on Carlo Bello and a second on Armani Bello."

"Text me his contact information and let me know where to meet him. We can head to New York shortly. I think Bello's guys are tracking us. One of them beat up a guy we met with yesterday."

"Why don't you come back here where we can protect you?"

"We'll be okay. We need to catch up with Agent Carter."

Miles started gathering up his things and turned to Bramley. "Let's get out of here. I don't think they have had time to track your phone yet, but we should play it on the safe side."

Miles dialed his old lawyer friend, Trevor. The call went to his voicemail. "Trevor, this is Miles. I'm headed to the Big Apple. Is your old Hatteras fishing boat down at the docks? If it is moored there, I wanted to know if I could stay there for a couple of days. Call me back at this number. I had to change phones. My other one got hacked."

They had their duffels and backpacks ready to go moments later. As they headed out the door she asked, "How are we going to get to New York City?"

"I think our best low-profile option is to take a bus."

The next scheduled departure for New York was in just twenty-five minutes. Bramley looked at her watch.

"Do the buses run on time?"

"No, they run on wheels." Miles quipped. She playfully punched him on the shoulder.

"Ouch! Hey, I'm just trying to lighten the mood," Miles said, rubbing his shoulder and pretending to be injured.

"Well, it hit the spot," Bramley smiled.

CHAPTER NINETEEN

ARMANI BELLO NOTICED HIS older half brother was once again in the society pages of the *New York Times* for helping with yet another charity fundraiser. He fumed and thought, *Benito is always being recognized for some do-good event. What does he think he's doing, running for saint?* The acclaim was yet one more insult in a lifetime of insults that Armani was forced to suffer in Benito's shadow.

Armani smiled. "Sometime in the very near future that will all change," he muttered under his breath.

Armani gazed out the fourteen-foot, second-story window of his well-appointed corner office. When the building project got underway, he decided to locate his office there because it gave him easy access to all points around the city. The polished glass and metal structure gave his construction company an upscale look. In reality, the office was only used for making compelling pitches and closing deals. All of the real work—the accounting, building design, supply logistics procurement, and construction management—took place either at trailers on the project site or in an old, rundown warehouse near the docks where his great-grandfather first started out.

A very faded black-and-white photograph of his great-grandfather adorned his desk. His mother had often told him that he was the spitting image of his great-grandfather. Armani felt that he had some of the old geezer's audacity and temerity as well. As he looked at the picture, he smiled, satisfied that the hour was close at hand for him to take his rightful place as the head of the Bello family. After all, the firstborn Benito didn't really know how the family business worked. Armani had studied it in great detail for years, and he knew where all the skeletons were buried.

Carlo always worked to keep his boys isolated from the illegitimate family business endeavors. Or at least he was under the illusion. From the time they were young, his edict had been that no one in or outside of his organization should involve the Bello boys in a criminal endeavor.

Benito had been sent to private schools and groomed to run the legitimate businesses the Bello family owned. However, Benito scoffed at the idea of having organized crime associations, so he struck out on his own. He not only refused the overtures of his father to run any of his businesses, he declined all of his offers to provide loans or capital contributions for any of his businesses. While Benito never said it outright to his father, he considered any funds the Bello family possessed as tainted, even if they had been generated by legitimate means.

Over time, Benito had become quite successful running and growing his own businesses. Starting with a small grubstake he cobbled together working at odd jobs while in school, he opened a restaurant supply business. It was small, but it was all his own. He worked long hours attending to every detail; he made sure deadlines were met and customers were happy. From the start, he plowed everything he made back into his budding enterprise. He lived a spartan lifestyle and worked almost nonstop.

Armani was supposed to follow the same path as Benito, but he had always liked to take shortcuts. He was fifteen years younger than his brother and always felt the need to be on par with his older sibling. In school he had stolen tests, paid others to take tests for him, bribed teachers, even paid a hacker to doctor his official record. He knew every way to work the system, including blackmailing the staff.

When Armani graduated, Carlo entrusted him with one of the family's legit businesses. However, Armani played by his father's rules, which meant that he employed many of the same strong-arm tactics to win construction contracts and stiff-arm suppliers. He wasn't too concerned about the quality of the materials as long as they were cheap and saved money. He would rig the bids to assure his company won the lucrative contracts. Armani also cultivated close ties with the labor unions. When they were working on competitors' jobs, things might not get done very fast, or accidents might delay the projects. All of these practices afforded Armani a lifestyle that would make even the rich and famous envious.

His mother was a brand-conscious socialite and thought that *Armani* would be the perfect name for a little boy, much to the chagrin of her husband, Carlo. At first it was cute, but as he grew up and realized the notoriety of his namesake fashion designer, he embraced it. He dressed in Armani clothing, shoes, and accessories. His wardrobe reflected the trappings of success, and it all fed his insatiable ego. The bar and dance club scenes were magnetic, drawing him out late every night. He used their specialty cocktails and energized atmosphere to seduce lovely young women. Another favorite pastime was dining at all the well-known restaurants, with gorgeous women, sometimes with one on each arm. He rode in his black, armored Hummer with security teams in front and behind him. He enjoyed a very conspicuous public persona, which annoyed his father.

As a youngster, Armani also learned the art of spy-craft. He often stayed in his room to avoid his father, who routinely berated the lad. To pass time, Armani eavesdropped on his father's private conversations, listening through vents and making notes about the various activities that his father directed or oversaw. Armani eventually figured out how to record Carlo's conversations and meetings while he was at school or playing with friends. To all concerned, he appeared very studious, retreating to his room right after dinner. However, instead of studying, he spent hours each night listening to his recordings and making notes in his journals. He noted every person and every activity, no matter how big or how small. At first, he didn't understand much of it, but over time he worked it out.

The first time his father ordered a hit, he didn't understand what had transpired. When the same guy his father had been talking about turned up dead the next day, he quickly put two and two together. In part, he played the role of the good son, but behind the scenes he used his knowledge to further his own endeavors and to build his own little secret empire.

Over the years, as his father became more paranoid about the authorities and their electronic listening devices, Armani had to get more creative to avoid detection. Needless to say, he found new ways to continue his long-standing habits. The other thing he had accumulated over the years was information that gave him leverage over some of Carlo's closest advisors and protectors. With blackmail or bribes, Carlo's closest advisors were turned into Armani's spies and moles.

Armani listened again to the muffled sounds that had been captured from a digital recorder hidden in a shoe. While the quality wasn't good, it was sufficient to make out his father's instructions about tracking down this West character and finding the location of the Stutz.

For years, he had been amused at his father's interest in Lefty Webber's Stutz; he considered his father's obsession with the mythical car to be folly. As much as the old man obsessed about finding it, he never explained to anyone why finding the car was so important or what exotic treasure it contained. Armani had paid close attention when his father mentioned to his lawyer that millions of dollars of gold certificates had been found with an antique car. Then, when his father dropped the inquiry like a hot potato, he decided the old man was off his rocker. But according to Armani's spies, his father was once again on his wild-goose chase. Armani had decided he could spare a few guys to keep tabs on this latest escapade. Besides, this little distraction might actually be very useful when it came time to execute his plan to take over his father's empire.

He looked back down at the newspaper and thought of Benito once again. Armani reflected on a couple of random memories from his childhood when Benito had visited and they played board games; he remembered Benito at a couple of his school activities. As they both grew older, their paths crossed less and less. Some of the estrangement was undoubtedly attributable to their fifteen-year age difference, but Armani sensed that his brother was wary of him. Now they rarely even spoke, and when they did his older brother seemed bent on telling Armani how his construction company was tarnishing its reputation by not treating its clients right.

On more than one occasion, Benito had passed along information about one of Armani's projects, where some client was aggravated by the poor quality, shoddy workmanship, billing surcharges, or any one of a host of other complaints. Armani told Benito in no uncertain terms that he should mind his own business and take care of his own disgruntled customers.

"Since you don't operate in the construction industry, you don't understand that there are always a few people that are never happy about anything you do."

Armani was sick of Benito's slights, the favoritism shown by their father, and the constant accolades in the press. Theirs was a Cain and Abel relationship. Although Benito seemed disinterested in assuming Carlo's role as boss, Armani wanted to make certain his older brother stayed out of the way. *Accidents happen all the time*, he thought as he tapped his fingers on his desk and smiled. He picked up a shot glass and toasted his great-grandfather's image, seeing his own reflection.

"Cheers!"

Armani's thoughts were once again on his father's empire and how he would manage it, change it and transform its scope and scale. He had been told that his father was being uncharacteristically neurotic. His gray hair was unkempt, his bushy gray eyebrows needed to be trimmed, his face was red, and his eyes bloodshot. All of these things gave him the air of a man possessed. Armani nodded when he heard this. *Yes indeed, he is possessed.* The search for Lefty Webber's Stutz haunted Carlo for too long. Now that it finally seemed within reach, he could think of nothing else. It was a sign of weakness, and Armani would find a way to turn the old man's obsession against him.

Armani had also been getting regular updates on Miles West's whereabouts. He too had people searching for West and the mysterious journal. He hoped to get one step ahead of his father and nab West first, and then figure out what West possessed that had his father so wound up. If Armani played his cards right, he might be able to use this farcical flap as part of his takeover plan. He drummed his fingers again; the timing might be right.

To celebrate his deviousness, Armani took out a Cuban cigar from the humidor perched on the credenza behind his desk. As he swiveled slowly back around, he held the unlit cigar under his nose and sniffed. He loved the aroma of the tobacco. He thought he could almost detect the slight scent of the Spanish cedar it had been stored in. The Hoyo de Monterrey

Hermosos were some of his favorite cigars—definitely a step up from those Montecristos that everyone seemed to have on hand. He picked up the cutter and cleaved off the tip of his stogie with a click and swish of the blades. Next to his humidor sat a small clay pot, which held a bundle of cedar slivers. Carefully, he plucked one of the rough-cut slivers at random.

He lit the sliver of cedar with his gold-plated lighter and twisted it in his fingers as he watched the fragment of wood ignite and start to glow with a bright-orange hue. He drew it close and blew on it softly to make the ember burn brighter. It was his ritual to use the lit piece of wood to ignite his cigar. He swore the practice made them taste better. Carefully he placed the glowing shred in his ash tray without extinguishing it, just letting the smoldering sliver of cedar continue to emit its smoky scent. He reflected on all the pieces of the carefully crafted plot that he had finagled into place over the years—the spies in his father's organization; the informants he paid to keep tabs on members of other organized crime families; the numerous civil servants he had in his pocket. His minions were planted in many of the public administrative offices in the city, from the police force to the public works department and everything in between.

The huge cost of building this elaborate covert network in some ways already paid for itself. They tipped him off about investigations detrimental to his interest, they gave him inside information on bids and contracts, they expedited paperwork, they could make complaints disappear and change information in a vast number of databases. He felt that he was pretty well wired into most of the important institutions in the city. He savored the thought that he was almost ready to execute his coup d'état. He had no illusions that overthrowing his father's little empire would be a cakewalk. It was the reason he was working to make sure he created the perfect environment for his rebellion to thrive, and to insure his takeover would firmly place him at the head of the Commission.

Now he just needed to decide how to best use the Stutz goose chase to his advantage. At this point, it seemed like it might be the perfect distraction. If his father was fully engaged in the hunt and deploying even more resources into this ridiculous pursuit, then he would be even less attentive to the affairs of his organization. However, the other more pressing and very big problem was neutralizing three particular individuals.

They were extremely loyal to Carlo and would fight Armani out of sheer vengeance with their last breath if he were to dethrone Carlo. Without them, the rest of the organization would fall into line, but he knew those three could not be free to interfere with his plans.

Since he had been collecting information on each of them, he knew their lives inside and out—what their routines were, where and what they ate, all of their special friends. He kept close tabs on them at all times. If he could only get them in the same place at the same time, that would make the plan much simpler and more effective.

Carlo rubbed the old Stutz emblem he kept in his pocket. It was like a special talisman at long last granting him its powers—a remnant from the very first Stutz he tore apart looking for the elusive journal.

For the past several days, his men had been scattered across the country running down dozens of leads on Miles West and the missing journal. These diversions meant that some of the routine activities of the organization were performed by underlings that were either overly zealous, seeing an opportunity to quickly advance up the organizational ladder, or dimwits.

Carlo contemplated how he might redeploy some of his men when the next Miles West sighting occurred. He would need to move quickly, as West had proven elusive. He wondered how long it would take Miles to decode the journal and figure out where the treasure was located. He reiterated his instructions to his crew. He wanted Miles West alive.

Bello warned them, "If you can't deliver him in good condition, then just shoot yourself and save me the trouble."

As he paced in his home, a thought occurred. *Maybe I'll let West do all the difficult recovery work and just take it from him.* He took out his phone and placed yet another call to check in on the status of the hunt.

"Have you found West yet?" Carlo fumed as he grilled one of his men over the static-filled cell phone connection.

"We followed his trail to the airport in Richmond, Virginia, where he caught a flight to Miami, but at that point his trail goes cold."

Carlo slammed his fist against the wall.

CHAPTER TWENTY

AFTER ARRIVING AT THE New York City bus station on what turned out to be an uneventful trip from Richmond, Miles and Bramley disembarked from their noisy, smelly bus and found a taxi stand. Trevor had returned Miles's call and offered the use of his boat for as long as they needed it. After a brief cab ride, they were dropped off a short distance from the marina.

Trevor told them where to find the extra set of keys and provided them with a code to disarm the alarm as well.

"I assume you remember where everything is on the old boat."

"Yes, I do. It hasn't been that long since we went fishing," Miles replied, trying to remember exactly when he had last stepped aboard the *Sea Estate*. "Thanks again. I really appreciate you letting us bunk here."

"No problem, man. It's really good to have you back in town. I'll drop over after work this evening."

The air was cool and held the briny smell of the harbor; the occasional bird squawked as it flew from post to post watching the new arrivals to the marina. The pair meandered down the desolate dock, admiring the various boats they passed. Their footfalls occasionally made the old dock squeak as they strode over its grayed and aging wooden planks.

"Have you ever been on a sportfishing boat before?" Miles asked.

"Not really, although when I lived here, I did take a ferry boat out to the Statue of Liberty. Somehow, I always missed the party boat excursions. Something always conflicted with my invitations for the dinner cruise."

"I'm not sure you missed much. Those floating bars are crowded, and the food is not that great. Trust me, due to my job I attended more than enough for both of us." He looked at the slip numbers and pointed ahead. "You don't walk on the boat deck with leather-soled shoes. Either go barefoot or wear rubber-soled shoes. The dark scuff marks leather shoes make are often hard to clean up; if you hit a wet spot, your feet will slide right out from under you."

"These shoes have white rubber soles. I didn't pack any shoes with heels."

"Those are fine, Bramley. The other little quirk with a boat is that its bathroom is actually called the *head*." She looked at him quizzically. "The term was originally derived from the days of sailing ships when the place for the crew to relieve themselves was all the way forward on either side of the bowsprit. That's the part of the hull to which the figurehead was fastened; thus the name for the toilet became the head."

"I am not going to even ask how you know that fact."

They stepped on board, feeling the slightest movement under their feet as the vessel moved in sync with the subtle shifts of the water below. Miles found the key lockbox and pressed the right combination of buttons to release the cover and retrieve the key. Next, he unlocked the door to the main cabin, turned the lights on, and disarmed the alarm system.

"This is quite lavish and surprisingly luxurious for a fishing boat. The opulent leather and wood almost give it a palatial feel. I'm not sure what I was expecting, but it definitely was not something this stately; it sure looks nothing like the old rusted ferry boat that runs out to Liberty Island."

Trevor had recently remodeled the salon; the old tired furniture Miles remembered was replaced with an L-shaped leather sofa and a blue water salon table, luxurious carpets, wooden blinds and a sophisticated entertainment system. The yellow-hued lighting gave a soft warmth to the large room. The galley had an under-counter refrigerator on one side and a matching subzero freezer on the other. The glossy granite counters were gorgeous and complimented the teak-and-holly floor.

"At the base of the stairs are two large cabins. You can take your pick." Miles indicated the direction with a tilt of his head as he placed his backpack on the couch in front of the coffee table and dropped his duffel beside it on the floor.

Bramley ventured down the stairs to select her cabin and check out the *head*. She selected the forward stateroom for the simple reason that it was the one right in front of her. When she stepped in the stateroom and turned the light on, she discovered the queen berth was actually larger than she expected. Suspended over the bed were a couple of small cabinets. She opened one of the lockers along the wall, concluding she could easily stow her meager collection of belongings and still have plenty of room to spare. It was well-appointed with a TV and stereo, and curtains over the porthole. The gentle movement of the boat was the only thing that was still a little bit unusual. It would take some time to adjust to that foreign sensation.

Returning to the main salon she said, "These accommodations are better than most hotels I have ever stayed in. I guess we can rough it here for a couple of days. What's first on our agenda?"

Miles pulled out his phone to check the signal strength and the battery level and replied, "I was just going to call Agent Carter."

When the FBI agent answered, Miles said, "Agent Carter, this is Miles West. We have just arrived in New York. I was checking in to see when you would like meet up."

"Mr. West, I was expecting your call. I am very interested to hear about your little encounter with Carlo's men. I want to meet with you in person, but it will have to be later this evening. We have a VIP we have to deal with this afternoon. I should be able to get away between seven and eight o'clock this evening. How does that work?"

"That will be fine. Call me later and we will figure out where to meet you."

They were preparing to depart when Miles spotted his old friend Trevor striding down the dock toward them. Friends called him "Mr. T" because of his large muscular frame. His strides were long and purposeful, his back straight, and he was still sporting the high-and-tight haircut he had always worn back in his college days.

"Hey, Trevor! Man, you're a sight for sore eyes. I didn't expect to see you until tonight. Let me introduce you to Bramley Ann Fairchild."

Trevor took her hand, which looked diminutive in his massive paw. "Delighted to meet you. Any friend of Miles is a friend of mine."

"Thanks, I am glad to meet you too."

"Miles, you old dog, it's great to see you. You're looking well. Man, it's been way too long. Things around here just haven't been the same without you. I told Myra you were going to be in town, and she said you need to come over for dinner sometime."

"I would enjoy seeing her too, T. How's she doing?" Going to the refrigerator, Miles pulled out a cold bottle of water. "Either of you want one?"

Bramley shook her head, "No, but thanks."

Trevor just waved him off, and then plowed on. "She's busy chasing after the youngsters and loving every minute of it. They are into sports, dancing, choir and band, so we eat late, on the go, or in shifts. Enough about me. Fill me in on this mystery you've gotten yourself mired in. Sounds like you two are on quite a journey."

Miles and Bramley got Trevor up to speed on their epic odyssey.

"What's your next move?"

"While we're waiting on Agent Carter to meet with us, I thought we would run out and grab a new laptop, and then see if we can get the decryption algorithm cranking on the coded journal."

Miles reached for a couple of his handwritten notes, then handed a page over to Trevor. "I have another request. Can you dig up information on Bello's real estate holdings? Specifically, I want to find out what companies he operates, as well as the properties he owns. I don't want to draw any attention to the fact that we are poking around. Given all the commercial real estate closings you guys do, I was curious if you could get a fix on him, shall we say, quietly."

"I think I could get at that information pretty easily with a couple of database searches. Most of it is public record anyway. What are you hoping to find?"

"I'm trying to get a better picture of what Bello is into. From a practical standpoint I want to steer clear of his domain, and avoid running into any more of his guys, if at all possible. They like to play a little rough."

Miles put his hand on his chin, thinking, then recited from memory, "If your enemy is secure at all points, be prepared for him. If he is superior in strength, evade him. If your opponent is temperamental, seek to irritate him. Pretend to be weak, that he may grow arrogant. If he is taking his ease, give him no rest. If his forces are united, separate them. If sovereign and subject are in accord, put division between them. Attack him where he is unprepared, appear where you are not expected."

Trevor chuckled as he winked at Bramley. "He's quoting Sun Tzu's *Art of War* again; the guy is *always* thinking in strategic terms."

"Not always. I am probably a little rusty. At any rate, I want to understand this character a little better—discover his strengths, weakness and motivations. I was definitely able to get under his skin a little when I called him from my office. Now he knows we have the journal, so I think he is more than a little irritated. I think we gave them a bit of misdirection when I bought the ticket to Miami, so hopefully they are looking for me in the wrong place, but that won't last long. If we are going to continue to evade him on his home turf, we need to know more about his endeavors here. I also want to better understand his organization and see if there is some way we can pit his own guys against him or divert his guys to go after one of the other crime families, while we stay out of the way. At any rate, I'm hoping he won't expect us to come into his backyard."

"Sounds like a game plan," Trevor said.

Miles rubbed his chin. "While you are looking into Carlo's holdings, can you also check out those of his sons as well? We need to know as much as we can about the whole Bello clan and also try to understand their family dynamics."

"No problem. That should be a pretty quick search." Trevor made a couple of additional notes to himself.

"We are headed out to get a replacement laptop and see about getting the decryption algorithm going again. Then we will also need to pick up a couple of other supplies as well. After we finish, we can meet you for dinner, if you're free."

"Sounds great. We'll see you in a bit. Be careful and keep your head down."

A quick search on the phone revealed several options for electronics purchases nearby. The day was partly cloudy and mild. Traffic was bustling along in its usual fits and starts. The din of the city traffic was occasionally interrupted by the roar of a jet plane flying low overhead or drowned out entirely by the drone of jackhammers tearing up the street. Sporting sunglasses, hats and collars turned up, Miles and Bramley melted into the anonymous crowds as they zigzagged toward the electronic shop.

Since the decryption program didn't require massive amounts of computational power, the whole thing could be done on a tablet computer as long as it had a slot for the USB thumb drive. Miles liked that solution, as it was very small and portable, weighing in at less than thirty ounces.

Getting a couple of bags of groceries and finding a new computer proved to be pretty simple. While they could have Ubered around, they both agreed that after the five-plus-hour bus ride, it would be nice to walk and get a little exercise. It was also a great way to get a feel for the area.

After they returned to the boat, Miles set up the new tablet, loading the decryption algorithm and data from the USB drive. Now the little computer would just have to sit around and perform its magical-black-box incantations and turn the gibberish into something coherent.

Bramley removed her shoes, plopped onto the sofa and booted up her laptop. She watched Miles stow groceries in the galley, radiating a strong confidence and the focus of a man on a mission.

"So, how are we going to proceed?" She reached into a plastic bag next to her on the sofa to pull out an apple and held it up. "Want one?"

"No, but thanks," he responded. "I'm betting that Trevor will be able to give us a little more background info on the Bello crime family and supplement the research you've done, which will give us a more complete picture of Bello and his organization. I'm not sure how much Agent Carter will give us. I suspect he will want all the information we can provide, but will not necessarily reciprocate in-kind. What I hope we will find are some weaknesses and division in the ranks. While we get a lay of the land, we can scoot over to one of the hobby stores and pick up a parabolic mic and a drone to surveil some of Bello's guys. We have to be very cautious on that front. We don't want to trip over the FBI guys. I also want to think through our options for strategically placing some additional false clues, disinformation and outright deceptions in order to send Bello's crew on more wild-goose chases and keep them away from us."

Bramley was seeing yet another side of Miles West. The guy was analytical, strategic, and attentive to detailed tactics.

"Have you ever heard of gaslighting?" he asked.

"No, not that I recall."

"It's a manipulative tactic that some people use to try and distort your reality. They try and convince you that something didn't happen, that you are imagining things, or that you're just plain crazy. In our phone conversation, Carlo was headed in that direction before I cut him off. Like a lot of people, he was trying to shift the blame onto someone else. The trait as well as his profession as a mobster gives us a couple of clues that he is probably a bit of a sociopath, which shouldn't be a surprise for a criminal. That insight might be important because at some point I will undoubtedly be negotiating with him.

"We have what he wants, and we know that he will go pretty far out on a limb to get it. I have witnessed this type of guy before, when doing merger or acquisition deals. They get so wrapped up in what they want that they go way beyond any normal bounds of ethics. They use deceptions, bluffs, misrepresentations and outright falsification. Sometimes they will even lie, cheat or steal to get what they want. The challenge becomes how little to trust and how much to verify. But that character flaw also works to our advantage, because we can lure him into a box. I have a feeling that the rewards hidden in our encrypted journal will be too tempting for him to resist. The uncertainty that we create for him will undoubtedly increase the likelihood he will do something very unethical, if not totally illegal. I hope Agent Carter will have an interest in backing our play and catch him in the act."

"How are we going to find Bello's guys?"

"That should be the easy part of this plan. Detective Miller thinks they've been using my credit card information. When we're ready, we will use one of those cards to check into a local hotel and see who shows up to find us. Then we'll turn the tables on them by following them back to their lair. Depending on the circumstance, we may be able to eavesdrop with our parabolic microphone; perhaps we can get a handle on what's going on."

"How are we going to move around the city unobserved?"

"Trevor has an electric motorcycle on the boat that we can use. The nice thing about riding a motorcycle is that you have to wear helmets, which has the added benefit of keeping our faces hidden. One other huge benefit is stealth. Since the bike is electric, it is super quiet. By the way, have you ever flown a drone or played one of those flight simulator video games?"

"No, I never really played video games." She chuckled as a long-forgotten memory surfaced. "Well, when I was in high school, I did play Pacman a few times while waiting on pizza. Why the question about video games?"

"Well, our next stop is to pick up a drone. Actually, I guess they're really called quadcopters. They're like little miniature helicopters, only they have four props instead of one. Last Christmas they demonstrated them at the mall in Winston-Salem. I was amazed how easy they are to use. Flying them is similar to playing a video game. We need to get one and let you get some practice flying it. I want to use it to track the guys who will attempt to follow us."

CHAPTER TWENTY-ONE

EVERY PLACE HAD UNIQUE rhythms and patterns—the ebb and flow of traffic, of people making their way to and from work and through their daily rituals. Whether stopping in a favorite eatery, coffee spot, or simply traveling the path to and from work, people tended to follow their routines. Their collective patterns generated the rhythms of their neighborhood, their borough, town, or city. Miles wanted to drive around getting a feel for the area and some of those cycles and patterns. He told Bramley they needed to know when and where the streets and sidewalks were most and least crowded and learn the surges and lulls in traffic in this part of the city.

They scoped out several prospective hotels they could use to lure their pursuers. Their goal was to figure out which hotel might be optimally positioned for discreet surveillance. After they had settled on one particular hotel that fit all of their criteria, they drove the nearby roads. They scouted each route for parking options, alleys, traffic patterns, and ease of access. They determined that they needed to have a couple of spots where they could observe people coming and going without being spotted themselves. More importantly, they needed a place where they could store and launch their quadcopter unnoticed. At last, they felt pretty confident they had identified the best location to spring their little ruse.

Their reconnaissance mission completed, they returned to the boat, noting almost no activity on any of the nearby vessels. As they stepped aboard, the fishing boat moved gently with the water, held in place by the four mooring lines securely tied to the dock. The fenders squeaked as the boat brushed against them, while a horn bellowed somewhere in the distance. Following a practice he picked up from Trevor, Miles gave both breast lines and spring lines a quick check. Though the setting sun was blotted out by clouds, it was still light outside with only a slight breeze. The conditions were perfect for a test flight of the funny looking quadcopter.

After they disconnected the quadcopter from the charger, they took it outside and set it down on the boat deck. Miles handed the controller to Bramley.

"According to the instructions, we can set this as a return point. If it runs low on battery power, it will automatically return to this spot." He pointed to the handheld controller. "That little joystick provides the direction of motion, forward, backward or to either side. The other little button controls assent and decent, while the last one is for the camera control."

Bramley powered it up. "Here goes nothing. I'm just a little nervous about my maiden voyage." It made a little whirring noise but was surprisingly quiet. "Up, up and away."

Gingerly, she shifted the controls; the little craft lifted with a smooth, even ascent. Then she made it move left and right, while she practiced shifting the camera to capture various images. She quickly gained confidence and proficiency, her jerky movements rapidly becoming more fluid. Purposefully, she started moving the camera around trying to follow boats moving in and out of the marina; she sent the little copter higher and it became easier because she gained a much wider vantage point.

Miles was still reading the instruction manual and looked up. "Hey, you're looking like an old pro."

She smiled and gave him a big thumbs-up.

"I was just reading that you can use the camera to lock onto an object in its viewfinder and it will automatically follow it. Let's try it and see how that works. Also, it is supposed to automatically avoid obstacles in its path." He talked her through the steps to engage the function. With a little practice they discovered how to quickly and easily engage and disengage the feature.

"This will undoubtedly be a very useful feature; it will make our tracking efforts almost hands free," Bramley noted. "I have to admit, I was a little bit worried and intimidated about using this thing while riding on the back of a moving motorcycle. But this quadcopter is so user friendly, it almost flies itself. The zoom feature on the camera works pretty well, although I am not sure we will be able to get very close to people before they hear it." She maneuvered the copter back and forth, up and down, noting the distance illuminated on the little screen. After testing it at a couple of different altitudes she said confidently, "With the minimal sounds we hear, I think we can keep it about 250 feet away without anyone noticing. On a noisy busy street, we may be able to get a little closer."

"Why don't you see what kind of images you can actually capture? Then we will see what they look like when we use the digital magnification feature."

She maneuvered the craft around, captured some boat names, then flew over the parking lot and captured images of cars and license plates to see how they turned out.

Miles looked at the image resolution on the screen and declared, "For what we need, I think this will be just fine, and given the high resolution of the pictures, I bet we can stay 300 to 400 feet away and still get what we need."

They enjoyed taking turns piloting the little craft around the harbor, gaining a new perspective of their surroundings.

"I think we found a mutual hobby," Bramley said with a wink.

"Fun, for sure," Miles replied. "Let's return it to the boat and recharge the batteries."

Miles's mind was cluttered with their plans, the questions he had for Trevor, and the instruction manual he was trying to digest. He closed his eyes and rubbed his temples.

"Are you okay?" Bramley asked.

"A thought just flashed through my head, but I can't remember what it was. I'm sure it will come to me in a minute."

"I hate it when that happens. I'm tired and hungry. Let's go back inside a grab a bite to eat."

They unlocked a storage compartment on the boat deck and found an electric bike, deck chairs, floats, beach towels and fishing gear all organized in their own sections, secured with Velcro ties or, in the case of the bike, a padded hydraulic arm.

Miles unplugged the trickle charger from the bike. After he had unlaced the ratchet straps securing the bike, he pressed the button to lift the hydraulic arm and roll it backwards.

Bramley stared at the wheels, then commented on the cloth wheel covers. "That's cute. I've never seen that before."

"It protects the deck from getting marred by any dirt, gravel or other debris that might be on the tires," Miles said as he rolled it toward the gangway and onto the gangplank, then onto the floating dock that led up to the pier.

"Grab a helmet. Let's go for a spin."

After securing their floating retreat, they donned gloves and helmets, then made their way silently across the dock into the adjacent parking lot.

"I should probably tell you, I have never been on a motorcycle before," Bramley said.

"Not to worry. It's like riding a bike. Just hold onto me and lean into the turns." He pointed out two rubber-covered metal pegs that folded down. "That's where you put your feet. Honestly, this is more like a bike and less like a motorcycle. The dang thing makes no noise. You don't have to worry about burning a leg on a hot muffler or exhaust pipe, and it doesn't have the bulk of a motorcycle."

"You sound a little disappointed. I guess you would prefer a big old gas-guzzling Harley Davidson?"

"Actually, what I would really like to have would be a classic 1937 Indian Sport Scout. Now that's a real motorcycle."

"I'm guessing there's a story behind that too."

"Yes, but we will save that story for another time," Miles said as he flipped down his visor and straddled the stealthy electric motorcycle. "Hop on."

Bramley wrapped her arms around Miles and peeked over his shoulder as they darted down the streets. As he turned, she leaned and followed his movements, and then began to relax and focus on the people, vehicles, and streets around them. It was nice to get lost in the anonymous crowds of the city. As they zipped past Central Park, they both were lost in various memories spanning their previous lives lived in the Big Apple. Their minds drifted until a fire truck with siren and horns blared across the intersection in front of them.

"That'll wake you up," Miles said.

They were riding around when Miles got a call from Trevor. He said, "Answer," and his earbud engaged. "Hey, T. What's going on?"

"Good news. I was able to track down almost all of the Bello properties. I have it all compiled for you on a couple dozen printed pages."

"That's great. I hope it wasn't too much trouble."

"Are you kidding me? It was a piece of cake, nooo problemo."

"We're not too far from your office. I can pop over and pick it up. We're zipping around on your super cool stealth motorcycle. Should be to you in about two minutes."

"I was just headed out, so I'll meet you on the street."

"I gotta tell you, I find this thing is even more fun than the last time I rode it."

"I don't think you were riding around with a beautiful woman on the back. Besides, every guy has to have a few cool toys."

"I'll second that idea!"

"See you in a few."

"Roger, over and out."

"And don't call me Roger!" Trevor joked. It was an exchange often repeated back in their college days. Miles smiled fondly at the memory.

The city skyline started to twinkle as lights popped on with the approaching sunset. The tall buildings took on a different hue and tone when the glass and steel structures became illuminated from within and began to reflect the light emitted from adjacent buildings. With the sky clearing, the red, orange and pink tones of the few clouds that remained in the dark-blue sky served as a colorful backdrop.

Another nice thing about the electric motorcycle was its small size, which enabled them to stack in right behind a car parked in front of the entrance to Trevor's building just as Trevor emerged with a briefcase in one hand and a large manila envelope in the other hand.

"Talk about perfect timing," Trevor said.

"Want to grab a bite to eat?" Miles asked as he pulled off his helmet.

"No, unfortunately I've got another meeting to attend, so I'm going to have to take a rain check. By the way, Carlo Bello has a sportfishing yacht. I checked and it's in a different marina. The information on his yacht is in the envelope, but I wanted to give you a heads-up; that way you could be on the lookout for it."

"Good to know. Thanks again, and I really appreciate all of your help with this sordid affair."

"Keep your head down. When are you meeting with the feds?"

"Hopefully later this evening."

"Okay, keep me in the loop. I'll check in with you a little later," Trevor replied as he flipped up his collar against the cool breeze blowing between the buildings.

"We're headed back to the *Sea Estate*," Miles said.

Trevor turned back and smiled as he thought of his pride and joy. He gave them a thumbs-up before he headed off to his next appointment.

As Miles watched his old friend walk away, he thought about how grateful he was to have such a steadfast and lifelong companion in his corner. No matter what the circumstance, or the distance between them, he knew that Trevor would always be there for him. And if Trevor ever needed him, all he had to do was ask and Miles would drop everything to help him out as well.

"I guess it just doesn't get any better than that," he mumbled.

Back on board the *Sea Estate*, Miles tore open the envelope and poured its contents on the table. They both grabbed pages, which were paper-clipped into assorted stacks, and perused the contents. Trevor had bound the holdings of each of the Carlo's real estate parcels into three respective stacks. There was a separate sheet of information on Carlo's yacht. It was called *Fishy Business*. Miles chuckled to himself and shared that little morsel of information with Bramley.

"More than a little bit of irony in that one, wouldn't you agree?"

"I had exactly the same thought," Miles admitted.

Still perched on the table was a stack of miscellaneous parcels owned by holding companies that had some association to the Bello family but whose ownership interest was not clearly defined. However, at the moment they were both still busy checking out the pages they had in hand.

Miles asked Bramley, "Would you get that travel map off the coffee table, and start identifying the various locations on the map?" Miles dug thorough his backpack. "I have a highlighter and a couple of Sharpie markers somewhere in here."

"Sure," she replied, a little distractedly as something had caught her attention.

"The other thing we should add is the location of that hotel we scouted out."

Bramley meticulously noted all the locations listed and then color-coded them according to which family member owned them. Miles made notes on a legal pad about the various holdings and any other people that were identified as associates of the Bello family. One interesting thing was how intermingled Armani's and Carlo's properties seemed to be, while Benito's businesses and personal holdings were held separately in his name only.

CHAPTER TWENTY-TWO

FOR SEVERAL YEARS, SPECIAL Agent Carter had been vigorously and methodically working to build a solid case against the Bello crime syndicate. His team had been busy following, eavesdropping, and building a network of informants. Slowly and meticulously they added substance and breadth to the growing list of corruption, racketeering, bribery, money laundering and tax evasion charges. The crime organization took great care to hide their activities with subterfuge, blinds, cutouts and encryption. Piercing the veil was a daunting task. However, in the last three days, law enforcers had identified and exploited a significant number of lapses in the organization's security measures.

Carter couldn't quite figure out what was going on. It now appeared that Armani Bello was surveilling Carlo Bello. Up to this point, it had always seemed that Carlo had two sets of men as a buffer to keep the feds and any other law enforcement guys from following them too closely. This practice had been going on for so long that Carter didn't even think of them as two distinct sets of criminals. But this new information made him rethink his premise. Why were Armani's guys keeping tabs on Carlo's guys? Was Armani plotting a coup of his father's organization? Carter would definitely have to contemplate the implications.

Carter also wondered how he could leverage these cracks in Carlo's armor to get a peek behind the curtain Armani Bello had pulled around his own organization. Armani's ruthless practices in his construction business had provided substantive evidence for warrants, but now Carter was wondering if there were other avenues of inquiry his investigators should pursue while building the case.

Miles looked over Bramley's shoulder at the map; she had compiled all of the locations of the Bello properties.

"The motel we liked is not far from several of these locations. I think after we meet with Agent Carter, we can put our plan into place tomorrow. First, we'll get a good night's rest," Miles said as he yawned and stretched left and right, twisting his body's core at the waist.

His cell buzzed. He hit the answer icon on the screen.

"Hello."

"This is Special Agent Carter calling for Miles West."

"You reached me. I have you on speaker. Bramley Ann Fairchild is here with me."

"I'm sorry for calling back so late. Are you folks still game to come down and visit?"

"Sure, just text me the location and we'll head on over."

"Our office is not far from you. It will probably take fifteen to twenty minutes this time of day. Just call me back when you get here, and I will expedite your entry. We have a few more security protocols than we had in the good old days."

"Okay, I got it. We'll see you shortly."

Bramley looked up at him. "That guy sounded wiped out."

"I guess we'll find out if that works to our advantage or disadvantage pretty quickly."

Bramley had already lined up an Uber ride. "Looks like our ride is pretty close. Should be here by the time we make it to the parking lot. Getting a ride sure is a lot more convenient than it used to be. Trying to get a cab in New York seems to be hit or miss. I think the Uber vehicles are a bit more comfortable than the cabs too."

They each grabbed a couple of things and headed for the door.

"I'll have to agree with that. I'm glad you showed me how to Uber around," he replied.

"Can I get you some coffee, tea or water? Perhaps a soda?" the driver asked when they climbed into the back seat.

"No thank you," they replied in stereo, looking at each other with slight grins. Spend enough time around someone, and it was no surprise to find oneself on the same wavelength.

At the FBI field office, they entered a stark room with bland walls, a generic conference room table, and lined with vinyl chairs common to every office environment. One wall had a whiteboard on it; other than that, all the walls were bare.

"I must get the name of your interior decorator," Bramley said with a bit of sarcasm.

Carter grimaced. "You're not the first person to mention that we have, shall we say, a minimalist decor. Honestly, I wish office decor was even on my list of problems." He sighed, then rubbed his temples. "Clark, can you give me a couple of Tylenol? I have got a screaming headache . . . Okay, what can you tell me about Bello? Why is he after you guys?"

Miles recounted the story, with Bramley filling in salient points. They spoke of the encrypted journal, Lefty Webber, the secret compartment on the Stutz and Carlo Bello's efforts to buy the car and then steal it.

"So where is this journal now?" asked Agent Carter.

"Right now, the computer is running a decryption algorithm. My guess is by the time we get back to the boat it should be about finished," Miles said. He sat doodling on his notepad, making notations, some of which were hardly legible.

Agent Carter perked up a bit. "We need to know what's in that journal. How about I send a couple guys over there to get it?"

Bramley volunteered. "I can tag along and show them where to find it. We can be back in about thirty minutes or so."

"That will give Mr. West and I a few more minutes to visit," Agent Carter said as he texted instructions to a couple of agents.

Miles was uneasy about Bramley heading off on her own, even though she would be with a couple of armed agents.

"What else do we need to discuss right now?" He stood with the intention of going along to get the tablet computer.

"Well, for one thing, your SUV was pulled out of the harbor in Annapolis."

Miles sat back down. "Somehow I doubted I'd see that vehicle again. I really thought it would end up in a chop shop someplace. Those guys looked like they were desperate for cash."

"Can you take me back over what happened when it was stolen? I would also like to get a better description of the punks that stole it . . . Wait! I think they sent over mug shots." He shuffled through one of the case files he had carried in. "We are pretty sure they're the same guys that were found inside."

"Inside? They had an accident?" Miles asked.

Two guys dressed in dark suits with plain, matching ties came into the room, and Carter instructed them to go with Bramley to the boat and retrieve the computer with the decrypted journal information on it.

After they left, Miles recapped the trip to get gas and coffee before recounting the details of the robbery.

"Were you being followed?" the FBI agent asked.

"No. I didn't specifically see anyone following me," Miles said.

At the conclusion of his narrative, Agent Carter launched into an explanation of what they had discovered at the scene of the wreck.

"Ballistics tests are still being performed, so it will be a while before we can figure out if the weapon used in that crime was associated with any other crimes." He also shared the information about the other car that was found at the scene. It was from New York and was registered to a criminal known to have ties to the Bello crime family.

"Looks like you were actually lucky to have your car stolen."

"The plot thickens," Miles said wryly. "So, what can you tell me about the Bello crime family?"

Agent Carter was quiet for a moment, debating how much to believe and how much to disclose. "I'm not at liberty to discuss all that we know."

"Agent Carter, please don't tell me that you're really not going to fill me in on anything I don't already know? I thought I would at least get a little more than the dribble you guys use for public relations."

"It's an ongoing investigation, and we can't compromise—"

Miles interrupted. "It's quite clear that it was Bello's guy who tried to steal my Stutz and kill me. Now you just told me about another one of Bello's guys putting shots into the back of *my* car, so we can assume he was trying to shoot at me. Given all that, don't you I think I'm entitled to a little bit more information than you hand out to the journalists? I do not appreciate being brushed off, especially when I am here trying to help you. Since I have what Bello wants, I am sure we can help you put this guy behind bars."

Agent Carter's phone rang.

"This is Carter . . . What?" His back went rigid as he sat bolt upright. "When? Okay, back up. Take it from the top. I can't believe this happened . . . Okay I'm headed to the ops center."

"Some guys just jumped my team and Bramley on their way to the boat. There was gunfire exchanged and she was captured."

Miles sat frozen, struggling to maintain his calm demeanor. He flashed back to the night that his wife was murdered. In a quivering voice he asked, "Did she get hit? Is she okay?"

"My guys don't think she was hit. One of my guys is headed to the hospital though."

"We gotta find her!"

"My guys will be pulling all the surveillance video from the cameras everywhere in that area. We will have a few leads in minutes, I'm sure."

By this time Miles was up and pacing around the room, clenching and unclenching his fist. He had to do something.

"Just stay here. I need to run down to the operations center. I'll be back in a few minutes to give you an update," Carter said as he dashed out the door.

Miles paced around a couple of more times; he was not sticking around. He peeked out the door and, when the coast was clear, he made a mad dash for the exit. Then he headed straight back to the boat.

CHAPTER
TWENTY-THREE

ARMANI'S GUYS HAD FOLLOWED Carlo's guys all the way to the Richmond Airport. There they bribed the ticket agent to get information about Miles's flight destination and discovered that he never boarded the plane. On a hunch, they decided to check the bus and train stations in Richmond. Their dark web guys found old pictures of both Fairchild and West from the archived web pages of their previous New York employers. Those pictures had been sent out to all of Armani's men.

The first place they searched was the Staples Mill Train Station. After making a few inquiries, they were confident the pair had not traveled through this location. Next, they journeyed to the bus station where they passed around the photos and a little cash. Their cash incentive elicited the information they needed; the couple was seen boarding a bus bound for New York.

Armani's foot soldiers called in and informed him that West and his travel companion had departed for New York City. When he received that information Armani immediately dispatched a couple of men to the bus station in New York to query some of the regular cabbies. It took a while, but eventually they found a driver who told them he was pretty sure he'd dropped the pair off at the marina.

"That's good news! Great work!" Armani had told his crew. "Head out to the marina and see if you can spot them. If you need to, stun them, but don't hurt them."

"Yeah, we got it." The urban hunters set off through the concrete jungle in search of their prey.

Two stalkers, Vinny and Duce, skulked around the docks trying to stay concealed while they figured out who was around. All in all, the place was pretty quiet. Only a couple of boats were illuminated from inside. They didn't see any lights on in the marina office, and the parking lot was almost empty.

"Hey, Duce, isn't that the girl we're looking for?" Vinny asked.

"Yeah, I think it is, but I thought there was only one guy with her. Who is the other guy?"

"I dunno, but they're headed for the boats. We can take them pretty easy when they pass by the little storage shed."

"Agreed. Let's get in behind them, and hit 'em with the stun guns. The boss don't want 'em hurt. They gotta be able to talk."

They spotted the woman with two men in suits and figured at least one was Miles West. The other, they reasoned, was probably the boat owner.

Vinny and Duce quickly exited their van and approached the two agents and Bramley.

"Excuse me," Vinny called. "We're lookin' for a Captain West. You guys know which boat he's on?"

Bramley and the agents froze, and Vinny and Duce blasted all three with the stun guns. They missed one of the agents, who pulled his pistol and managed to get off a shot before being stunned on a second volley. The agent shot Vinny in the chest. Bramley took a direct hit from one of the stun guns and collapsed, smacking her head.

When the bullets started flying, Duce drew his pistol and returned fire, hitting one of the agents and sending the other diving for cover. He grabbed Bramley, threw her in the van and sped off.

She moaned as she tried to recover from the blow to her head.

"Don't worry, lady. Armani Bello only wants to talk to you."

It was the last thing she heard before she blacked out.

Duce called Armani as he drove off with Bramley.

"Vinny's hit. I think he bought it. I got the girl, but the guys she was with pulled guns and started firing. I had to get outta there."

"Just get back here fast. I want to see the girl right away. We can use her as leverage to get to this Miles West guy. Does she have a cell phone?" Armani asked. He heard some scuffling on the other end of the phone.

"Yeah, and a small purse with some ID."

"Bring it to me, then take her to the warehouse and put her under lock and key."

"Uh, she's going to be out of it for a while boss. She took a nasty hit to the head on one of those pilings."

"How bad is it?"

"Small gash and a couple of big knots, but I think she should be fine."

Armani said something indistinguishable under his breath, then said, "I have some leverage now, and when the girl wakes up, I can get some answers to this mystery." He drummed his fingers on his desk, trying to expel restless tension. "Bring me her phone," he repeated, "We will use it to draw West to us."

"All right then," Armani said to himself once he'd hung up. "Carlo doesn't know that West is in town yet. So, I think we can still nab West and get the journal before the old man even knows what happened."

Agent Carter walked into the special operations center to get an update on the shoot-out at the marina.

"What do you have so far?"

"Ramsey got hit once with a stun gun, then he took a bullet to the leg—nothing vital. He's on his way to the hospital now. Sanderson is still at the scene. One tango went down; he's dead. We're checking his ID. We have his weapon, and, no surprise, the serial number has been filed off. The other tango escaped with the woman. She appeared to have been knocked out."

"Have you pulled the surveillance video yet?"

Another agent chimed in. "We have some of it. We're piecing the rest of it together. So far, we have a couple of stills capturing each of the tangos. We're running those images through facial recognition software right now.

In addition, we have a still shot of the vehicle they were using. We're trying to find other cameras in the area to figure out where they went. The only problem is that there is very little coverage in that area. All we really know at this point is that they started out in a southward direction."

"What do you have on signals?"

"We have isolated the victim's cell phone signal, but it went down shortly after they left the parking lot."

"They probably destroyed it, but keep a trace going on it. We may get lucky if they power it back up to check it out or get something off of it."

One of the guys across the room piped up. "We got a print match from the tango that was shot at the dock."

"Put it on the main screen."

"His name is Vincent Moretti. His sheet is filled with a variety of small-time charges. We also have a list of known associates. Looks like he's part of the Bello organization."

"Which Bello?"

"Armani Bello."

"Are you sure? We've never seen Armani's guys working with Carlo's guys before."

"Maybe they're not working together," the analyst suggested.

"Put the HRT on standby." With a little luck they might have a location for the hostage rescue team to target in short order. Carter wanted to be able to react quickly when they got a hit.

Miles raced out of the building and back to the boat. He was frantic and furious at himself for letting Bramley tag along on this crazy quest. *What am I doing in the middle of this anyway?* His rage was building; it had been simmering for a long time.

The police had never found out who murdered his wife; an anger he suppressed for years welled up. He had finally let another woman into his life and now she was in jeopardy—possibly dead.

What was I thinking? This isn't a game. These are killers.

He approached the marina cautiously; there were people everywhere. The crime scene had to be cordoned off and his pathway to access the boat was closed. He was going to have to find another way to get back to the *Sea Estate*.

After sizing up the situation, he decided to leapfrog along moored boats. He had just put his foot up on the side of a boat to get an extra spring when he slipped and crashed into the side rail with his torso taking the brunt of the hit. Despite having the wind knocked out of him, he clung to the rail. He held there just a moment to catch his breath and then pulled himself up and over the edge. When he made it over, he poked at his rib cage. From the searing pain in his side, it felt like he had broken every rib, but as his fingers traced over the impact spot, he could not feel any fractures.

The last two hops were short enough that he could almost walk across. It took him a lot longer than he anticipated to reach the old sportfishing boat. No one was this far out on the pier, so he could move freely without drawing unwanted attention. He didn't cut the lights on, instead moving around the cabin under the dim illumination of the dock lights. The challenge of getting to the boat had settled him somewhat. He realized that he needed to think straight and keep his wits about him. Most of all, he needed to keep his emotions bottled up. Bramley was depending on him; he needed to be logical and smart to find and rescue her.

His first order of business was to gather all their stuff and get off the boat. He packed up his backpack, got the computer tablet from behind the TV, pulled all the notes and maps together. He left the excess clothes and toiletries. He grabbed the first aid kit, then spotted the flare kit and strapped it on his backpack. He turned slowly as he looked around the dark room. When the refrigerator came into view, he strode over, opened it and grabbed a couple of bottles of water and the bag of granola that was on the counter.

He hauled all the gear to the gangway at the back of the boat. Looking around, he still didn't see anyone nearby, so he climbed the ladder to the bridge and peered over the other boats. No one was on this end of the pier. The few people that were around crowded the crime scene, trying to get a glimpse at what was transpiring, all the while whispering the latest rumor to neighbors or talking on their cells. It was bizarre how these things drew the curious like moths to light.

Miles went to the storage compartment and pulled out the *Sea Estate*'s inflatable dingy and grabbed a paddle. He slowly twisted the valve on the compressed air tank, and the little rubber boat unfolded as the air hissed and raced into its sealed compartments. The noise seemed loud; he kept looking up, expecting to find someone standing there asking him what he was doing. When it was filled to capacity, he lifted the craft over the side and gently lowered it to the water without a sound. Next, he lowered the quadcopter case, then his backpack.

He paddled to the water's edge and hiked to the spot where they had left the electric motorcycle in the parking lot. As he stood there contemplating his next move, his phone buzzed with a text message from Bramley's phone.

Trade you the girl for the journal, Central Park, 20 minutes, come alone. The location was marked with a digital pin. He typed *OK*, thought about it for a second, then hit send.

"Okay, boys, let's play ball," Miles said with cold malice as he powered down his phone. "I am not going to make it easy."

He pulled a second phone out of his backpack and powered it up. Then he brought up a map of New York City and zoomed in on Central Park, scrolled up, then down, then side to side. Then he smiled as he thought of his eye in the sky.

"We have a hit on Fairchild's phone!" an agent at the FBI operations center announced. "It was just powered on."

"How long until you get a fix on it?"

"Working on it. A text message was just sent from the phone."

"I want to know what was sent and who it was sent to!" demanded Carter.

"We don't have access to see the text message yet, but we will work on it."

"We have a location."

"Spin up HRT!" Carter barked. "We need to get them deployed to that location ASAP!"

"HRT Alert confirmed."

CHAPTER
TWENTY-FOUR

MILES ZIPPED THROUGH THE streets on the electric motorcycle, the whir of the little motor drowned out by surrounding traffic. Quickly, he worked his way over to a street running parallel to Central Park, turned in and cut off his headlight. Miles knew Central Park pretty well, despite it being spread over 600-plus acres. Bramley's captors wanted to meet at Bow Bridge for the exchange. Miles found a spot under cover close to the turtle pond. This would be a good place to launch the drone and get a lay of the land.

"We got the text message," an FBI analyst announced as he put it on the main screen and everyone read. *Trade you the girl for the journal, Central Park, 20 minutes, come alone.* The location was marked with a digital pin. The reply was just two letters, *OK.*

"That location is in the middle of Central Park."

"Tommy, you and Keith get over there and see if you can intercept them," Agent Carter said.

Miles looked at his watch; they would be expecting him to make contact in about five minutes. He quickly unpacked the drone from its padded carrying case. After powering up and checking the flight controls, he sent it straight up, over 400 feet in the air. Then he slowly moved it toward Bow Bridge. Once he spotted the bridge, he started flying concentric loops around the spot. He spotted one person standing there, looking around, smoking a cigarette. He knew others had to be close. On his next pass, just as he anticipated he spotted a pair of people behind some rocks, just north of the path that he would've taken to reach the bridge. He kept moving farther away, but at no point did he see any women who even slightly resembled Bramley. That pretty much confirmed his suspicion; they intended to trap him.

After finding the pair stationed on the north side of the bridge, Miles returned to the south side, making several trips back and forth. He noticed another pair of guys moving slowly toward a grove of trees. Just before they entered, he saw them separate and move in two different directions.

"Okay, they plan to take up positions on each of the four compass points around the meeting location. They're here to capture me and not make the exchange. Well, fellows, that is your first mistake," Miles whispered.

He hit the button to recall the drone to his location. In less than a minute the drone returned. He repacked and strapped the drone case onto the motorcycle while checking out his surroundings. For a moment, he debated the merits of leaving his backpack and hiding it with the motorcycle, then decided to take it with him. From his backpack he removed a small metal bar wrapped with cloth and tape. He had found it in the storage compartment on the boat and had taken it to use as a truncheon; he had no idea of its real purpose. He would have to ask Trevor about that, because he was really curious.

Quickly but quietly, he made his way to the backside of the rocks. As he approached, he moved from tree to tree, staying directly behind the one man still hiding in the rocks. He slowly scanned 360 degrees to make sure he wasn't being flanked. Adrenaline surged as he redoubled his efforts to slow down and maintain a stealthy approach. His plan was to put the guy in a sleeper hold; then he noticed something laying on a rock next to his adversary that he couldn't identify. *Is that a gun?* He made a misstep, and the guy turned his way with a startled look and launched at Miles, who easily deflected him and hit him on the side of the head with his makeshift truncheon. The cretin looked dazed.

"Where's your buddy?" Miles asked.

"Oh, my head," the man groaned. Miles balled up his fist and knocked him out cold. He looked around to make sure their little scuffle had not been noticed. Miles removed a couple of zip ties from his backpack and confiscated the guy's phone and gun. He then went back over to the rock where he saw the dark object. It turned out, the thing on the rock was a stun gun. The only other thing his foe had was an old wallet, which Miles left with him.

"They're using stun guns to capture me. Well, I guess that's one positive note," Miles mumbled. He thought, *One down, three to go.* He needed to get one of these guys alone so he could find out where they were holding Bramley.

After backtracking, he made an arc to the northwest side of the meeting location, where he anticipated he would be behind the second guy. With his borrowed stun gun, he quickly subdued the thug and left him securely gagged and tied up. He was making his way back to the electric motorcycle when he heard someone yelling. Two guys were running up the path toward him, and they were chasing a third guy.

Miles quickly surmised, "Shit, someone was mistaken for me."

Miles pulled on his helmet to race toward the ruckus. As soon as he engaged the motor at full throttle, the back wheel threw dirt in a big, brown rooster tail as it sought to gain traction. He came out of the trees like a possessed, black-clad wraith. The first two guys never knew what hit them as he sped past, clubbing one in the head with his metal bar and launching the other assailant into the air with a direct hit from a head-on collision that sent the guy sprawling. He fought to regain control from the collision and quickly stopped and turned around to see if he needed to make another pass. He saw a muzzle flash and then a large, dark SUV bucking as it hit assorted obstacles coming over the rise. Miles hit the accelerator again, making a spinning U-turn and once again spraying dirt backward as he shot off in the opposite direction like a rocket. The SUV stopped to pick up the lone gunman.

Miles got way ahead, racing down the path, and then darted through a wooded area. The small motorcycle easily maneuvered between the clustered grove of trees. This little stand would also hopefully provide protection from a stray bullet. In the distance, he heard police sirens. Reaching the other side, he found another pathway. Slowly, he maneuvered through the parking lot and stopped before moving back on the street. He pulled out his cell phone and called Carlo. The message went to voicemail.

"You just tried to double-cross me, and that was a really big mistake. If you ever want to see this journal, you better make sure that nothing happens to her. Next time it will be on my turf and my terms." He powered his phone back down and rode off into the night.

"Sir, Agent Jones is reporting that local police are responding to an incident in the park."

"What is going on?" Agent Carter said, exasperated because Miles wasn't responding to his phone calls. He tried to have the phone traced, but it was currently powered down. Yet he was sure that Miles had gone to that park.

"What's the status of HRT?"

"They just arrived at the phone's active location, and they are getting ready to deploy."

Carter thought for a minute. "Get them to hold position." He looked up at the text message about the exchange and its location in the park, which was not where the hostage rescue team was currently being deployed.

"Give me Agent Jones."

"Sir, there are four tangos down, with various injuries, none of them life-threatening. Two of them were bound with commercial zip ties normally used for ductwork, and they had duct tape over their mouths. We are running IDs on all of them right now. There was a civilian who said he was being chased by two men. As he was running down the path, a guy on a stealth motorcycle came out of nowhere and ran them over. A third guy pulled a gun and started shooting at him. That's when the man on the motorcycle wheeled around and fled. The dark SUV came roaring through the park, collected the gunman, and took off after him. The local police pursued the SUV but lost it."

"Did you find Miss Fairchild?"

"There is no sign of her." Agent Carter heard rustling in the background. "One more thing: these guys were carrying stun guns as well as firearms."

"That's something you don't usually see," Agent Carter replied. "Let me know when you get IDs."

He switched his communication gear so he could talk to the HRT leader.

"Sir, I have the HRT leader for you. His name is Pat O'Brian."

"Sit rep?" Carter asked sharply, condensing the question "Hey, O'Brian, how's it going down there? Can you give me a situation report?" into two succinct syllables.

"We are staged outside the target location; it's a residence. We've identified five tangos, but we have not seen the hostage. We are doing some recon. Do you have any additional information?"

"Wait one." Agent Carter looked at his analyst and snapped his fingers. "Is Fairchild's phone still at that location?"

"Yes, it's still there. Just sent another text."

Carter replied to the HRT leader, "The hostage's phone is still at your location, and it is being used. Continue to hold position. Alert me if you spot the hostage."

Carlo had been stomping around his home, waiting for an update on the search for Miles West, when one of his informants called and said that the FBI had one of Armani's men.

Carlo only trusted three men. One was simply known as Conti. Carlo waved him over, and whispered, "The FBI has one of Armani's people. Get over there find out what's going on." Conti nodded and left the room.

Carlo had recently become more paranoid that he had a leak in his organization, and he suspected his son Armani might know more about his business than he should know. Now that the FBI had one of Armani's guys, Carlo wanted to know what was going on. He knew Armani had a couple of problems because he had rigged some contracts. But was Armani working with the feds? Would he try and cop a deal to sell out his own father? Carlo didn't think so, but he had to consider the possibility.

Carlo looked down at his vibrating phone. *Finally, a report on West,* he thought. When he listened to the message he was flabbergasted and called on another of his top three guys.

"Roman, come here. Listen to this message." Carlo set the phone on his desk, pressed the speaker icon, then played the message.

"You just tried to double-cross me, and that was a really big mistake. If you ever want to see this journal, you better make sure that nothing happens to her. Next time it will be on my turf and my terms."

He played it a third time.

Roman said, "Somebody's got the girl, and they are trying to trade her for the journal."

"My thoughts exactly," replied Carlo. "I think we've got a mole in our house. I also suspect that Armani has the girl." He was livid at the thought that his son was trying steal the journal out from under him. He had given him everything. He helped him start his business, and now he was being betrayed by his own flesh and blood.

The old mob patriarch clenched his fist as his face glowed beet red.

"Roman, go and figure out where he's holding the girl, get her and bring her to me. We need her to get that journal!"

"I don't get it. Why isn't he responding to our text?" Armani asked in frustration.

Paolo sipped his Coke and wiped his mouth on his sleeve. "We will get him. We have five guys at the meeting location."

"What did you find out about Vinny? How bad was he hit?"

"I sent the kid over to the marina. He said the coroner was there, and Vinny had a sheet over him. He's dead."

Well, at least I don't have to worry about him running his mouth, Armani thought.

Armani's phone rang.

"He got away, boss! We were chasing him toward Mikey and Tito and this dude came out of nowhere on a black bike and runs over Frankie and Knuckles. I tried to cap him, but he was too far away. We started to chase the guy on the motorbike, but the cops showed up."

"What happened to Frankie and Knuckles?"

"We didn't see 'em and they're not answering their phones, so I dunno know what happened to them."

Armani fumed silently and swore under his breath. "I am surrounded by incompetent morons. I told them not to kill him." Barely restraining his rising anger, he barked, "Just stay put. I'll get back to you."

"Have you got IDs on those guys from the park yet?" Agent Carter asked.

An analyst replied, "I am putting them up now. As we suspected, these guys are also tied to Armani Bello. We got a couple of phones and weapons off them. The weapons that were recovered had the serial numbers removed, so we will run them though ballistics and see if anything pops. The phones gave us a bit more information. We plugged them into the system and are logging their locations and call lists." He tapped a few keys and a new image popped onto the central screen. "You are looking at call clusters attached to each of the three phones recovered so far." The image looked like a spider web combined with a flowchart. "As you can see, there are calls linked to a dozen other phones and each other and at the very center of them is Armani Bello."

"What is that outlier?" Agent Carter asked.

"That is a link to one Eddie Lorenzo, who just happens to be a known associate with Carlo Bello."

"Damn," the special agent huffed.

He mentally ticked off charges that could be brought up against these guys: kidnapping; extortion; assault with a deadly weapon. This evening was turning out to be full of surprises. He checked his phone to see if he had any new messages. None had appeared since the last time he looked at it. He thought, *Where the hell is West and why isn't he returning my calls?* The more he thought about it, the more confident he became that Miles West was the one on the motorcycle. He was trying to get Fairchild back on his own.

CHAPTER
TWENTY-FIVE

MILES INSPECTED THE PHONES he had taken off the guys that he subdued at the park. The simple flip phones had a short list of phone numbers, and only first names were associated with each of the numbers. He wrote down all the names and numbers. When he finished, he compared the lists. Most of the phone numbers were duplicates. After recording all the useful information they contained, he dropped each phone on the ground and crushed it with the heel of his shoe, pulverizing the little pieces of plastic, glass and metal. He looked at his notes, then circled Armani. *So, it must be Armani Bello who has Bramley.*

Miles pulled out his map and looked at all the locations they had previously identified as Armani Bello's locations, marked with *AB* on the map. There were seven to choose from.

"Where to begin?" he muttered. It seemed unlikely that Armani would be keeping her at his home; that just didn't make sense. There was a construction site that would be empty given that it was a Saturday evening. That might be a good place to start. The warehouse might also be a good location. He decided to start with the construction site.

Miles held the disposable phone on which Armani had texted him earlier. He debated the merits of turning it on to check new messages, but he didn't like the idea that someone might locate him with it. He thought about what he would say to the person holding Bramley's phone. As he played out various conversations in his head, he didn't like the outcomes of any of them. He had to stay in control and be logical. He took some deep breaths, which made his bruised ribs ache.

Tossing the phone up in the air, he watched it flip end over end, then caught it and stuffed it back into his pocket. No, he wouldn't engage them until he was good and ready, and next time they would have to bring her to him. He was going to make them put her on the phone, and he would be someplace where he could observe everything that was happening. He would figure out a way to make sure he got her back safely. Miles put on the helmet and climbed back on the motorcycle, heading out into the crisp, cool night.

His first stop was a pharmacy to get pain pills for his ribs. As he walked through the sliding glass door, he ended up in front of a makeup counter. He spotted a lady's compact hand mirror, which sparked an idea. He went up and down the aisles collecting a couple of odds and ends. He most definitely would be able to make use of the paracord. *Better get two packages of them.* Steel wool, 9-volt battery, Bluetooth speaker, a volleyball, and of course some maximum-strength pain relief.

If this construction site location was not where Bramley was located, it might be the perfect place to draw them in and make the exchange. Miles would need to find a spot where he could set up the mirror. He figured he could use his red laser pointer, bounce it off the mirror and give his adversaries the impression that someone had them targeted in their sights. He would give them very specific instructions not to move from the spot. That would be where the computer/journal would be lowered, suspended with paracord attached to the drone. He hoped the drone could carry the extra weight; he would need to test that assumption. A well-placed shot to the volleyball marking their spot would demonstrate his marksmanship and give them pause to test his resolve.

Miles would use the Bluetooth speaker to communicate with them from ground zero, so they wouldn't be able to tell where he was positioned. He could also use the drone to scout out their car on the way in and make sure there were no tagalong guys. His insurance policy would be a threat—if either he or Bramley were killed, the information would be released on the internet. He had to work out more of the details, but he felt confident that he had a pretty good plan for the exchange.

"This is O'Brian,"

"Go ahead," said Carter.

"Sir, we've got another player that showed up to the party. Only he's not going straight in; it's like he's casing the joint."

"Oh shit! That must be West trying to find Fairchild. He's going to screw everything up." He paced over to another workstation to view the location via a remote camera that had been set up. "Can you apprehend him without alerting Armani and company? We need to use nonlethal force, as he is a civilian and not one of the bad guys."

"Roger, wait one."

They actually waited several minutes before he came back on the line.

"Three members of my team got him, but not without a struggle. We had to take him down with a sleeper hold, and one of my guys almost got cut. The target went for a knife and started slashing. Turns out the tango is not West; according to his New York driver's license, his name is Michael Conti."

Agent Carter smiled. "Well, this day just keeps getting better and better. That's Carlo Bello's number two guy. Keep him on ice. We'll convey him down here. I would like to have a little talk with him. Does he have a phone on him?"

"He had a phone and a Glock 9mm, no serial number."

"Bingo."

Before he could ask, his analyst said, "I'm on it." He would get the information off of that phone and add it to his growing database of numbers, calls and geolocation tags.

"Damn it!" Carlo had been trying to get Conti with no response. He called Roman for an update. "What's going on?"

"I am on my way to a bar Armani's guys frequent, to see if I can squeeze some information out of one of them."

"Conti's not answering his phone."

"Do you think they took him out?"

Carlo had been asking himself the same question, but he didn't want to say it out loud. "Nobody could get the drop on Conti, but he is not responding, and I don't like it. Get some more guys and get back here. We need to gun up and figure out just what's going down."

"I'll call in the other boys and have them meet me at your house. Just stay low. I'll be there in a bit."

Carlo was once again pacing back and forth, trying to decide just how far his son might go. He had survived two other attempted coups, one in the '70s and the other in the '90s. Those had been attempted by rival mob families. He never envisioned being betrayed by his own son.

Carlo played a scenario out in his head as his naturally suspicious nature overrode his familial bonds. Armani knew that Conti was Carlo's key man. In fact, he knew almost all of Carlo's men. Taking Conti out would be a logical move if Armani were plotting a takeover. *But how does the little punk think he can get away with it? What will he do next?*

Miles parked the electric motorcycle behind a dumpster outside of the perimeter fence. The dumpster served as a convenient entry point to the construction site. After looking around to make sure he was alone, he climbed on top of the dumpster, then looked over the fence. There were piles of building materials everywhere. His perch on top of the dumpster extended his field of view across the construction site, and he still didn't see anyone nearby, so he decided to jump the fence. Fortunately, there was small pile of construction sand on the opposite side that would make a decent landing spot. He landed awkwardly on one knee, then got up and dusted himself off.

He made his way toward the construction trailer. The loose dirt was dry and helped him make a silent approach as he cut a circuitous path to avoid the lighted areas as much as possible. The steps were sturdy but well worn. He tried the first door, but it was securely locked. He made his way to the next door, which was also locked. Using his flashlight, he examined it more closely. It wasn't dead-bolted, so he pulled out his pocket knife and pushed the tip of the slender blade down just behind the lock. The gap of the opening between the door and the jam was just wide enough that he could wiggle it. The latch bolt was slowly pushed back into the lock, and the door popped open.

After he checked his surroundings once more, he made his way in and looked around the place. It just had a couple of desks and a big table in the center with plans stretched all over it. The doors to each of the restrooms were angled open. *Why did they even bother to lock it?* Flashing his light over the table, he performed a quick inspection of the building floor plan. He tried to assess any spots they might use to hide someone. Once he had committed the plan to memory, he exited the trailer. Relocking the door, he set out to canvass the site.

Miles froze mid-step. He was certain he had heard a noise. Moving between the stacks of cinderblocks, pallets of concrete mix, and heavy equipment, he slowly made his way toward the main portion of the partially completed building. He spotted two men prowling around. *Probably vagrants,* he thought. He had covered most of the site but came up with nothing, and it didn't seem like a good spot to set up his own ambush. *Bramley's not here. Better get out of here before I get spotted.* As Miles rode away from the site, he heard an explosion. One of the vagrants had tossed his cigarette onto a pallet full of five-gallon stain buckets, one of which was leaking.

A call came in about fifteen minutes after the explosion.

"What is happening?" Armani asked. *Is someone trying to send me a message? Who?* It occurred to Armani that one of the other crime families might be out to take over his operation. But he was powerful and that seemed very unlikely. Something wasn't right, though. He had lost four more guys at the Central Park meet site and one at the marina. Now, someone blew up one of his construction sites.

"How many men do we have here?"

"Four of us plus you," Paolo replied.

"Call Nucci and get him to bring his boys over here. We need some reinforcements. Break out the heavy guns too. I'm not sure what's going on, but I want to be ready for anything."

One of his men called back from the other room. "Nucci wants to know if he should bring the woman here?"

Armani thought about it for a minute, "No, leave her locked up at the warehouse." He grabbed his phone and sent a text off to Eddie. *R U up?*

Yes. Place buzzing. Everybody here. Getting ready.

He typed, *GOING WHERE?*

IDK your old man keeps whispering to Roman.

He tapped *K* and hit send.

What are you up to old man? Armani stood spellbound. *What made you call everybody in? Why are you getting everyone geared up?*

"Sir, you have another call from O'Brian."

Carter said, "Go ahead, O'Brian."

"We have parabolic mics on the target residence. We just picked up a couple of conversations. First, the target was notified of an explosion at one of his construction sites. The second was a call to a man named Nucci about getting additional men and coming here to provide additional manpower. During that conversation the question was asked, 'Should we bring the woman back here?' The response was, 'No leave her locked up at the warehouse.' It appears that the hostage is at a third location."

Before Agent Carter had a chance to respond, O'Brian interjected, "One more thing; these guys are gunning up, like they're going to war. They have started passing out machine guns. Whatever is going to go down, it could get very messy."

Now it looks like we will have to get the ATF in on this little party. Agent Carter grimaced at the thought of adding the Bureau of Alcohol, Tobacco, and Firearms to his case. It would complicate his life exponentially.

"Did they mention the location of the warehouse?"

"No, I was hoping you had some information on where that might be located."

"We will check it out, and get back to you. Can you guys keep eyes and ears on the site, without getting compromised?" He thought for a moment, then he added, "Without getting yourself in the middle of a mob war?"

"We are secure for the moment. Just get me a location for that hostage. If I hear anything, we will let you know. At the point this place starts getting overrun, we're going to fall back and make a retreat."

Carter's eyes were drawn to a workstation, where one of the analysts had a couple of screenshots of a raging fire. "Where's that inferno? Is that the Bello construction site we just heard about?" he asked.

"Yes," the analyst replied with cold efficiency. Her fingers danced across her keyboard as she worked to quickly capture as many newsfeeds of the unfolding event as she could find.

"So, what do you want to do? Should we call Armani?" Roman asked his boss.

"No, I think we'll go over there with overwhelming force. I think he is trying to pick off a few guys at a time or make them disappear and blame it on someone else. I just made a call to someone who keeps watch on his place for me. He says Armani's place is all lit up, and he is definitely not having a party. It seems that there is a lot of activity over there with people coming and going, and some of the guys are openly walking around with weapons slung over their shoulders. So, Roman, what do you think he is doing up in the middle of the night? And why does he have his guys armed to the teeth?"

Roman shrugged. "None of this makes any sense."

As Carlo continued to pace, he said, "We still haven't heard from Conti. I'm thinking about heading over there, surrounding his place, and then having a little conversation. I want to know what he has been doing behind my back. How many guys do we have available?"

Roman had just been doing a headcount. "We have nine guys here. I can get a couple more to meet us if we need them."

"Anybody you worried about?"

"You read my mind. Eddie Lorenzo. He and Armani grew up together. Eddie's always been loyal to us. So, do we take him or leave him?"

The old, gray-haired mob patriarch leaned in and whispered, "Keep your friends close, and your enemies closer. Make sure he's right out front, especially if it gets loud."

Roman checked his 9 mm. "You know, if we go over there, they got the home court advantage." He dropped the clip and confirmed it was fully loaded. Then he popped it back in. Finished with his check, he returned the matte-black gun to his underarm holster.

Carlo ticked off a list of suspicious activities that, when viewed together, suggested that his son was plotting against him.

"From where I'm standing, it looks like he's trying to make a move on me. Do you disagree?"

"No, boss. It doesn't look good."

"Let's load up. Get those other guys to meet us over there."

Armani was ready and waiting. He texted Eddie again but didn't get a reply. The lack of a response made him particularly nervous.

"Tell everyone to be alert. We may be getting some unexpected visitors. Put the guys in the defensive positions too. That way, if anyone comes at us, we can hit 'em from two directions."

One of the sentries called in.

"Hey, we have some people moving in out here. They are all around the house. I think I see Carlo's SUV."

"How many?" Armani asked.

The radio squawked a bit before the reply came through. "I'm not sure. I can only see a couple of guys from here."

Carlo and Roman sat on the street in his bulletproof SUV, waiting for everyone to get in position before they made the final turn into the driveway. One by one, each of Roman's guys checked in. They were just getting in position to have the place surrounded.

A neighbor, old Mr. Potter, had fallen asleep and was snoozing when he heard a crash in his backyard. He had put up fishing line tied to garbage cans and other countermeasures to alert him of intruders. He bolted upright out of a dead sleep and said, "I got you little shits now."

This time he was prepared for those little hoodlums vandalizing his yard. He had his shotgun loaded with rock salt. His mind was groggy, but one thought was clear: *Since the police can't stop them, maybe this will scare the little twerps.* As fast as he could move his old bones, he made his way to his back door and peeked out. He made out someone with his back to him peering over his back fence into his neighbor's yard. If he had been more alert, not having been roused out of a dead sleep, Mr. Potter might have stopped to ask himself why the guy was looking the other way over the fence. He swung the door wide open, stepped outside, took aim, and fired.

Ka-boom! The shotgun erupted with a ferocity that would rouse the dead.

That single shot was the spark that lit the fuse and ignited a mob war. After the first shot, everyone else opened up on their targets. Armani's guys were firing at Carlo's guys and vice versa. Half a dozen guys on each side went down in the first few seconds with the first volley of shots. Then it turned into pure chaos as people tried to acquire other targets by focusing on muzzle flashes anywhere in their view line.

Shots pinged off the sides of Carlo's SUV.

"That's coming from behind us!" Roman yelled. "Get outta here! Go! Go! Go!" He slammed the back of the driver's headrest.

Carlo's faithful driver, Mateo, punched the gas pedal to the floor, and the wheels squealed as he peeled out. He tried to keep it straight, racing down the street to escape the line of fire.

HRT leader O'Brien said, "Aw shit." He cursed himself for not pulling back sooner. As much as he didn't like it, it looked like he was going to have to clean up this mess.

"Hold positions. Make sure all the tangos are in the box. We don't want to get caught in the crossfire."

He switched coms channels. "Carter, get reinforcements over here pronto. We have a mob war and it's gone loud."

Men scattered in every direction. Those caught in the crossfire were either dead or hunkering down in place trying to stay out of the line of fire. Those positioned inside the house continued firing. Muzzle flashes illuminated their positions. Meanwhile, lights inside the house were rapidly extinguished to make it more difficult to be seen. Windows splintered and glass shattered as lead fell like windblown hail. After the initial flurry of volleys back and forth, the firefight quickly diminished. Most of the men were wounded or dead. Only a few remained in the fight. Consequently, only sporadic shots were being made.

O'Brien used a bullhorn.

"This is the FBI. You are surrounded. Put your weapons down. Lay down on the ground with your arms away from you." He had already briefed his team on their ROE, or the rules of engagement, for this scenario. Over his coms he queried his men to sound off and give him a status report. One by one, each of his team members provided an update. Only two men had to return fire on noncompliant targets.

"One and four, start securing the tangos. Two, three, five and six, provide overwatch and cover. If anyone twitches, give 'em a warning shot; anything else, put 'em down."

All of the mobsters were caught off guard. No one had been prepared for the FBI to be on site. A few guys tried to make an escape, but a couple of well-placed shots put them down on the ground, writhing in pain. Those two examples swiftly took the fight out of the rest of them.

In the house, Armani was cursing like a drunken sailor. Hurriedly, he moved around behind his desk, opened up his safe and pulled out the duffel bag that he had stashed in it for a speedy departure. He told the couple of guys who were uninjured to follow him. They moved toward the kitchen, then down a back staircase. When he had built the house, a tunnel was installed to serve as his escape route if he ever had to make an abrupt, covert exit. He never thought he would have to use it. He couldn't believe he was using it now.

Where did the FBI come from? The more astounding realization, which he was having trouble understanding, was that the old man was actually gunning for him. Armani would just have to send a message right back. He knew exactly where he was going right after he made one little detour to a storage locker that he had rented.

CHAPTER TWENTY-SIX

FISHY BUSINESS WAS CARLO'S pride and joy. The old man used it often. As soon as the weather was favorable, he would head out. The yacht was not only outfitted as a sportfishing boat but had all the scuba gear for diving and underwater exploration.

Armani's boys had long ago planted tracking devices on the boat to be able to follow it from discreet distances. The destination was always in the same general area—just off the coast of Newport. In the early years, they had started close to shore with their rectangular routes. But as time passed, each successive trip ventured farther south, out into a new quadrant of the ocean, where they would make crosshatch trips back and forth. Armani was certain that they were looking for something, but that was one of his father's secrets he had not been able to discover. He wrote it off as one of his father's eccentricities, as he could not fathom what might hold such appeal.

He knew where the *Fishy Business* was docked, and also knew that no one would be around at this hour. Dawn was rapidly approaching, so he needed to hurry. He wanted to take full advantage of the darkness and the cover it provided for his nefarious task.

He had always liked the yacht, and for a time he thought he might keep it when he took over the family empire. But as more time passed, the less enamored he was with the old boat. To have the kind of yacht he envisioned, it would need to be totally rebuilt. All of that useless equipment would have to be torn out, and decks would need to be replaced. Even the staterooms needed to be refurbished to make the ship inhabitable. No, given all the refitting that would be needed, he concluded he would be much better off with a new yacht. That realization made his course of retribution an easy decision.

Armani and his little crew arrived at the marina before dawn. The eastern sky was just beginning to get a little lighter.

"Okay, we need to get in and get out. Does everyone know what you're doing?" Armani asked.

They all nodded their affirmations. One by one, they climbed out of the minivan and went around back to pick up several large, black duffel bags. One of the bags made a little noise because it had cans of paint thinner. The metal cans clanked as the bag shifted. Armani grabbed the smaller duffel with the explosives and detonators. While he didn't know much about the details of his construction business, he had learned everything he needed to know to blast those pesky rocks that needed to be removed before one of his buildings could go up. He loved blowing things up.

The three men moved silently across the boardwalk and out to the yacht without being noticed. Quickly they entered through the main door and moved to perform their assigned tasks. Armani went to the engine room to place two devices near the main fuel lines. Little Anthony disabled the fire suppression system built into the engine room.

"Ant, are you finished yet?" Armani asked as he secured the last detonator.

"Yeah, boss," he grunted. Something cracked as it was ripped off the wall. "Just want to disable this last sensor." Another crack and ripping sound emanated from the far side of the engine bay.

"Okay, let's go."

As they walked back through the main stateroom, the fumes from the paint thinner they were using as an accelerant almost knocked them out.

"It's going to go up like a rocket," whispered one of the confederates as he grabbed the duffel with the empty cans and made a hasty retreat.

Armani smiled, anticipating the impending inferno.

"Let's find a spot to watch this little show." He wished he had a camera to capture the moment. He would love to send it to the old man. "This is what you get for shooting up my place," he said under his breath.

An impressive fireball erupted. Floating fuel ignited and spread the roaring inferno to neighboring boats.

Agent Carter walked through the exterior crime scene and into the house, taking note of all the bullet holes. He thought, *The CSI guys are going to be here a long time getting everything documented.* The few wounded had been stabilized and hauled away. The dead lay covered in white sheets ready for the coroner to process them. The place looked more like a war zone than a typical residential neighborhood. With the exception of the neighbor, Mr. Potter, who admitted to firing the first shot, all parties involved had been either associated with Carlo or Armani.

Agent Carter peered around the corner of the kitchen to the stairs that led to the basement escape tunnel. "He had this planned out," he mumbled. He retraced his footsteps back to the office and the open, empty safe. He looked around the room and noted that a couple of cabinet doors had been left ajar. He tried to divine what Armani had been doing.

"Okay, so you had to make a hasty getaway. You grabbed stuff out of the safe and out of a couple of these cabinets, then dashed out the escape tunnel. You had to leave in a hurry, and you couldn't take everything, so what did you leave me?"

Something was bothering him, but he couldn't put his finger on what didn't fit. He paced the office and then walked into the adjacent room and back toward the kitchen again. It had been a very long day; he had been up for almost twenty-four hours, so his mind was a little fuzzy.

Thankfully, the last cup of high-test coffee was starting to kick in and clear his mental fog. He looked at the wall to his right, envisioning the office behind it. Then he became very excited as it dawned on him that the office was too small. He had to make sure. Quickly, he returned to the office and counted off the paces from one side of the room to the other. Then he walked through the doorway into the next room, the living room.

He paced off the exact number of steps he made in the office and realized there was eight feet unaccounted for between the office and the kitchen.

He returned to the office, yet again, and this time started looking at the wall that should back up to the kitchen. It was lined with bookcases and cabinets. He pulled out his phone and turned on its flashlight. He dropped to the floor, getting on his hands and knees. Surely, there would be some scratches on the floor near a doorway. He moved back and forth; then he found it right in front of the middle bookcase: scratches going under the molding. The base of the molding had a gap that was just a little larger than the shoe molding next to it. He was sure he had located the hidden door to access a room behind that bookcase. Now, if he could just figure out how it opened.

Agent Carter called one of the techs over.

"I think we have a hidden room here, and this bookcase is somehow covering the doorway that will allow us to access it. How do we get it open?"

The technician looked around, then noticed the thermostat on the wall. "What do you want to bet that the thermostat is not really a thermostat?" He went over pulled off the cover and examined it. He took the thing off the wall. "Well, I'll be a monkey's uncle," murmured the tech in surprise.

"What?" asked Carter.

"I was right and wrong. I mean, it actually is a thermostat. Do you see this extra bundle of wires? Those don't go to the HVAC unit, so they must operate the door. The thermostat touch pad initiates an open and close function like a switch. We just don't know the code." Carter deflated at that statement. "However, I think I could just cut the wires and sort of hotwire it. It's just a fancy switch."

"Give it a try," prompted Carter.

The tech cut the wires and then stripped them and touched the first pair together. Nothing happened. Then he tried another combination, and the bookcase moved backwards. When it had recessed about eight inches, a light inside automatically came on. The bookcase started to swing left. When it reached about forty-five degrees, it stopped. Everything was quiet. Carter had pulled out his 9 mm as soon as the door started to open.

"Well, well, well, what do we have here, Armani? Were you spying on Carlo?"

A bulletin board was full of pictures. Most of Carlo's associates were pinned up with various notes posted under them. On a nearby bookshelf were a couple of journals. He glanced around the room, and he spotted a box with microcassettes and another with silver CDs. There were stacks of CDs with notations on them piled in one corner.

"Son of a bitch!" Agent Carter said as he plopped down into the big black swivel desk chair. He thought he must be dreaming; there was no way he could be this lucky. He slowly spun the chair around the room and took it all in. If he was right, he had just stumbled onto a record of the Bello family's greatest hits. He had no doubt this stuff could put the crime family behind bars for a couple of lifetimes. He texted Miles West.

We have all we need to take down the Bellos.

Armani pulled out his phone. A text message alerted him that an additional silent alarm had been triggered at his home: *Safe Room Breach.*

Damn! How did they find my secret room? Much less breech it. He needed to leave the country, immediately.

Much of his illegal wealth had long ago been moved to accounts in the Caribbean and Switzerland. He could access them from anywhere. He would need to find a country without an extradition treaty. How had everything fallen apart so fast? He was so close to taking over his father's empire.

He dropped his guys off at one of the subway lines and told them, "Go get some sleep. I'll call you later." However, he had no intention of ever talking to any of them again.

He turned north and headed for Canada. He had a Canadian passport and from there he could head to one of the Caribbean islands and figure out his next steps.

CHAPTER
TWENTY-SEVEN

BENITO THREW DOWN THE newspaper in disgust. His shortsighted half brother had sullied the family name again. Another headline touted new allegations of price-fixing on a contracting bid for yet another public works project that Armani's construction firm was trying to secure. Benito sighed. *It just never ends.* He had been working for years to restore the Bello family name. Recently, he had hosted a successful fundraiser for the Polycystic Kidney Disease Foundation to help find a cure for that lesser known disease. It seemed like it was always two steps forward and one step backward. *If the bloody fool would just keep a low profile, my life would be so much easier.*

It seemed to Benito that he had been trying to atone for his family's sins his entire lifetime. No matter how many philanthropies he supported, or good works he did, he always felt guilty and ashamed. He had never married because he didn't want to bring anybody else into his world, fearing that at any moment he would be drawn into the web of his father's crime syndicate.

His longtime girlfriend constantly tried to reassure him that he was his own man, a good man, a man that always made sound choices. She admonished him, "Stop living in your father's shadow."

The thought of *restorations* brought him back to the moment and to one of his recent projects. He picked up the paperwork on an old warehouse that he had just purchased at auction. He needed to visit the warehouse location and ascertain what needed to be done to convert the decaying structure into modern condominiums that would draw young urban professionals into an old, rundown part of the city. The new blood would help revitalize the neighborhood; young people had the energy to bring it back to life. He glanced at his watch. He had some extra time before he needed to meet his girlfriend, so he decided now would be a great time to visit the old warehouse and give it the once-over. He looked down at the headline, thinking, *Maybe it will even help me forget about Armani and his antics, at least for a few minutes.*

Bramley emerged from her unconscious state in a first-rate fog. Not only was she having trouble focusing on things, her memory was all muddled; she didn't know where she was, or what she had been doing.

Where am I? Why does my head hurt so bad? What time is it? What day is it?

She touched the tender lump on her head and winced at the pain. Her hand came away with a little sticky blood on it. She was subconsciously taking inventory as her brain performed its reboot procedure. Everything seemed to work, sort of. The room seemed to be spinning. She was moving slowly, and her head was throbbing, so she closed her eyes and tried to remain still to let things settle into place. The stillness made her feel better. Slowly and gingerly she lowered her head back onto her arm. "I think I'll just lay here for a couple of minutes." Then she was out again just as if a switch had been turned off.

Benito tried to focus on the good he was attempting to achieve. Bringing this old place back to life would provide homes and jobs. It would also help reverse the decay and decline of this little corner of the city. He shook his head as he surveyed the rustic exterior of the building. *This is going to be a bit more challenging than the last one.*

The old warehouse was dark and musty. The further into the structure he went, the more he recognized that it was definitely in a state of severe disrepair. Water stains and peeling paint were typical problems, but this building had exposed wires, holes in walls and floors, lots of trash and debris, and rodents darting everywhere. Benito had been in some rundown buildings before, but this had to be one of the worst piles of bricks still standing.

He moved his flashlight around in a methodical pattern, taking in the enormity of the task. Restoring this old warehouse would be a huge undertaking. If he didn't decide to demolish it and start over, it would become his most ambitious restoration yet. On his way in, he noted the rough exterior and the building's old sign painted on the weathered brickwork. It had such wonderful character that would be very difficult to replicate. Part of what made these places attractive to young people was the authentic, rustic feel.

He continued through the old hallways and passages, peering into the various storage rooms and old offices. He turned the corner and found an old door with a brand-new padlock on it. He examined the old solid oak door. It was big and beefy, and worn and scarred where it had been used for shooting practice. As he approached it, the LED beam of his flashlight highlighted gashes and pits in the wood, as well as the holes. It appeared that someone had been throwing knives at it too.

He stopped when he heard something. There it was again.

That was someone moaning, he thought. He pressed the light up to one of the holes, trying to peer inside. He could just make out the form of a person lying on the floor. *What in the world is going on? Someone is being held captive.*

He grabbed the lock and yanked it. The fasteners didn't even budge. He backtracked to a previous room where he had seen some scrap metal, and he grabbed a heavy iron bar and an old iron rail spike. He went back to the lock, put the spike in the lock and then used the heavy iron bar as a lever. The first time he tried to pry it apart, the makeshift crowbar slipped, and he busted his knuckles.

"Ouch!" he yelped as his knuckles scraped the rough wood grain. He shook his hands, then repositioned his lever and started applying steady, even pressure. Holding his flashlight in his mouth, he saw his makeshift pry bar pulling the metal clasp over the heads of the screws in the old oak door. With one final push, it popped off, allowing the door to swing open.

The room was empty except for a woman on the floor with hands and feet bound. He approached her cautiously.

"Are you okay?"

The woman tried to kick him.

"Whoa! Wait a minute. I'm trying to help you."

She stopped struggling. "Then get this off of me," she said as she stuck out her hands.

"How did you get here?" he asked.

"A couple of guys grabbed me, then one of them hit me and the next thing I know I am here . . . err, wherever here is."

He worked at the plastic zip tie with his little red Swiss Army knife.

"You're in an old warehouse. I am thinking about restoring it and converting it into apartments. I had a little extra time in my schedule this morning, so I just happened to stop in to look around." He started working on the restraints binding her feet.

"What time is it?" she inquired with both hands holding her head as she tried to stop the spinning sensation. She was feeling a bit of nausea.

He looked at his watch. "Just after seven. I guess you're probably a little hungry."

"No," she said sharply. "I am trying not to vomit. Who are you?"

"Oh yes, forgot to introduce myself. I am Benito Bello."

She jerked. "Your brother's men brought me here. What do you want?"

"I don't have anything to do with my *half* brother." He said it with such disdain that she was taken aback. Then he bent down and resumed working on the zip tie restraining her feet.

"What are you going to do with me?"

"I think the first thing we should do is get you to a hospital and have someone look at that nasty bump on your head. I'm not an expert, but it looks like that wound may need a couple of stitches. We should also contact the police. Then I want you to explain to me why Armani would want to kidnap you and tie you up."

"I need to call a friend."

He took out his phone and looked at it, then he turned the display in her direction; he wanted her to be able to see the screen.

"We don't have any service in here. You'll have to wait until we get out to the car. Can you walk?"

"I think so," she replied tentatively. "I just need to sit here for a minute."

"Can you make it to my car, or do you want me to call an ambulance?"

"Let's go to your car."

They made their way to his Toyota SUV. He opened the passenger door and helped her slide in. As he made his way around the front of the car, he pulled his cell out of his pocket. He opened the door and fell into the seat, simultaneously hitting the speed dial for Tommy.

"Hey, Tommy, it's Ben. I need your help. Can you meet me at the emergency room? Armani's guys hit a lady over the head, and I think she might have a concussion. She definitely has a gash on her head that I am guessing will need stitches. I want you to take a look at her."

"Get here as soon as you can. I'll meet you at the emergency entrance."

Bramley watched him. He looked distant, like he wasn't really there. He got out his wallet and pulled out a faded, wrinkled and worn picture of a woman holding a child. He rubbed it with his finger. A single teardrop rolled down his cheek.

She asked in a soft, gentle voice, "Who is she?"

He looked at her with a blank expression and stuffed the picture back into his wallet. "She was my mother. She died when I was almost seven."

"Oh, I'm sorry."

He started the engine.

"Who is Tommy?" she inquired.

Benito smiled. "Dr. Thomas John, perhaps the best friend a guy could ever have in the whole world. He is more of a brother to me than my own sibling."

They rode quietly for a few minutes as Bramley watched Benito out of the corner of her eye, not sure whether she could trust him.

"So, do you prefer Ben over Benito?"

"The only person that calls me Ben is Tommy. Everyone else calls me Benito."

CHAPTER
TWENTY-EIGHT

MILES FOUND AN ALL-NIGHT diner and persuaded the manager to let him run a power cord out the door to the motorcycle so that he could charge it. While he waited for it to charge, he finally made it to the restroom. His order of eggs, sausage, grits, toast and coffee came in short order. To anyone watching, it appeared that he had inhaled it, as it disappeared so fast. Someone flipped the channel from the soccer match to the news channel. The seven o'clock *Rise and Shine News Report* was just beginning. The lead story was about a fire and explosion at a Bello Contracting construction site. The fire was still burning, but it was under control and expected to be extinguished shortly.

The news commentator said, "Police have not yet determined if a shoot-out that occurred at the residence of Armani Bello is related to the explosion at his construction site. Multiple casualties were reported. We are awaiting more details from the official briefing that is expected later this morning. It's been rumored that Bello is part of a crime syndicate. The FBI agent at the site said that they would have a statement for us shortly."

Miles fumbled to power up his phone. He had several messages from Agent Carter but none from Bramley. One of the text messages that Carter sent said they were going to nail the Bellos. *But where is Bramley?*

In a flash, he threw a fifty on the counter. "Keep the change. Thanks for the charge." He unhooked the power cord, then mounted the bike. After he consulted his map and typed in the location for Armani Bello's residence into his GPS, he put in his earbud and donned his helmet. In seconds, he was speeding for the location they had simply marked as *AB residence*. He tried to call Carter back, but it went straight to voicemail.

A chirp emanated from his Bluetooth earpiece. He realized he was getting a call, although he couldn't tell who was calling. He said "Answer" to activate his earbud.

"Hello," he said tentatively.

"Miles," Bramley said with relief. "I was worried about you."

At the sound of Bramley's voice, he slammed on his brakes and came to a dead stop in the middle of the street. "Are you okay? Where are you? I was so worried about you. What happened?"

"Slow down. I got a hit on the head, but I am okay. I'm at the hospital."

A horn sounded from behind him, and he quickly maneuvered off the street and onto the sidewalk.

"Tell me where you are. I'll be right there!"

After she hung up, he bowed his head, said a prayer, and started to cry.

Miles made it to the hospital, though half the time he could barely see through the tears streaming down his cheeks. At one point, he flipped his visor up to let the cool morning air dry his face.

When he arrived outside room 315, he overheard Bramley having a stern discussion with a doctor. He knocked on the door and walked in. The swelling had gone down; she was no longer dizzy, and she was ready to go.

"Look, Doc, I really appreciate you fixing me up, but I am not going to stay in here overnight."

"All I'm saying is that concussions are difficult to diagnose. They present a variety of different effects, and the best way to ascertain your recovery is observation."

"Well, he can observe me for the next twenty-four hours," she said as she pointed to Miles.

"Oh. Is this your doctor?" he inquired.

"No, he's my new best friend!"

Miles smiled warmly at her sarcasm.

"Is she always this cooperative?" the doctor joked.

"Always," Miles smiled. "Pure attitude. Between you and me, Doc, I never win these little arguments."

"Come here," Bramley said, pointing to Miles. "Boy, am I glad to see you." She gave him a hug.

"Owee!" Miles said, flinching from Bramley's tight hug.

"Maybe you're the one who should be in the hospital. What happened to you?"

"It's a long story, but along the way I think I bruised or maybe cracked a couple of ribs," Miles said.

Dr. John said, "Off with the shirt. Let's have a look at you. Hop up on that other bed."

Dr. John noticed the bandage wrapped around Miles's ribcage and advised, "We don't recommend wrapping the chest with compression bandages anymore. We find that it prevents people from breathing deeply, which can in some cases lead to pneumonia."

"I was just trying to get through the night. I was trying to find her," he pointed in Bramley's direction with an unsteady hand.

"That's a pretty wicked bruise. How did you get it?"

"Would you believe she punched me?"

"Hey, don't blame it on me!" she cried.

"Actually, I slipped jumping from one boat to another boat and hit the railing, square across my chest. It knocked the wind out of me, but I managed to pull myself on board."

The doctor was poking and prodding, producing grimaces, grunts, and groans.

"They make it look so easy in the movies," Miles opined.

"Well, they also have stunt men for the action shots," replied the doctor.

"Touché."

"Looks like you have some bruising to go along with those cracks, but I don't feel any serious fractures. I would have to do an X-ray to confirm the diagnosis, but it won't change the treatment."

"Then I vote no for the X-ray," Miles replied.

"I am going to give you a prescription for some pain relievers. I really want you to take them at least for the first couple of days. It will make it much easier to take deep breaths. I can't stress enough how important it is that you take deep breaths. The risk of pneumonia is significantly reduced; otherwise, just take it easy. They should be fully healed in about two months. Shall I take a look at the leg and hand too?"

"You're pretty observant, Doc."

"Goes with the job. And you got this little gash how?"

"Well, I was scaling a wire fence, looking for her," he said as he glanced Bramley's way.

Sounds like he went to a lot of trouble to find me. That was a very pleasant thought, which warmed her heart. She actually said, "Sure you were. I bet you were just gallivanting around town having a good time without me." She used her best pouty expression to convey her disappointment. She started to ask him a question, but then stopped when she noticed Benito in the hallway.

He was carrying a large hot tea in a disposable brown cup with a plastic lid on it.

"I brought you a little bread and honey to go with your tea. I thought you might want to get a little something on your stomach," he said as he came through the door.

"Room service?" Miles asked.

Bramley replied, "Miles, let me introduce you to the man who found me, Benito Bello. After he found me, he phoned his friend, Dr. John, to meet us here, have a look at me, and fix me up. If he hadn't come along, I would still be locked in an old warehouse."

"Thank you for finding her and bringing her to the hospital," Miles said. "So, how did you just happen to be in *that* particular warehouse?"

"I just bought the abandoned warehouse from the city; we closed on it Friday. I'm going to refurbish it, much like I've done with other warehouses in that neighborhood."

Dr. John picked up on the tone and inquiry. "He is not part of his father's empire, if that's what you're thinking. He's had to live under that dark shadow his entire life and has paid a huge price."

"Ah, well, I'm sorry, but your father has been, shall we say, difficult to deal with. I am not privy to your family dynamics," Miles said.

Benito turned to Bramley. "I thought you said Armani's guys kidnapped you."

"I did; they did. It's a long story."

"Why don't you two come over to my place and fill me in? I'll fix you something to eat, and you can tell me about the latest saga of how my family is trying to wreck my life yet again. Armani and Carlo are the bane of my existence."

They arrived at Benito's and entered his modest but tasteful residence with an awkward silence.

"Let me start by offering you a cup of coffee or tea. Come on into the kitchen and I will brew you something. Do you have a preference? I have a variety of flavors."

Bramley responded, "If you have any Earl Grey, that would be perfect."

Miles took in the place and thought it looked pretty sparse. He couldn't put his finger on it. Then it came to him: it definitely didn't have a woman's touch. It wasn't messy or unorganized, and all of the furniture was proportional and coordinated with the other pieces and general decor. However, there were no throw pillows or knickknacks on the shelves. There was really nothing that gave the place any personality. He was so distracted by the spartan decor that he didn't realize they weren't alone until he saw shadows shifting behind them.

Benito had pulled a couple of boxes out of the cabinet. "Yes, I . . ." His voice trailed off as he turned and saw a very unexpected guest standing across the room. "What are you doing here?" he snarled.

Bramley turned and saw Carlo, his men, and the guns. In a heartbeat, she launched at Benito and yelled, "You liar! You lured us here so he could get the journal. I can't believe I fell for it."

"Stop!" barked Carlo. There were guns pointed at each of them. Roman stood in the other doorway with a weapon trained on them from yet another direction.

"Sit down! All of you," Carlo commanded.

Benito, Bramley and Miles all took seats around a circular wooden kitchen table. Each of them was secured to one of the four cane-bottom armchairs around the table. Roman tied all three of them quickly and efficiently with zip ties.

When they were all fixed in place, Carlo said, "Actually, my dear, Benito didn't lure you here to be snared by me. He had no idea I would be here. I had never planned to be here." Then he looked at Benito and announced, "Your brother tried to kill me last night."

"What?" asked a stunned Benito. His lip was bleeding from the punch Bramley landed. His father plucked a fancy paper cocktail napkin from its pewter holder in the center of the table and dabbed at the superficial wound.

The old man ambled around the room slowly. His shoulders were hunched, and he had a bit of a shuffle as he walked. With his slow, low, gravelly voice and a tired, thick Italian accent, he summarized.

"Apparently, Armani has been plotting against me and I didn't even know it. Imagine my surprise when I received a voice message from Mr. West telling me that if I let anything happened to Miss Fairchild, it would be his personal mission to make me regret it."

My knight in shining armor, Bramley thought.

Carlo rambled on. "Only, I wasn't the one who kidnapped her. Then it occurred to me that only a couple of people even knew about the journal, so I knew I must have a mole in my organization."

"What journal?" Benito asked with a puzzled expression.

"We will come to that in a minute," Carlo said as he picked up where he left off. "Then when I reflected on some of the offhand comments that Armani had mentioned in a couple of prior conversations, I realized he had referred to things that I had never shared with him. That's when it occurred to me that he had to be the one spying on me. I sent Conti over to find out what was going on. Only, Conti disappeared and never reported back in. I still have not been able to find him.

"The only course of action at that point was to confront Armani. I gathered a bunch of the fellows and went over to visit with Armani. Before we could get the location secured, Armani's guys started shooting, and we found that we had unwittingly sauntered into the middle of an ambush." He shook his head, still not believing the turn of events. "If I had not been there myself, I wouldn't have believed it. I lost most of my men last night at Armani's house. Fortunately, I was still in my bulletproof car when the lead started flying. Roman and I just managed to escape his little trap. I returned home and collected some things, since we will need to lay low for a while. When we get to the marina, we discovered that Armani blew up my yacht and burned up half the marina with it."

"So, you just decided to come to my place, and drag me into your little war? Tie me and my guests up? Do you really think I had anything to do with it?" Benito vented. "I knew you were going to drag me into your corrupt world one of these days. That's why I never married Sara. I didn't want to ruin her life. Why are you doing this? Why did you lock me in that closet and not let me out?"

Carlo was taken aback. "What are you talking about? What closet?"

"When I was seven, just before mother died, you locked me in a closet and wouldn't let me out. When Mom came home, you both started arguing. Not long after that, she died, and you sent me away to a boarding school. I spent more time with Tommy's dad and with his family than I spent with you."

"I was trying to protect you, Son. I promised your mother that you would never be involved in the business. I meant it, and I still do. At any rate, I have something I need you to hold for me, given that Armani is burning down everything in sight."

"I am not going to become an accomplice to your sinister machinations!" Benito yelled.

"Calm down. I'm not drawing you into anything."

Roman returned carrying a couple of banker's boxes. "Dump them out on the table. Look, it's just memorabilia. Stuff about you and some things that remind me of your mother."

Pictures, newspaper clippings, reel-to-reel video spools, slides, scraps of cloth, tattered papers all spilled out across the table. Benito was silent. His eyes fell on a picture of his mother, then a clipping about the most recent fundraiser Benito had chaired. Carlo could tell what he was looking at.

"Your mother would be so proud of you, how you have turned out and all the good things you have done over your lifetime and what you are still doing. I know it doesn't mean anything to you, but I am proud of you too."

The old man teared up. As he placed his hand gently on a dried flower, his voice cracked. He leaned on the back of the chair, swaying just a little bit. The years had worn him down.

"Anyway, I came here to tell you, I might be leaving for a while. I just wanted you to know how proud I am of how you turned out. I have only had a couple of good things in my life. Really, just you and your mother," he said wistfully. Benito was still and quiet, looking at the pile of memorabilia and memories from two lifetimes splayed out like debris from a car accident.

"Okay, Carlo, how about letting us go?" Miles said.

"No, this is for your own protection. If you weren't bound up, one of you would try and do something heroic and then it would all go to shit, and someone would get hurt. I'll call someone to come cut you free as soon as we leave here. And . . . where is that journal?"

"So, you're still going to take the journal?"

"That journal belonged to my family. It was stolen from my grandfather by Jimmy O'Connor. Jimmy stashed it in a bank in Indiana, then Lefty Webber robbed that bank in 1928; thus, it was pilfered once again. My grandfather spent two years trying to track it down. By the time he caught up with Webber, the fool was dead in a failed bank robbery. He searched for years trying to find it, but never did. He went all over the country to every place that Webber ever was suspected of visiting. Then, he discovered from an outfit in Chicago that Webber had a 1928 Stutz customized. He knew at that point that's where the journal had to have been stored.

"Before my grandfather died, he passed his secret on to me, and I took over his quest to recover our journal. Over the years I bought five different Stutz cars looking for that book. Yours would have made six. Why didn't you just sell it to me? Oh, never mind. Where is it?"

"In my backpack, on the tablet computer."

Roman went to the backpack and pulled it out.

"I never looked at it after it was decrypted. What does the journal contain?"

Carlo smiled. "So, you saved me the trouble of decrypting it. I have the key." He pulled a small cipher wheel out from under his shirt where he kept it on a small chain around his neck. "It's the final location of the tsar's gold. A shipment of gold coins that the United States government was sending to Russia on the HMS *Republic* in order to support the Russian tsar. Everyone thought the *Republic* sank with the gold aboard, but it was actually transferred to a fishing trawler that was headed back to Newport.

On the rough seas, the overloaded boat took on water and sank, with a fortune in gold that is now estimated at over a couple billion dollars. I intend to recover it."

Benito was so shell-shocked from the contents spread across the table that it had taken a couple of minutes to process it. Finally, he uttered, "I don't understand. Why didn't you just get out?"

"I couldn't. I guess I sold my soul to the devil, and he will never let it go. I don't expect you to understand, but I had to see you one more time, and pass along some of your mother's mementos." He scanned the text of the decoded journal, and then smiled. He was at last triumphant. Like a modern-day Dr. Jekyll and Mr. Hyde, Carlo kept morphing back and forth from a repentant man to an obsessed, maniacal gangster.

"I got an unexpected bonus." He patted the tablet in his hand. "Goodbye, my son." He glanced at his wife's picture, then took one last look at his son. "You do look so much like your mother," he said as he patted Benito's shoulder.

When they heard the door close, Benito, Bramley and Miles looked at each other. All had disbelief etched on their faces. Miles started struggling, twisting his left leg. He had shifted his foot just before the zip tie went on to leave just a little bit of slack. He leaned his chair backward by pushing his toes down. "Looks . . . like . . . I am going to . . . owe you a new chair."

"What?" Benito asked, a bit confused.

With his now loose foot, Miles launched himself up and backward at an angle. All of his weight and momentum came crashing down on the back-right corner of the chair. The leg cracked and splintered; then, as the corner of the seat of the chair contacted the tile floor, the rest of the chair disintegrated into pieces. The impact knocked the wind out of Miles and sent another round of searing pain through his body; this time it was across his back. For a moment, he thought he was going to blackout.

"Are you okay?" Bramley asked tentatively.

Miles moaned. "Yep," he gasped, and then he groaned as he bit his lip to avoid audibly yelling a curse. With slow, agonizing movements, he worked his limbs out of some of the restraints and debris. Gradually, he managed to get to his feet; one part of the chair base was still bound to his right leg, while a portion of its arm dangled from his left wrist.

Benito pointed with his head to the wood block on the granite counter. "There are some knives and scissors in that wood block."

Miles made his way to the counter and grabbed the scissors and cut the zip ties binding Bramley and then handed her the scissors as he made a sluggish dash out the door.

When he got to the street, Carlo and his people were long gone. He limped back inside and dialed Agent Carter.

"West, where are you?"

Miles filled him in on their recent run-in with Carlo and their current situation.

"I'll get an APB out on him immediately," Agent Carter responded. "Hopefully we can catch him before he gets too far. He's going to have a lot of charges to plead when we catch him."

Then he filled Miles in on the night's events.

Bramley felt a little awkward. "Benito, I'm really sorry about busting your lip."

"Don't worry about it. It's nothing. I probably would have done the same thing if I was in your shoes." He searched around for his remote so he could turn on the TV in the far corner of the kitchen. He walked to the hall and looked into the mirror at his lip and jaw, which was already turning black and blue.

"Hey, you throw a pretty good punch. I haven't had a shiner like this since high school. Guess you've never met a more messed up family than mine. I suppose some psychologist would say I've got daddy issues. And they probably would be right."

Bramley looked at the clippings on the table as she tried to clean up the stuff strewn haphazardly across its weathered surface. She noticed a full-sized picture of a mother and son that she had seen earlier. She shifted the pile around and picked it up. She admired the old, slightly faded black-and-white photograph.

"You really do look a lot like your mother," she observed. "What's your given name?"

"Benito Leonardo Fontana Bello. Why?"

"Have you ever considered that perhaps the only name that really matters is yours, Benito Leonardo Fontana Bello? It's quite obvious that over the years *you* have created a legacy that no one can tarnish but you. A legacy about which any mother would be proud to brag. A legacy that some kindred soul would be proud to share."

"My girlfriend, Sara, told me the same thing, repeatedly," he added. A tear ran down his cheek from the outside corner of his eye.

"Why don't you listen to her?"

"Maybe I will after I get through this cabal, brouhaha or whatever this thing is." He threw up his hands with frustration. "Since I am apparently the last person that knows what's going on, could you at least fill me in and tell me how you ended up getting kidnapped by Armani and what the rest of this story is all about? I feel like I walked into a play in the middle of the second act."

She told the whole story from the beginning. After she had finished, he was momentarily dumbstruck; then he broke the silence.

"I am not sure how I can help, but I would like to try. I want—no, I need you to know that not everyone in my family is a corrupt, Neanderthal thug or a deplorable, nefarious miscreant. I am no saint, but I do try and do the right things and stay on the moral high ground."

"Your father and brother need to have their day in court and answer for their crimes," Miles said.

"I agree," said Benito as he held Miles's gaze and gave a slight nod.

"How do we find them?" Miles asked.

"I doubt either one of them would respond if I contacted them directly. We could always try it, though. They are both very cagey, and they tend to work through surrogates. I don't know many of their men—maybe just one or two in each camp. I can tell you about some of the construction projects Armani has built over the years; I know where they are located. I heard far too many complaints from various people about their dissatisfaction with Armani's construction projects. I don't know about Carlo's businesses, and I never wanted to know. He had a yacht, but apparently that's gone. Maybe if you guys asked me questions, it would help. What do you want to know?"

Sara burst through the front door with a wire cutter in hand. Breathless, she yelped, "Benito, Benito, are you okay?" While trying to refill her lungs with air, she slid around the corner, then stopped dead in her tracks. Breathing hard and leaning on her knees she said, "I got a call from Carlo that said you were all tied up, and he told me to get some wire cutters and release you. What happened?"

Benito stepped up, pulled her close and gave her a bear hug and a long kiss.

"In fact, we were all trussed up. But that didn't appeal to Mr. West, who quite literally broke out of his bonds to free us." He pointed to the pile of scrap wood on the floor that once had been a sturdy armchair. "Let me introduce you to Miles West and Bramley Fairchild." Then he pointed to his right. "This is my girlfriend, Sara Twiss."

"What number did Carlo use to call you?" Miles asked. Sara pulled out her phone and gave him the number. He quickly passed this additional information on to Carter, hoping that he might be able track it. Benito then told Sara the sordid saga.

CHAPTER TWENTY-NINE

CARLO HOISTED HIMSELF UP into the back of the delivery truck and plopped down into the sagging seat with a deep sigh. He finally had it in his hands. He patted the tablet computer that he still held under his arm and thought about the gold that he might finally see. The brakes squeaked as the worn-out service vehicle eased to stops, and the engine growled and sputtered as it fought to gain speed again. He was rocked and bounced as the aging vehicle headed toward its destination.

Carlo felt like he was floating; he was drifting along in a trance-like state somewhere between sleep and full consciousness. He had always had trouble sleeping; he was constantly tormented by his demons. Sometimes he would wake at night in a cold sweat, with the vision of dead eyes staring back at him, two dark, glazed eyes on a ghastly white face—the distinct image of a dark hole in the center of the forehead with just a trickle of blood dripping down. It was the first time he ever shot someone. The imbecile had been embezzling from his grandfather. *What a moron*. Carlo's grandfather had told the then sixteen-year-old, "You need to make an example of the swindler so that people respect and fear us."

After the deed was discovered, everyone looked at him differently; they were wary. He knew things were whispered about him, but he didn't care. His old chums from school steered clear of him. He decided he didn't need to waste time hanging around with them. His grandfather put him in charge of the finances, and he could not believe how much cash they were generating and accumulating. He made more money in a month than he made the whole time he worked at the docks, and he didn't even have to break a sweat. He decided he was going to stick with his grandfather and make his fortune. That's how it all began.

Now, all these years later, he could still hear his grandfather talking to him with that scratchy wheeze drifting out of his feeble lungs in a voice scarred from years of smoking. The admonitions, instructions, and cryptic sayings all still echoed in his mind.

Another thought occurred to him; with his newfound billions, he could atone for all his sins. He would go to his priest and confess, pay his penance. Then he would be free from the demons that haunted him. He would build a hospital, and they would name it after him. He would be admired for his benevolence and generous gifts. He would at last be able to sleep like a baby.

The truck hit a bump in the road, jostling him. He sensed a dark, black shadow cross over him. The pleasant thoughts vanished like the vapor escaping his mouth on a cold morning; he knew it didn't work that way. He was deluding himself. The torment flooded back in, gnawing at his gut, so he reached for the antacids he kept in his pocket. These days he chewed them like candy.

His reflections were cut short when he caught the sound of police sirens in the distance. The wailing grew closer. His pulse quickened as he removed his pistol from his coat pocket. He didn't have time to be stopped. He had things to do. He was so close to recovering the gold. No one was going to stand in his way now.

Roman saw his actions and automatically knew what was expected of him. The driver slowed to make a turn, and the sirens raced past.

Agent Carter found his smoking gun in Armani's hidden room and worked the phones to coordinate efforts from multiple law enforcement agencies to find and capture both Carlo and Armani. He had his agents running down every sighting and every lead. Concurrently, he worked to get the authorizations necessary to freeze all the Bellos' assets. Back at the office, Carter had his team compile a list of all the people associated with either Carlo or Armani. They were tracking down where each and every one of them was located to start the process of serving warrants and making arrests as they worked their way through the ever-expanding tally of offenses and offenders.

The music was playing low as Matteo finished his second cup of coffee. It had been a long night, and he was tired. He was waiting on a call from Carlo or Roman to let him know where they wanted him to go next. When they left him, he had been told that he might need to serve as a diversion until Carlo could get into place. "So stay on the move and keep your phone handy." Given what Armani had done at the marina and at his home, Matteo wouldn't be foolish enough to stay in one place too long. His eyes darted to his rearview mirror, and he spotted the NYPD cruiser easing up behind him. He decided to maneuver out into the street and get on down the avenue. He wasn't too excited about trying to answer any questions about his pockmarked car. He put it into gear and made a quick right turn out of the ally and onto a street that intersected Central Park.

Immediately the flashing lights came on behind him. Matteo smiled to himself. "This is just like the old days. I can lose this guy in a heartbeat." Long ago, he made sure Carlo's SUV had a little extra horsepower under the hood, as well as a nitrous booster, not that he ever had to resort to that cheating tactic. He preferred to race old school, on just plain horsepower and skill, but it never hurt to hedge his bets.

With so little traffic on the streets, they wove between cars and hit some decent speeds before having to suddenly slow down. As they approached a red light, Matteo slammed on his brakes and turned slightly right. The patrol car came sliding up beside him. He stuck his shotgun out of the window and fired at the front tire and quarter panel but missed as the officer reversed and maneuvered in just behind him. He mashed the pedal to the floor and took another right turn, spinning tires and burning rubber. This street was right next to Central Park. He liked the option of going off-roading if needed.

Carlo wanted him to create a diversion, and he was doing just that. Police in another patrol car spotted the SUV plowing through the park and hit their siren as they lit out in pursuit of the fleeing vehicle.

One of Agent Carter's guys popped his head in the door and said, "NYPD has spotted Carlo and is in pursuit. Shots have been fired at the pursuing officer."

At the same time, Carter was getting a call from Miles West.

"Carlo has been spotted at his old warehouse down at the docks."

"That must be an older sighting. At this very moment the NYPD is pursuing him near Central Park. Shots were just fired at the pursuing officer. I'll have to call you back in a little bit," Agent Carter replied hurriedly as he ended the call.

Miles looked at the phone and then repeated what he had been told.

"Agent Carter claims the NYPD is currently in hot pursuit of Carlo over near Central Park." Miles looked at Benito. "I need to borrow your car."

"I'll drive. I know where the warehouse is located. That's where my great-grandfather started his first business," replied Benito.

"Then I'm going!" Sara and Bramley responded in unison. They looked at each other with a knowing glance and a slight nod, then back at Miles and Benito respectively.

Miles rolled his eyes. He didn't want to have *this* argument and knew how it would end before it began. Before he could think about all the countless things that could possibly go wrong, he said, "Let's go."

Matteo veered left and right as he sped around cars. His pulse quickened; he felt the old thrill of street racing, the titillating sensation he knew from his youth. Once again, he felt invincible knowing that he could outrun anyone. With precision, he clipped a couple of cars in an effort to spin them out and slow the other vehicles in pursuit. As he passed each intersection, more patrol cars materialized. Knowing they would soon be ahead of him blocking the street, Matteo slowed, cut right up onto the sidewalk and then accelerated back into Central Park.

He was alone on the wide pathway, sliding around a turn as he raced toward the interior of the park. He spotted his opening and felt confident he could elude his pursuers with a little off-roading. Yanking the wheel to the left, he tore over the sidewalk, bouncing the vehicle like a bucking bronco, barely avoiding blowouts to his tires as he pounded the unyielding concrete curb. Several shots were fired from officers who had taken an intercept course. He slid around on the grass, spinning his wheels, sending twin streams of dirt, grass and other debris flying behind him as he careened wildly over the uneven terrain.

He was approaching eighty miles per hour when he started drifting sideways on the damp grass. The wheels caught and sent the top-heavy SUV into a barrel roll, crushing metal and glass, flinging parts in all directions before slamming to a stop on a pile of landscape boulders. The gas tank was punctured, and the leaking fuel was ignited by the heat of the exhaust system. The flames followed the fuel trails, the yellow, red, and blue-hued flames lapping at everything they touched. Black smoke rose quickly from the expanding fire. The scorching flames eventually made their way toward the nitrous oxide tank. The safety valve that should have relieved the pressure building up with each lapping flame had been damaged in the crash.

Eventually, the tank could no longer contain the expanding gasses. It exploded like a mortar, putting a large crater in the bottom of the big SUV and sending plumes of gas from the ruptured fuel tank in all directions. The park was rocked with a brilliant hot flash and a deafening explosion. Metal, plastic and glass shards rained down all around the inferno. In the distance, fire, police and rescue sirens wailed as they converged on the conflagration.

Carlo ended the call with one of the policemen on his payroll. His informant kept him apprised whenever an investigation got close to one of his guys or some of his business interests. This call was about Matteo and numerous other rumors racing around the precinct.

For years, Carlo's informants had managed to help him stay one step ahead of the legal beagles that were trying to hunt him down. With their assistance, he made witnesses disappear or lose their memories. Sometimes he would pay them off; other times he used threats to keep them quiet. Today, the news was not good. The cops had an APB out for both he and Armani. There was also gossip that the Internal Affairs Department had been called in; that never happened on a Sunday morning, and it had his inside guys very nervous. His informants told him that at this point none of the law enforcement agencies knew where either of the Bellos were hiding. The informant said that some people suspected that Carlo and his driver had perished in the explosive crash in Central Park. The SUV had rolled, flipped and exploded while trying to evade the police; no one escaped before the explosion. Carlo sighed. Of all the guys he had around him, he always had a soft spot for Matteo.

"Damn it!" he swore. "How can this be happening to me now, just when I have the journal in hand?" He was puzzled at this drastic shift of fortune. He would find out who else had betrayed him and how this had fallen apart later. Right now, he needed to flee his warehouse and move quickly to recover the gold before anyone else could find it.

Carlo hoped that Armani had not learned about his purchase of the old, rusted-out utility vessel docked across from the warehouse. It was larger than his sportfishing boat, but, more importantly, it had a crane and would be large enough to transport the gold he recovered. It had only cost him $300,000, which he thought was a pretty good deal, especially considering that the cost of the new sportfishing yacht he wanted was well over a million dollars. In reality, the meaningless comparison was like contrasting apples to peanuts, because they were entirely different types of boats.

After getting his temper under control, he walked over to a work table where his accountant pounded away on his laptop computer. The bookish accountant with thick glasses and a beaked nose had met him at the warehouse with a carton of files. Together they were reviewing various holdings and account summaries.

"We don't have a lot of cash on hand, but I can aggregate some of the accounts together and generate a couple hundred thousand pretty quickly. Where would you like me to move the cash?"

"I am not sure, but we should get it offshore somewhere. We don't want the feds to locate it. Is there a location that you can use in the Caribbean?"

"I'm pretty sure I know just the place. However, let me check a couple of things. These banks are not open on the weekend, so we can't complete the transactions until tomorrow morning. But I can go ahead and aggregate the funds we already have on hand into one account. Then the wire transfers will be ready to relay right when their offices open in the morning."

Carlo nodded. "That should be good." He turned to Roman. "How much of the gear has been loaded onto the freighter?"

"All of the dive gear was transferred as soon as the ship arrived. The food supplies were loaded this morning. We just have a couple more boxes of things to put onto the ship that are still at the front door of the warehouse. As well as the things you brought from your home."

"Good, good. Get the rest of the stuff put on board. I want to get out of here soon."

Benito eased to a stop a short distance from the warehouse.

Miles said, "Okay, give me a lay of the land. Specifically, where is his warehouse?" He already had his iPad out and the map program up; he switched to satellite view and saw the blue dot where they were sitting. Benito leaned over and pointed with his pen.

"Here you can see the outline of the building; as you can tell, it has open space all the way around. Its construction is very old. All the floors are concrete; the walls are a mix of corrugated tin and aluminum sheets, and the old single-pane windows are flimsy. I think we could get in pretty easily. That old section is timber frame. The new section over here is steel framed. The roof extends over the front where an old gantry crane was used to unload trailers." He pointed out each of the other buildings in the area as well as other features. Then he asked, "What are you thinking?"

"First, we need to determine if Carlo is in there, and also how many other men are in there with him. I would like to find something definitive to convince Agent Carter to get down here and arrest these guys."

While he talked, he put together the parabolic microphone that he and Bramley had procured the previous day.

"What is that?" asked Sara.

"It's a parabolic microphone. I hope we can pick up something from one of their conversations." He handed the device to Bramley and said, "Roll your window down just a little bit and let's see what you can hear. These tinted windows should keep us pretty well hidden; however, this type of car is probably a bit unusual around here. Sara, would you mind keeping your eyes peeled for anyone that looks like they're checking us out? We need to stay vigilant."

Bramley held her hand up, trying to silence the conversation. The listening device was pointed at two guys talking in front of the warehouse. One of them had been leaning on an old, rusty, fifty-five-gallon barrel, vaping one of those newfangled electronic cigarettes, when the other emerged from the warehouse and approached him. Bramley had the microphone's receiver in her ear and concentrated on the discussion across the dockyard.

"Carlo wants the last of those boxes inside, loaded onto the freighter. Don't forget to get the stuff we brought from his house out of the panel truck and load it on board too. He wants to cast off before too much longer."

"He's here," she said excitedly, "but we have a problem. It sounds like they're going to finish packing stuff onto that boat and head out before too much longer."

Sara piped up. "Why don't we just block them in with the car, and wait for the police to arrive?"

"I can tell you from personal experience that's not a very sound strategy," Miles said. "Their bullets can penetrate that siding and this vehicle like it's paper. When this is all over, I'll tell you about it."

Miles's mind raced, quickly formulating plans. While it was unlikely anyone could see them behind the stacks of pallets, movement between the open slats might be noticed.

"Benito, back up a bit, just around the corner."

Benito slowly backed around the corner of an adjacent building.

"Bramley, call Agent Carter and tell him we have confirmed that Carlo is here. Then have him get some guys over here ASAP. I'm going to see if I can take a peek inside. Benito, I'm going to be further in your debt," he said as he reached up and grabbed the rearview mirror, yanking it off the windshield with one good pull.

"What the hell are you doing?" Benito yelled in surprise.

"I need it for a periscope," Miles said as he pulled duct tape and a pocket knife out of his backpack. The recycle bin they were parked beside had a couple of long, skinny boxes lying on top of the heap. Miles got out of the car, grabbed one of them, and cut a square hole in the bottom. He taped the flap back on a forty-five-degree angle. Benito came up beside him as he flipped the box over and did the same thing at the top on the opposite side.

"That's pretty resourceful," Benito said as he caught onto what Miles was doing.

"Tear off some duct tape and fold it back on itself to create a double-sided sticker," Miles said while he disassembled the mirror and split it into two halves. "Ouch!" he grunted when he cut his finger. "Give me another piece of tape." He wrapped his bleeding appendage with the strip of duct tape; while it was not an antiseptic bandage, it would have to suffice for the moment. They installed the mirrors in the box openings on the angle and quickly but quietly crossed to the nearest window.

"Keep an eye out for anyone headed in our direction. Since we're only armed with a couple of questionable pistols, we don't need anyone sneaking up on us," Miles whispered. The two pistols he had recovered from the thugs at the park who tried to ambush him were both loaded, but since he had not fired them, he had no idea how reliable they were. At the moment, they were still wrapped in a hand towel stuffed in his backpack.

Carefully, Miles moved the makeshift periscope up to the bottom of the dirty window. He used the building to keep his quick-and-dirty periscope from moving and drawing attention, but he didn't feel comfortable leaning on the tin wall too hard.

He could barely make out the people inside because of the layers of dust, dirt, and grime accumulated on the glass. He shifted the periscope and saw boxes stacked at the front door. At first, he only spotted two figures walking near the door; on his second pass he made out a couple more figures hunched over a work table toward the back of the building. Most of the building was vacant. Pallet racks on the far wall were mostly empty.

After surveying the interior Miles whispered, "There are four guys inside, plus the one we saw outside moving stuff to the ship. I take it the only doors are on the front of the warehouse?"

"Yes," whispered Benito. He held out his hand, and Miles handed over the periscope. Benito made his own survey as Miles quickly moved to the back of the building to see if he could spot anyone doing a patrol. Seeing no one, he darted to the front corner of the building to check the status of the guy that had been loading the ship. Miles moved slowly behind the stacks of pallets to find a good sight line that would still keep him hidden. From that vantage point, he could just barely see the guy toting another box to the ship and then disappearing as he continued down the gangplank. Looking back toward the warehouse door, Miles spotted the drum of recycled oil and had another idea. He silently retreated to Benito and signaled to him that they should make their way back to the car.

"I am positive that's Carlo," announced Benito.

"How close is Agent Carter?"

"I couldn't get him on the phone. Every time I called, his line was busy. I left him a voicemail and told him we found Carlo and asked him to send his guys," Bramley replied.

"We need to slow these guys down. We can't let them get away," Miles said as he reached into his backpack and found the zip ties that he had in the bottom. "Okay, when the tote guy takes the next box over to the freighter, let's subdue him, and then we'll only have four guys to contain. Sara, get behind the wheel and keep an eye on us; we may need you to speed in, give us a hasty ride out of here if they come out of the door too soon. Benito, let's get behind that container, wait until he's boarding the vessel, and then we'll take him down." Miles tucked one of the pistols in his waistband at the small of his back, then grabbed the stun gun.

Benito and Miles moved into position. Miles gave the zip ties to Benito and turned the stun gun over in his hand. He had not examined it since retrieving it off of the brute behind the tree. *Wow, that was just last night. Feels like a week ago,* he thought. He was tired, sore, and he needed another couple of pain relievers. The adrenaline had kicked in again, and his senses were on full alert; he noticed every sound. He flipped the switch on and was relieved to see the LED display indicate that it was fully charged.

The guy loading the rusty old work boat looked tough and pretty fit, although he was undoubtedly a little worn out from all of his trips back and forth. Even though the temperature was still a little cool, sweat was pouring off the thug. Fortunately, he seemed distracted by the oversized box in his arms; he never noticed them coming up behind him. Miles got closer, then fired. Two prongs shot straight and true, going through the sweaty T-shirt to pierce his back. The charge caused him to freeze and convulse. The electricity and spasms shot through his body, causing paralysis. Benito grabbed the box as the big brute collapsed.

"This guy weighs a ton." They dragged him onto the vessel and bound him, then wrapped his shirt around his face as a gag. When they peered over the front edge of the freighter's deck to survey the warehouse, Sara gave the all-clear signal. Benito and Miles made their way back around the container to Bramley and Sara.

Benito was panting. Miles gave out guidance and instructions for the next part of the plan.

"I want to tip that container of recycled oil over and spread it all over the concrete in front of that door. We're going to get them to come out, then blast them with the high-pressure water streaming out of that firehose, which will put them down. We need to create an explosion at the back of the building or toss a couple of smoke grenades into the warehouse to drive them out. Before we put the oil down, let's string that fishing net up over the door."

Benito shook his head in amazement. "That sounds like a good plan, but where are we going to get the explosives and smoke grenades?"

"There was a five-gallon bucket of hull cleaner on the freighter. If we can get a gallon or two of ammonia cleaner from that restaurant we passed on the way in, we can use the combination to gas the warehouse; it will drive them out. As for an explosion, a container of gas and a delayed fuse would create a pretty big bang. But I really don't want to worry about a lot of collateral damage, so maybe we'll just have to fumigate the place. Sara, go see if you can round up some ammonium from the diner. Bramley, you and Benito help me stretch out that fishing net over the doorway. We're lucky all this rigging is still intact. It will make releasing the net a lot easier. Benito, go grab that hull cleaner. Bramley, unspool the firehose; I'm going to create a little oil slick."

Miles rolled the partially filled oil barrel toward the door, the thin metal edge at its base grinding into the brittle concrete with each rotation.

Then he tipped it over to spill oil in several directions. Backing away, he poured a widening pool of oil across the concrete. He used a rope to spread the pools more evenly and fill in the spots he missed. Once Sara had returned with ammonia, they retreated to their position just around the corner.

"We need to stay concealed; they may start firing weapons, and these walls are paper thin. So, you need to make sure to stay behind that steel trash dumpster or one of those steel shipping containers," instructed Miles. "Get some glass jars out of the recycle bin and fill half of them with the ammonia and the other half with the boat cleaner. Put the little glass jars with ammonia in the big glass jars with boat cleaner. Then, I want you to pitch them into the window, while staying concealed behind that steel trash dumpster. When they hit the floor and mix, they'll give off a noxious gas that will drive them out. Benito, here's my knife. Stay positioned behind those iron girders when they come out, cut the rope and drop the fishing net on them. I will keep them subdued with the firehose. Everyone good? Last chance to change your mind." He looked each of them in the eye, then nodded. "Okay, everyone get into your positions."

They moved to their respective assignments. Miles signaled for the siege to begin.

Before Carlo and his men knew what was happening, over half a dozen jars had been tossed through the windows and broken on the concrete floor inside. It didn't take long for the chemicals to create a noxious fog. They heard the men inside yelling; then Carlo's men started coughing and hacking. A couple of shots were fired through the wall, just as Miles predicted. The shots pierced through the warehouse and ricocheted off the steel dumpster. Then shots started coming through the front wall. Three men raced out the door, firing weapons randomly. They were soon sliding across the oil slick with their arms spinning like windmills.

Benito cut the rope, and the fishing net came down on them just as Carlo emerged. Carlo's slow pace kept him from being snared. Miles had the water flowing at full volume, and he doused the men wriggling on the ground like soaked rats. He turned the spray on Carlo just as Carlo raised his gun to fire. The wave of water pushed him back toward the wall of electrical distribution panels, which sparked and arced as the water made contact. Carlo grabbed at one of the boxes, trying to remain upright, and started convulsing. Miles stopped the high-pressure flow of water and pulled his gun from his waist.

Bramley stood right beside him with the other weapon trained on the men under the net. Miles ordered, "Everybody, just freeze where you are. Benito, Sara, get their weapons." As Benito and Sara started peeling back the net, one of the men made a move. A shot rang out. Bramley said, "I wouldn't do that if I were you."

Her shot had hit Roman's weapon, sending shards of concrete into his hand. Roman pulled back like he'd been bitten by a rattlesnake and gave her a venomous stare.

Carlo started to come around. He grunted, then spat. In a hoarse voice he asked gruffly, "So, you're going to steal the journal back?"

"This is not about the journal. You and your boys have a lot of legal issues you need to address. The FBI has been looking for you, and I have a feeling you will be going away for a long time. Apparently, Armani had been spying on you for quite a while; some of his tapes are going to be hard to refute."

Carlo swore under his breath. "I'm not going to be locked up. Just wait, you'll see; they have never been able to make anything stick."

Sara had never told Benito her deepest secret. It was one of the reasons she started dating him. She wanted to get close to Carlo—not out of admiration, but for revenge.

Her father and her uncle Bobby had been dockworkers for decades and, by all accounts, were lawful men. Her father, Phillip, was tragically killed; safety inspectors ruled it an accident, but she and her uncle Bobby always suspected his death was more sinister.

Her uncle had kept a close watch over Sara and she secretly kept in touch with him, sharing information about Carlo and his antics. She had spoken to him hours earlier, in private, and it was Uncle Bobby who informed her that Carlo likely was headed to the docks for his escape.

"Be careful, lassie. He's a dangerous man."

With Carlo now immobilized and unprotected, it was time for Sara to exact her revenge. She would extract the truth, once and for all.

"I want to know, why did you have my father killed? Everyone tried to convince me that when the container crushed him, it was an accident, but I never believed it." She held the big gun with both hands, aiming just over his head. She pulled the trigger; the .45 boomed and made a huge hole in the wall above Carlo.

Benito was shocked. "Sara!" he cried out. "Put the gun down. What are you doing?"

Sara repeated her question, her voice was filled with rage and laced with desperation. "Why did you have my father killed?" she yelled.

Benito moved toward her. "This is not the way. Don't do something you'll regret."

She looked over her shoulder and said, "Stop, don't come any closer. I grew up around these docks. I still come down here for breakfast with my uncle. I know what I heard. Some of Carlo's guys were talking about the 'accident.'"

Carlo said, "I have always said, keep your friends close and your enemies closer."

"That's a rather cryptic response," replied Sara. "Does that mean I am an enemy?"

"Well, you're the one holding a gun on me." He pushed himself up into a sitting position and inched slightly closer to his pistol. "Some people shouldn't go poking their noses into other people's business," he added.

"You're saying my dad was poking around in your business?"

Benito looked down at his father with a look of pure contempt. "For once in your life, can you just tell the truth?"

Carlo looked down. His eyes came to rest on the tablet that he dropped, and he wondered if the water and electricity had destroyed it. The words Miles uttered finally sank in. Undoubtedly, Armani had sealed his fate. Carlo sighed. There was no way they were going to lock him up. *If I can distract them, I think I can reach my gun.*

"He poked his nose into a major arms transaction that was none of his business. It was a multi-million-dollar deal with the South American drug cartels. Actually, a bit of bad luck was really what got your father killed; one of the wooden crates fell off a pallet and cracked open, spilling out part of the arms shipment. He might not have even been killed if he had not let his curiosity get the better of him. The fatal mistake he made was that he snuck into my warehouse and discovered our connection to the cartel. So, now you know. I suppose you are going to kill me. I have four people pointing guns at me, with four different reasons to kill me. It's like an old-fashioned Western shoot-out."

He smirked at her. Then, with surprising speed, he reached for his sidearm, grabbed it and was just bringing it up when a lone shot rang out with a boom that reverberated off the metal siding. A small red spot the size of a dime bloomed in the center of Carlo's chest. He looked down at it in surprise before he slumped over.

All four of them turned to see Sara's uncle Bob holding a rifle.

"I couldn't take a chance on him shooting someone," he said as he lowered the weapon.

Sara was shaking and sobbing, barely holding onto her own gun. Benito lumbered over to take her in his arms. His feet felt like lead. He was dazed by the whole ordeal.

In a quivering, small voice she asked her uncle, "Did you hear him admit that his guys killed Dad?"

"Yes, lassie, I heard it," Uncle Bobby replied as he removed his frayed Yankees ball cap and wiped his face with his sleeve. "You were right. I'm sorry we could never prove it."

Bramley reacquired her targets as she stood sentry with her pistol ready to fire at anyone that moved. Water streaked with oil snaked a path away from the warehouse.

Miles wandered over to pick up the tablet computer and, not surprisingly, discovered it was ruined. Computers didn't often stand up to the combined effects of water and excessive amounts of electricity. Miles shook his head with a grimace. He was not having too much luck with his electronic devices.

Bramley watched him out of the corner of her eye. From his expression she could tell that the device was damaged beyond repair. "What's the old saying? The third time's the charm."

Agent Carter's car was the first to come sliding around the corner. He jumped out as it skidded to a stop. In his methodical way, he surveyed the area, taking in the whole scene instantly. He holstered his weapon as it became apparent that the skirmish was over and the bad guys were out of the fight.

"Well, Mr. West, do you want to fill me in on what transpired here?"

Miles proceeded to recount their efforts to prevent Carlo from escaping on the old freighter.

Benito was filled with a mix of emotions. On one level, he felt a sense of relief that he had never experienced before. He was considering the faint possibility that he might yet have a shot at happiness. He would no longer have to live in the shadow of an evil man who bore the same last name.

Then, he had a sense of dread. *Was Sara just using me all this time to find an answer about her father's death?* Benito was deeply ashamed of the terrible pain his father had inflicted on Sara and her family. Yet, here she was crying on his shoulder and holding onto him for comfort. He was confused; his whole world had been turned upside down and inside out. He looked at the man who was supposed to be his father, hunched over dead, and couldn't really understand what he was feeling.

A couple of agents pulled the wet, oily men out from under the fishing net. The riffraff they uncovered smelled like dead fish, old rags and oil. Everyone got dirty and messy as the agents tried to find a clean spot to hold onto while they cuffed the filthy criminals for transport. Needless to say, none of them liked drawing that particular assignment. Each hoped one of the other agents would volunteer; in the end, as was often the case, the low man on the totem pole got first dibs.

Bramley looked up at Miles.

"Why do you think Carlo said, 'I have four people pointing guns at me, with four different reasons to kill me?'"

"Maybe he was taunting us. I didn't want to kill him—just get him locked up," Miles said.

Agent Carter approached Miles with a serious expression.

"I need to fill you in on something we found. There is no easy way to say this, so I'm just going to lay out the facts. It appears that one of Carlo's guys killed your wife, because she stumbled upon Carlo presenting an open briefcase full of money to that senator that had a heart attack and died last year. We know the identity of the killer and we have him in custody. One of the counts we charged him with was your wife's murder. I promise you, if he doesn't get the death penalty, with all of the other charges we have on him, he will never ever see the light of day."

Miles was thunderstruck. Stumbling a couple of steps back, he plopped down on a little concrete wall; a tear rolled down his cheek. Bramley moved to his side and pulled his head to her chest and rubbed the back of his neck and head as he started to cry. All of the pain that had been bottled up for so long rushed to the surface.

Agent Carter walked away to give them some space and to keep his own emotions under control. No matter how often he delivered such news, it always tore him up inside. He felt the pain of those who mourned the loss of loved ones, of the lives that had been cut short far too soon, of those left behind to pick up the pieces.

CHAPTER THIRTY

IT TOOK A WHILE to collect all the statements and evidence. Afterward, Agent Carter told the four civilians to "go get some sleep. We'll catch up on the rest of this tomorrow morning." He was running on fumes himself, feeling the effect of too much caffeine and too little rest.

Miles was dog-tired, but with all the adrenaline still working its way out of his system, he doubted he would be able to sleep anytime soon.

"Let's swing by the electronics store on the way back to the boat."

Bramley patted his leg. "I guess we already know what's going to be revealed. Now it's just a matter of seeing a translated copy."

"Well, actually, there is another whole section that we never decrypted the first time around. Remember, when we were back in Richmond, I pointed out the variations in the codes in the last half of the journal, as well as the distinct ways they were written?"

"Now that you mention it, I had forgotten about that part of the journal."

"I suspect that part will actually reveal where the rest of Lefty's cache was stashed. Perhaps after we get some sleep we can see about solving the rest of this mystery." Miles yawned. "I haven't pulled an all-nighter like this since my college days."

Bramley leaned over and put her head on his shoulder. "I think I could use some more pain relievers and some rest too."

"How's your head?"

"Just a mild headache. In case you haven't noticed, I have a pretty hard head. It will take more than a little bump to knock me off my game."

He kissed the top of her head. "Thank you."

"For what?" she asked as she shifted and looked into his eyes.

"For coming along on this wild adventure and . . ." He paused, thinking about grieving for his slain wife. "For just being there when I needed a friend."

"Anytime. After all, that's what friends are for." She squeezed his arm with her left hand. His eyes were still watery. She was sure the pain of his loss was still at the top of his mind. "Anytime," she repeated.

They arrived at the marina to find Trevor working on some minor boat maintenance. He was eager to hear their tale and astounded by the events that unfolded in such a few short hours. They found the recap a cathartic way to unwind and decompress after a long, harrowing and stressful night. It was also the first chance that they really had to compare notes about their individual odysseys through the previous night's trials and tribulations.

Even though it was only mid-afternoon, Trevor could tell they both were fatigued. "I'm gonna head out and let you guys get some rest."

"Thanks again, T. We really appreciate your hos-pi-tal-i-*TEE.*"

"Ooh, that's a bad one. Now I know you're wiped out. Go catch some z's," Trevor replied with a big grin.

With the speed of a sloth, Bramley got up and moved toward the stairway. "You're not going to have to tell me twice. I'll see you later. Not sure I have the energy to get a shower before I get in bed, but I feel grungy."

"Sleeping over in an old musty warehouse can do that to you," Miles teased. She threw him a mean look and would have sent a pillow that way too if she wasn't so wiped out.

Treavor leaned over and whispered in Miles's ear, "A piece of advice: don't let that one get away!"

Miles just nodded and smiled as his old friend disappeared out the door.

After decoding the journal section that outlined the location of the tsar's lost treasure, Miles turned the information over to the FBI. The federal government would want to launch an effort to recover the long-lost gold that was technically still part of the United States gold reserves.

Running the decryption algorithm on the last set of coded pages provided yet another interesting revelation. And, as Miles suspected, the new information also provided additional clues to the whereabouts of the rest of Lefty Webber's hidden treasure. And those clues led them right back to where they began—or, rather, very close to it.

"Well, this is it. It's more than a little ironic that this property is right next to the Vogel estate, where this whole thing began," Bramley observed with a wry note in her voice. "Wow, it seems like so long ago, yet it's only been eight weeks. Have you talked to Agent Carter?"

"I caught up with him yesterday. They tracked Armani to the island of Antigua, but his trail went cold there. They are still processing all of the evidence they recovered at his home, but they were unable to seize all of the money he sent offshore. By the time they found the accounts, they had been emptied."

"At least he's out of the country." Subconsciously, she felt for her weapon secured in her fanny pack; she was always reassured knowing that it was in easy reach. Her run-in with Armani's goons had prompted her to take a self-defense course, and she enjoyed the martial arts moves that she was learning.

They stopped just after turning onto a sandy driveway. Miles hopped out of the truck, grabbed the faded *For Sale* sign, pulled it up and placed it in the bed of the pickup. After he jumped back in, they made their way up the weed-covered path toward their destination. It was a simple plot of ground—an old family graveyard surrounded by a knee-high metal fence that was mostly rusted and broken. Miles cut the engine off.

"The property was owned by the estate of Tammy Mills. It had been on the market for quite a while, and they were happy to sell it to me. Since she had no heirs, the proceeds of the land sale will go back to the state. She and her husband purchased it from the Vogel sisters in the late 1930s. They lived on the property until they passed, never having any children. The property they purchased had this old family graveyard on it, and, as you can see, it's overgrown."

"Do you really think his treasure is still here?" Bramley asked as she picked up a shovel and a rake out of the back of the truck.

Miles grabbed the weed eater, which he had already topped off with a gas-and-oil mixture. "There's only one way to find out."

Miles cut a wide swath as they made their way to the graveyard. It had not been maintained for many years. With effort, he cut through all of the old, dried grasses and bramble that had not yet been replaced by the new growth springing up through the dense thicket of dried stems. He took his time clearing the detritus around the old tombstones. Bramley raked the fallen debris away from the area.

"One bad thing about a weed eater is that the assault on one's ears can be deafening," Miles said after he switched it off. They both welcomed the relative silence. The only sounds now were the birds chirping a cheerful melody. Occasionally, they heard the gentle rustling of new leaves on the limbs above their heads.

They approached the tombstones with a solemn demeanor. Miles looked down at the markers they had uncovered.

"I've arranged to have any remains and the tombstones moved to the graveyard by the church on the top of the hill. At least that way these graves will be maintained in the future."

Bramley walked around, noting the dates on each of the markers. "Looks like they all predate the Vogel family with the exception of this one."

"The other odd thing is the brass plate on this headstone." Miles dug his knife out of his pocket; the little screwdriver head matched the screws holding the plate in place. He started unscrewing them. The last one was unyielding. As he struggled to twist it, his hand slipped, and the plate shifted a bit. He pushed it around to reveal a small hole carved in the stone.

Using the light on his phone, he peered into the little hole, which was just larger than an old silver dollar. As he moved the light around, he noticed a metallic reflection. He went back to the truck, opened the back door, and grabbed a shirt on a metal hanger still covered with plastic from the dry cleaners. He removed the freshly cleaned and pressed shirt and plastic from the hanger, then tossed it carelessly into a disheveled pile on the back seat.

As he walked back to the tombstone, he fashioned the metal wire into a double hook. Carefully, he slid it down the granite hole. When he had it under the object, he pulled at it carefully. It didn't budge. He kept the tension on it, wriggled it left, then right, and it popped free. When he removed it, they found themselves looking at another gold coin, just like the ones he found in the old Stutz.

"I would say we have our answer." Miles turned the coin over in his hand and tossed it to Bramley. "That's actually pretty ingenious," Miles said as he realized what Webber had done. "He drilled a tube on the inside of this tombstone that goes down to a vault in the ground. Each time he wanted to hide more diamonds or gold coins, all he had to do was remove these three screws, pivot the plate, make the deposit and then put the screws back in place."

He got up, went over and grabbed the shovel. "Shall we find out what he has stashed down there?"

CHAPTER THIRTY-ONE

JEDIAH WAS THE FIFTH Fletcher to work the family farmstead outside of Decatur, Illinois. It was hard but satisfying work trying to raise his crops on this unforgiving land. Once in a while, bad weather and disease seemed to conspire to ruin his crops and empty his coffers. The family had sustained two such occurrences in the last three years, and that had wiped out their family savings.

People thought he was wealthy because he had large tractors, trucks, planters, combines and wagons, silos and elevators and a large tract of land. What they didn't realize was that no one could be a small farmer anymore. Those types of operations barely made enough to support a family, much less produce crops at a competitive price necessary to generate a profit. His family learned long ago that they had to expand their farming operations and produce more crops more efficiently just to remain competitive.

They scrimped and saved to buy more land as other farmers sold out. Additional land required building bigger grain elevators and silos, which in turn required new loans and more working capital. When they had good seasons, they invested in better equipment to enable them to plant, spray and fertilize, or harvest more rows of crops at once, saving time, fuel and labor. As cutting-edge farmers, they followed the best practices for land management, crop rotation, and sought out the best-yielding seed stock. Yet, after doing all of this, working long days and sometimes into the night, they would still be tossed against the ropes by a cycle of drought over which they had little control.

His grandfather managed to survive the Dust Bowl era. His father survived the trifecta of floods, droughts and disease. As they had been able, they installed irrigation in some fields, but that too was an expensive proposition. Now, yet again, they faced looming bank notices that would quickly come due at the end of this crop season. Without a bumper crop, they would be wiped out.

He contemplated his fortunes and misfortunes as he made his way from the machine shop back to his house to grab a bite of breakfast and a cup of coffee. He loved this time of year. It was always filled with so much promise. He would prepare the soil and savor the aroma of the rich, loamy earth. Monitoring the soil temperatures to get the seeds in the ground at the perfect time was another favorite pastime. Most of all, he enjoyed the simple pleasure of watching all of his crops grow. Some evenings he could count on one or two light shows, as lighting streaked across the sky and thunder echoed over the plains with the rains soaking the thirsty crops. He shook his head and chuckled about a long-ago memory. He envisioned an unusually colorful evening sky, while he and Kathy sat rocking in the chairs on the front porch, sharing a humorous story, and watching the sun sink below the horizon.

The screen door squeaked as he pulled it open; the old, rusty spring groaned as it stretched wide. He always let it go just a touch too soon, and it would *thwack* the frame. Walking into the kitchen, Jediah smiled admiringly at his wife, then kissed her on the cheek as he passed.

"Morning, sweetheart. Something sure smells good."

Kathy had an invincible spirit and an infectious, energizing personality. Jediah thought for the millionth time how lucky he was that she married him. Not that there was really any doubt; they were high school sweethearts and their friendship went all the way back to grade school. Now, twenty-five years later, they had their own school-age kids. For a moment, he wondered what he would do, and where they would go, if they had to sell the farm this fall. His wife said that it didn't really matter, just as long as they were all together. She had offered to go back to teaching this fall. Since all of their children would be in school, she could work it in pretty easily. He hated for her to give up her weekly Bible study; she really enjoyed the fellowship she shared with the other women.

He sniffed the air, breathing in the wonderful aroma drifting from the oven as he washed his hands.

"I thought you might want a hearty breakfast, especially with your long laundry list of chores that you have planned for today. You sure got started mighty early."

"When I woke up at four, I just couldn't get back to sleep, so I decided I may as well get something done. Since the tractor was already parked in the machine shop, I figured I'd get that part I need to replace unbolted. Now, I can be first in line when they open up the service counter."

She poured him a tall thermos cup of strong, black coffee, the way he always liked it—straight up, nothing added. "You didn't forget about those people coming by to see us this morning, did you?"

"Well, as a matter of fact I did. It plum slipped my mind." He smiled. "Guess that's the reason for the cinnamon buns I smell. You only make 'em for special occasions. What are their names again? They didn't give you any clue as to why they were coming?"

"I have no clue why they want to visit." She glanced at the bulletin board next to the phone where she posted the reminder. "Their names are Miles West and Bramley Ann Fairchild." They both turned toward the big window over the sink as they heard the crunch of gravel under the wheels of an approaching car. "Suppose that's them," she added.

Jediah walked to the door, swung it open and waved their guest in. As they approached, he slid the old John Deere cap off his balding head and tossed it on a hook. His face was weathered from constant exposure to the sun and the wind, but his blue eyes twinkled with the reflected light of the rising sunbeams. "Welcome, folks. Come on in. I am Jed Fletcher, and this is my wife, Kathy."

Bramley was a bit surprised at that revelation. She and Miles introduced themselves.

She said, "I thought your name was Antony. Are you named for your grandfather?"

"Well, my given name is Antony Jediah Fletcher. When I was a kid, everybody called me AJ, but Kathy always called me Jed ever since we were in high school; it caught on and stuck. Jediah was actually my great-grandfather, but how did you guess that?" he inquired with mild curiosity.

In response, Miles asked, "Have you ever heard of Lefty Webber?"

"Yeah, he was that old bank robber that stole my great-granddad's truck, back in 1929 or 1930." He paused, scratching his head as he tried to remember the story. "At least I think that's when it happened."

"Let me tell you a part of the tale that was just recently discovered and unraveled."

Both of the Fletchers were spellbound as Miles and Bramley relayed the story of the old Stutz and its mysterious cargo. When it ended, Kathy declared, "That's the most extraordinarily interesting story I've ever heard."

Miles reached into his inside pocket and pulled out a check that was folded in half.

"We tried to track down the people that Lefty Webber robbed. For the most part, he stole from banks and not individuals. However, the last day of his life he stole several different vehicles. We never discovered who owned the Auburn Phaeton Sedan. The second vehicle that was stolen was owned by J. J. Moran. It was a brand-new 1931 Chevrolet McCabe Powers dual-purpose ambulance/hearse. The bank robbers also stole a 1930 Model AA Ford pickup truck. That vehicle was owned by your great-grandfather, Jediah Fletcher, which led us here to you.

"To make a long story short, Webber had exchanged much of his stolen loot for diamonds and gold coins, which he stashed in a most unusual way. Nevertheless, we found out where his treasure was buried and recovered it. We had hoped to return it to its rightful owners, but that has not proven feasible after all this time. At any rate, we would like to give you a check from some of the proceeds that we recovered to compensate your family for the vehicle that was stolen by Lefty Webber. We added the compounded interest for the last ninety years and have made this check out to you."

Miles handed the check to Jed. When he opened it and looked at it, he couldn't believe his eyes.

"This can't be right. It's too much!" he exclaimed.

"We rounded it up, but it's pretty close. We took the value of the truck purchased new in 1930, and added the compounded interest for ninety years, and it came out to almost two million, so we just rounded it up."

Jed looked at Kathy in disbelief. "Honey, I think I'm dreaming."

She was speechless; her mouth kept moving, but no sounds emerged. She looked a little like a guppy.

"We can't accept it," he said.

"Why not?" Miles asked. "I don't know if your great-grandfather had insurance to cover the loss, and it really doesn't make any difference. We are giving it to you to use as you see fit. If you don't want it, you are welcome to give it away. When Bramley and I discussed this issue, we too grappled with the decision of what to do with this windfall. In the end, we relied on a little wisdom gleaned from an old saying. The maxim states, 'If you give a man a fish, you feed him for a day. If you teach a man to fish, you feed him for a lifetime.' Consequently, we decided to put most of what we recovered into an education fund held by our community foundation to provide matching scholarships and grants for kids working to earn their degrees. A couple of scholarships are earmarked specifically for kids wanting to learn the art of restoring old cars, old antiques and paintings. We believe that it's important to preserve the past and pass on that legacy to future generations. However, in your case, we felt that it was more important to restore something that was stolen from your family."

Both Fletchers started to cry.

"Kathy, we won't have to put the farm on the auction block next fall." Jed paused and patted her knee. His excitement growing at the possible implications. "We could pay off the note on the farm, and still have a little to start a college fund for the kids. You've been praying for a miracle; I think we just got it."

It was a beautiful, sunny afternoon when Bramley pulled up in her 1957 Ford Thunderbird. The warm weather was ideal for riding around with the top down. As she meandered down the gravel driveway, she spotted Miles sitting in his freshly painted double swing, a glass of tea in hand.

She slipped out of the car and grabbed a couple of boxes off the other seat. Turning around she declared, "The place looks fantastic! All the new paint, mulch and flowers give the place so much charm! *And*, I have to tell you, I especially like those new cushions you added to the swing."

She noticed he was rubbing his midsection toward the bottom of his left ribs.

"Well, I'm glad you approve. After all, you helped me pick them out. Come join me. Care for a glass of tea?"

"Thanks for the offer, but I'm fine." Bramley looked at Miles with a sly grin. "So, are you checking for a spare rib?" she prodded.

He shook his head in amusement, contemplating a smart retort.

"So, really, how are your ribs by now?"

"Well, I would have say . . . having broken ribs is not all it's cracked up to be."

"Oh, that was soooo bad! Do you want me to break them again?" Then she admitted, "I guess I set myself up for that one."

"Seriously," replied Miles, "the doctor was right. The two-month mark was the magical milestone. They feel pretty good at this point."

She handed him a stack of wrapped boxes.

"Something for my ribs?" he asked as he gently shook the boxes.

"No, more like a souvenir to commemorate the third-month anniversary of our little adventure."

Miles retrieved his handy pocket knife and opened the blade to cut the tape sealing the wrapping paper.

She looked at him and proclaimed with mock disdain and exaggeration, "I can't believe that you are one of *those* kind of people."

A confused Miles wrinkled his forehead. "Uh, one of what kind of people?"

"There are only two ways to open a present: you either cut it open or you rip it open. I have to tell you, I'm a ripper!" she declared as she reached over and pulled a loose seam with a big *riiiip*. "It's much more fun!"

He removed the lid to reveal a unique diamond-weave suit; the double-breasted coat had a white shirt tucked inside with a snazzy bow tie. The lapels were the widest he had ever seen. The worsted wool felt thick and sturdy. He unfolded the dark-blue jacket to reveal cuffed pants.

"It was all the rage in 1928. I couldn't see you sporting around in that old Stutz without the proper attire."

"Don't you think that you'll look a little out of place sitting next to me in my retro duds?" he countered.

In a singsong lilt and an exaggerated Southern accent she said, "Well, it just so happens that I found this gorgeous flat-crepe dress. It's lovely, all silk flat crepe with a chic kerchief collar, box-pleated skirt, hand-embroidered motif on the bodice, and smart, contrasting silk crepe with trimming in the *perfect* dark-orchid color." She batted her eyelashes. "Plus, I found a hat, handbag and shoes too!"

He was not at all sure what she just said, but it was all Greek to him anyway. "Ah, that sounds . . . lovely."

She stopped and looked at him as if she were peering over a pair of reading glasses. "You have no idea what I'm talking about, do you?"

"Not a clue," he admitted.

"Pick me up at six and you'll see," she said playfully, then added, "I've got another surprise for you too."

He waited. "Hey, come on. Don't keep me in suspense."

"Well," she said, tapping one finger on her lip as if weighing the implications of her response, "I didn't want to tell you until dinner, but—"

"Out with it already!"

"Do you remember when we were in New York sitting on that electric bike? You said that what you would really enjoy riding would be a classic 1937 Indian Sport Scout. It just so happens that someone you know . . . that would be me," she exclaimed with gleeful excitement in her voice, "found one for sale out west. Since we have a four-day weekend coming up, I thought we could take a trip to go look at it. Then maybe I can finally get you to tell me the story that's linked with that classic ride."

ACKNOWLEDGMENTS

A special thanks to my test readers for wading through my drafts. Mary, Judy, David, Brooke and Sydney, thanks for your time. I really appreciate your support and encouragement.

Joe, thanks for all of your efforts to polish this novel with your wonderful edits and for helping me become a better writer. Thanks to rest of the team at Koehler. Without you this book wouldn't exist.

CPSIA information can be obtained
at www.ICGtesting.com
Printed in the USA
LVHW111959150419
614195LV00004B/289/P